The Butterfly Box

Nora Naish was born in India, one of seven children of an Irish father in the Indian Civil Service, and did not come to England until she was eight years old. She was educated at a convent in Wimbledon and London University before qualifying as a doctor at King's College Hospital during the war. She married and brought up four children in Gloucestershire. In middle life she went back to medicine as a GP in Avon. Her elder brother was the late P.R. Reid, the author of *The Colditz Story*. *The Butterfly Box* is her second novel.

Also by Nora Naish
and available in Mandarin

Sunday Lunch

NORA NAISH

The Butterfly Box

Mandarin

Singin' in the Rain © 1929 EMI Catalogue Partnership/EMI Robbins
Catalog Inc, USA. Reprinted by permission of CPP/Belwin, Europe,
Surrey, England

I Can't Give You Anything But Love: music by Jimmy McHugh and
words by Dorothy Fields © 1928, Mills Music Inc, SA. Reproduced
by permission of Lawrence Wright Music Co Ltd, London WC2H 0EA

J'attendrai (R. Marbot, Reisfield, Olivier) © Lille Stiebel. Reproduced by
permission of Lille Stiebel.

A Mandarin Paperback
THE BUTTERFLY BOX

First published in Great Britain 1994
by William Heinemann Ltd
This edition published 1995
by Mandarin Paperbacks
an imprint of Reed Consumer Books Ltd
Michelin House, 81 Fulham Road, London SW3 6RB
and Auckland, Melbourne, Singapore and Toronto

Reprinted 1995

Copyright © Nora Naish 1994
The author has asserted her moral rights

A CIP catalogue record for this title
is available from the British Library
ISBN 0 7493 1559 8

Printed and bound in Great Britain by BPC Paperbacks Ltd
Member of The British Printing Company Ltd

The Butterfly Box

ONE

Saturday

October had always been Lucy's favourite month, in child-hood because that was when her birthday fell with all its celebrations: the pink-iced cake with candles served in the cool dining room on the shady side of the bungalow in Patna by Bearer dressed in his long brown coat, a crimson cummerbund round his corpulent middle, and a big white turban wound on top of his head making him look even taller than he was, the presents from Mummy and Daddy – a wonderful doll which uttered 'Ma-ma!' when you tipped her forward, and a tiny brush and comb for her wig, which was made of real hair and didn't come out when you pulled it, and the garland of flowers that Ayah hung round her neck to mark her special importance on this day when she became the Babamemsahib. She had, she remembered, certainly enjoyed queening it in those days. Later, when they all came Home from India and she saw for the first time the glorious colours of an English autumn in west country woods, and the red and gold promise of riches hanging on the branches of apple trees in a Gloucestershire orchard on her tenth (or was it eleventh?) birthday she was almost bursting with joy. And now that she would reach her eightieth birthday tomorrow, which everybody at High House was making such a fuss about –

presumably because they all thought she might not have another – she was enjoying again that sense of happy fulfilment, the soft golden sunshine in the garden, the long shadows of this Saturday afternoon, and the great burn of colours from the stand of Japanese maples planted by her mother, all that belonged especially to October.

She was glad to be able to snatch a little peace and quiet here among the trees before guests began to arrive for the houseparty. She knew she could leave all the management of caterers and cleaners in the competent hands of her daughter Beena: good, kind, well-meaning but sometimes infuriating Beena. Lucy sat on the stone plinth of a statue of a scantily draped girl in the brooding shade cast by a pair of evergreen holm oaks. They were planted by Louise, it must be nearly seventy years ago, when they first came to High House. She could see through the natural archway between the trees the green vale of Frenester sloping away towards the little town with its church tower, from which on this still afternoon a single bell slowly tolled its message: someone in Frenester had reached the allotted span. Donne's famous words boomed in her head with the bell: 'Never send to know for whom the bell tolls. It tolls for thee.' She remembered the first time she heard them. She was fifteen then, and just home from school, still in her gym-slip and black stockings. She was pushing her father's wheelchair across the lawn when they heard the church bell tolling; and he suddenly quoted Donne in his staccato, clockwork voice, adding 'For – me! For – me!' A few months later he was dead.

Lucy shook herself, stood up, and began to walk back to the house. Joanna (sweet child!) would be arriving soon, Beena's once unwanted baby who had brought them both so much joy. Lucy felt a twinge in her stomach as she imagined Joanna driving down the motorway, and momentarily remembered the crash which years ago had devastated her own life. Now this golden girl was bringing

2

a man, undoubtedly a lover, to her grandmother's birthday party; and Lucy was apprehensive. She asked herself why, when she should be delighted to share in Joanna's happiness in love, to look forward perhaps to her successful marriage and family life. That was what she herself always wanted more than anything; and so did poor Beena. No doubt Joanna would want it too; but if she chose the wrong man there would be years of pain and regret ahead of her. The fact is, Lucy told herself, all the women of my family have been afraid of love, less on account of the sexual taboos held by past generations than because of their own experiences. Old Grandmama Dambresac used to talk of the madness of passion. *'L'amour, c'est une maladie,'* she used to say; and this for her was what it was. In her own case Lucy had certainly loved passionately and with joy; but it had all been much too brief. For Beena the experience had been a disaster. Was there, she wondered, some flaw in the family character which prevented the full flowering of love? Was it the very nature of love to be transient, or had they simply been unlucky? It was not marriage, she decided, but the hurts of love she feared for Joanna.

She tried to sweep all these anxieties out of her mind. Prejudice is what they are, she scolded herself. I must meet her boyfriend with an open mind. I must not be hostile or I will antagonise not only him but also Joanna. I must not be jealous, nor possessive, nor over-exacting. I must try to see things from his point of view. It will be hard enough for this poor young man to meet so many of Joanna's family knowing they are putting him through all sorts of testing hoops. He might even feel like Daniel in the lions' den, so I must not be like a wild cat, ready to pounce. She resolved to be friendly and encouraging, to try to draw out the best in him; but all the same she couldn't help hoping that Joanna had no intention of marrying him – not yet awhile anyway, not before she'd finished her training and established herself professionally.

'You'd better go and change, Lucy,' Beena greeted her mother in the hall. 'They'll all be arriving soon.'

Lucy went upstairs meekly, although she couldn't resist remarking as she did so: 'It won't take me long Beena – not as long as it's going to take you.' Beena was still wearing a soiled apron, and her hair was as usual looking like the irregular matted fringe of an old, much walked-over rug.

'You make it sound more like an ordeal than a celebration,' Joss said as he overtook a battered van, its number plate askew, its paint of many coloured coats flaking to display rust, and a bit of torn curtain swaying inside the rear window. 'Hippies! Best steer clear of them!' Unreliable citizens that they were, living unregulated lives, accident-prone, a health hazard to their neighbours and a danger to other drivers on the M4. 'I suppose they're the remnants of the now almost obsolete Great Unwashed.'

His attitude to drop-outs always made Joanna feel uncomfortable.

'They do provide homes for themselves – even if only in old vans,' she said. 'They don't add to the homeless statistics, you know.' She had been brought up with a commitment to fair play.

They both fell silent as they watched the Wiltshire landscape roll away from the windscreen: fields of stubble, ploughed earth across which cloud shadows moved like stately galleons, and then wave after wave of unploughed, windswept, rainswept grassland. They both breathed more deeply, relishing the sight of so much uncluttered space and the prospect of fresh air.

'I wonder you don't go home more often,' he said. 'Just looking at all that lovely space must be good for health. Don't you agree, Doctor?'

'I have a lot of work to do at weekends, you know,' she said primly. 'And I haven't got a Volvo like yours to make the journey easier.'

4

He smiled indulgently. The Volvo came with the job. It wasn't really his, but he hadn't told her that. She was after all still only a student, a good deal younger, poorer, and less worldly-wise than himself; and it would be a few years before she became a real doctor and earned anything at all, and many years before she would earn as much as him.

'As a matter of fact,' she admitted, 'it's a bit of an ordeal even for me – going home.' She fell silent, seeing her mother through his eyes, and feeling ashamed of her, and then guilty of feeling ashamed. To Joanna, that her mother cared nothing for her appearance, and indeed sometimes looked like a homeless tramp, that she lived in her own arcadian world of home, garden, animals and church, was a bit of an eccentric, were all facts she accepted because she'd grown up with them; but she feared that Joss, with his sophisticated taste and dedication to design, and the importance he gave to Art with a capital A would pronounce Beena a fool and a frightful old frump. And what about Lucy? Lucy with her Raj accent, her outward shell of old-fashioned manners and the self-discipline which did not allow her to burden others with too excessive an expression of her own feelings? All that was out of fashion today. And would he condemn her reluctance to spend money foolishly, thinking her mean? She considered he would appreciate her dislike of gaudy, meaningless ornamentation, which was a reprehensible vulgarity to both of them. But would he even guess – and this was perhaps the most out-of-date aspect of her whole character – the altruism which was her inner guiding star? Joanna was afraid Joss would find her grandmother difficult to understand and hard to take.

'They're rather old-fashioned I suppose,' she said, 'my mother and grandmother. They're country people. They'd certainly stick out a mile in town.'

He nodded, smiling, glad that he could enjoy a little feeling of superiority over them in London at least. 'They'll all be weighing you up, of course; but why should you worry? You'll be doing the same. That's your job, isn't it? Appraisal, as the Yanks call it.'

'Appraisal, yes. But I make value judgements about things, *objets d'art*, paintings and so forth: static things, not moving, living, changing people.'

All the same, he thought, the mother will be hearing wedding bells in her head, seeing me dressed up as a bridegroom, and the rich grandmother will be wanting to have a look at my bank balance. Joss had no intention of marrying; that was the last thing he wanted: to tie himself down to a life sentence. One of the reasons he was enjoying this affair with Joanna so much was just because she wasn't on the lookout for a husband. She still had another year of study ahead of her before she qualified as a doctor, and after that there were her internships to work through. All this work and study filled a large part of her life making her, he believed, less demanding in love than most women. That was one of the things he liked about her: her independence. He believed her attitude to love was like his own: a grateful acceptance of present pleasure; with no commitment to the future. But he did know and relish the knowledge that her family was fairly well-heeled; and should the time come when he wanted to settle down to marriage and family life she could bring with her as a wife a tidy capital sum. For the time being there was the weekend to face with its monstrous regiment of women. Most of the men seemed to have died off or disappeared. Women outlasted their men so often there was always a glut of them in old age. He just hoped there'd be one or two male survivors to bolster up his courage.

'I suppose it was a bit unusual being brought up in a household of women only,' said Joanna, reading some of his thoughts. 'But I don't think I missed much. I know they – Beena and Lucy, my Mum and Gran – refused to send me away to boarding school (which I longed for when

6

I was twelve) because they said I needed some males in my background. I went to the Primary School in Frenester, and later to the local Comprehensive, and later still I did go away to boarding school when Lucy got me into the Sixth Form at Chesborough. I was sixteen by then.'

'Plenty of upper crust males there!' laughed Joss.

'It wasn't for them I went there. It was because I wanted to do Medicine, and Lucy thought a big public school which had more money to spend on labs and scientific equipment, and perhaps Science teachers too, would get me through my A-levels more easily than the Frenester Comprehensive.

'Did you always fancy yourself as a doctor?'

'Oh no!' This time Joanna laughed. 'I always wanted to be an actress.'

'To join the eighty per cent unemployed?'

'Well I didn't know much about the facts when I was a kid, did I? I just loved acting. I used to get carried away on the school stage by the words I had to spout. I could even weep real tears to order – believe it or not!' She paused for a few seconds as Joss manoeuvred his way into the fast lane to overtake a juggernaut lorry. 'Once,' she said, when they were safely past, 'when I played the King in *Richard II* – abridged version it was. And I don't know why I was chosen for the part when there were plenty of boys. Perhaps I was taller at fourteen than the boys in my class; or perhaps it was my loud voice – anyway, there was I in the middle of the stage spouting:

> For God's sake let us sit up on the ground
> And tell sad stories of the death of Kings . . .

and as I began to describe their sad deaths a lump came into my throat and tears poured down my cheeks. I couldn't speak. There was a sudden awful hush. The prompter kept hissing from the wings: "Some poisoned by their wives ... Some poisoned by their wives' ..." It was an agonising moment.'

'What happened?'

'The audience began to titter. That brought me to my senses. I suddenly rushed on, gabbled the words to make up for lost time. My great moment of triumph as an emotional actress thrown away!'

He gave her thigh a little sympathetic squeeze with his left hand.

'Poor Joanna! What a shame!'

'It didn't matter much. Everybody was very kind about it; but I wasn't asked to take such a big part again. I loved school, you know. Had a wonderful childhood really. Beena, my mum, was marvellous when I was little. She ran a small riding school with a string of Shetland ponies. One of them, and elderly quiet mare called Sheila, was mine; and when, at five, I was allowed to ride her round the field without being led it was a solemn occasion. It was also, I remember, absolute bliss. Lucy used to say riding Sheila was as good as a religious education for me. It gave me the heavenly expression of one of Fra Lippi's angels.'

'Strange cove: Fra Lippi!' said Joss. 'Did you know he was a monk who ran off with a nun? And all those lovely cherubs he painted crowding round the knees of the madonna were modelled on this nun and their children?'

'No!'

'Oh yes. Very romantic – a true love story. Fra Lippi was himself an unwanted child brought up in a Carmelite Convent; and I suppose he had no choice but to take vows; but he wasn't a very good monk. When he caught sight of pretty Lucrezia Buti (he was Chaplain in the convent where she was a novice) he asked permission to use her as his model for the Virgin. And perhaps because he was already a famous painter he was not refused. No doubt he prolonged the sittings. They fell in love. And then they ran away. Terrible scandal of course. Rumours reached the

8

Vatican. They were forcibly separated, although by this time she was pregnant. Somehow they met again, and ran away again, only to be separated once more. But in the end the Pope annulled their vows, so they were able to marry at last. The course of true love was a very bumpy ride for them.'

'I suppose they were freed to keep the Pope's painter happy,' said Joanna.

'I've always suspected it was owing to the appealing look on the cherubs' faces.' He glanced sideways at Joanna and decided that she did have something of that Lippi look: the short, curly, copper-coloured hair, the perfectly balanced features, and a certain innocence spiked with a glint of mischief.

He could see in his wing-mirror a low red car coming up behind him with the speed of a Scud Missile, and possibly as inaccurately aimed, and moved out of the fast lane quickly. Joanna asked herself how many obstacles Joss would be able to overcome for her sake, and then suppressed the question.

'Beena was great when I was little,' she said. 'I lived with all her animals at that stage. It was only later it dawned on me that she actually loved animals more than human beings. When I was a teenager it was to my grandmother that I turned for understanding. We used to go for long walks together and talk about everything under the sun. Funnily enough the age difference didn't seem to matter then. She was always so fit and seemed so young – well certainly till a few years ago.'

They were nearing the end of the journey when she said: 'You'll like High House. It's a Grade II listed building – interesting architecturally and all that. In a lovely spot too.' She glanced at his hands on the driving wheel: beautiful hands, fine but strong; and then she looked sideways at his profile. It still gave her a small shock of surprise. He really was so good-looking that nobody could help but admire

9

him. And that little curl of hair at the nape of his neck made him seem so boyish and vulnerable that her heart lurched every time she noticed it. She knew she'd be proud of him at High House; she knew, too, that underneath his handsome confident shell he was socially shy, so she tried to reassure him.

'The other men there? Well, there's a Canadian family coming. Some sort of cousins of Lucy's who happen to be on holiday in the UK. I've never met them and I don't believe Lucy has either. They wrote saying they wanted to become acquainted with their relatives in Britain. The father is called Duncan; and there are two teenage kids, I believe. Then there's Charlotte. She's a first cousin, and a very old friend of Lucy's. They'll all be staying in the house over the weekend.'

The entrance to the house fulfilled his expectations. An avenue of beeches flanked the driveway, and beneath them on the rich mould formed by the rotting of many years of leaf-fall the first russet-gold of autumn was sparsely scattered. He got out of the car stretching his long legs with relief after the drive from London, and stood admiring the beeches, untouched by the hurricanes which had left so many trees in the south-east sprawling.

'They were planted by my great-grandmother in the Thirties,' said Joanna. 'She was the real gardener in the family.'

Four identikit women in bright yellow overalls skipped out of the house towards a yellow van which advertised MOPITUPPERS in black letters on its side. They were rosy and plump and might have been quads fed on full-cream milk from babyhood. They were carrying cleaning apparatus of various sorts which they pushed into the van, then climbed in smiling and waving in unison.

Joanna's mother was at the door. She was wearing a none-too-clean apron and looked harassed, her hair inexpertly dyed blonde, not a blush of make-up on her face.

Her hands, which she spread out over Joanna's back as she hugged her, were knobbled and parched, with split nails like an old gardener's. She grinned at Joss over Joanna's shoulder. 'I'm Beena,' she said.

'I'm Joss.' He offered his hand as she freed herself from Joanna's embrace.

Beena would have liked to know if Joss was short for Joseph, which might suggest a Catholic in his parenthood, or for Joshua which would reveal a rabbi in the background, or perhaps Josiah with some distant link to the pottery families; but she didn't want to appear to be too inquisitive so early in their acquaintance.

'Show him upstairs, Joanna darling,' she said, sticking to practical matters, which was always safer. 'I've put you in the attic rooms. Being young you won't mind climbing all those stairs.'

The hall was rather dark, but at the end of a shadowed recess at one side of the staircase there were glints of gold and silver. They must have come from the frame, or even the glittering paint on the famous portrait Joanna had described. It was what he'd come to see as much as the relatives. He would examine it at leisure during the weekend. It would give him an excuse to escape a good deal of the inevitable socialising and paying of respects to the old girl whose eightieth birthday they had come to celebrate, the rather formidable grandmother, held in considerable awe by her descendants, not least because she was the possessor of all this wealth: old wealth, not excessive, not made in a flash and flashily squandered, but earned and saved by the skills and hard work of middle-class generations of craftsmen, traders and professional people. It had been based solidly and solidly invested, and now, since somebody during the preceding generations had had the sense to put it into land and property, was indestructible. He smiled as he watched Joanna's back ahead of him on the stairs. It wasn't only her body he admired; he appreci-

11

ated the clothes she wore as well. The way she dressed was so much an extension of her personality: no frills, uncluttered and rather austere, but revealing a strong sense of design and a sneaking affection for vivid colours. Those black pants she was wearing outlined her round buttocks and slim thighs, and ending as they did just below the knee, defined, with a sort of flourish as elegant as Japanese calligraphy, the shape and surface of her sun-tanned calves. Her shirt of corn-gold silk showed off to perfection her marvellous hair. He knew they were the kind of deceptively simple clothes which only a well-filled purse could buy. What she had to live on was not much more than her student grant. That was her grandmother's edict. So how could she afford these fashionable, expensive clothes? He wondered if they could have been a present from her dowdy mother. It made him hope his sweet Joanna would inherit quite a lot in the not-too-distant future. That would make her even more desirable. Of course he was not pursuing her for her money. Of course he loved her. 'Well, for heaven's sake – !' he exclaimed aloud, drying his hands on a small towel with a very deep soft pile in the attic bathroom they were going to share; but he finished his thoughts silently. Money is – let's face it – inevitably an attribute of charisma just as much as a beautiful body, or Joanna's very individual red-gold hair, which she wore like a copper helmet, the tight curls cut close to the head. He had often thought she resembled an antique Greek warrior. Come to think of it she did look rather masculine till she took off her clothes. There were certainly plenty of reasons apart from her family's money why he found her so attractive, though he was aware that she was unlike the women he usually fancied: good natured, pretty girls who didn't think much, but who were intelligent enough to listen to him without looking bored, who were willing to do more or less what he wanted and took pains to please him in small ways. The trouble with that sort was they usually wanted him for keeps. Joanna was different: independent and outspoken. Sometimes her independence, and especially her difference from himself alarmed him and made him wonder why he loved her. Was the bond a simple sexual one, or was the affair useful to his getting on in the world? He had learned to hide so much of his true feelings in his upwardly mobile social climb that he was sometimes unsure which of his feelings were spontaneous and which were learned. But he was reassured by the thought that Joanna, being a good deal younger and less sexually experienced than himself, seemed to be willing to be taught by him, and often to be led by him. He didn't ask himself if this would always be so.

He wondered if Beena had put them together on the top floor on purpose. Separate bedrooms but very easy access. Nobody else in the bathroom or corridor to get in the way. Probably not, probably the arrangements were entirely practical, providing two single rooms (undoubtedly the servants' quarters of earlier times) for two single people. Joanna had once described her mother as an out-of-the-world Christian, living in a self-made garden of Eden carefully fenced off from rude reality and the wriggling in of any wily Serpent, so Beena probably didn't guess what he and Joanna got up to. But you couldn't be too sure. These religious people were usually pretty hot on the scent of sin.

But what fabulous views she had provided of the outside world! He stood at the window and gazed down upon the great space extending south-westwards, and had to lean on the window frame to steady himself against feeling giddy. High House was built on the outermost ridge of those limestone undulations that stretch across middle England fifty miles or more north-eastwards from where he stood. The steep Cotswold escarpment had been thrown up, full of shell fossils, out of the sea hundreds of million years ago. From here on its crest he could see part of the garden sloping towards a fringe of trees whose shadows, like long fingers in the late afternoon light, pointed up towards the house. Beyond them lay chequered fields spotted with sheep, and more distantly the huddled roofs of Frenester. The horizon was blurred with mist, but he knew that there the Severn slid on its way to the Bristol Channel.

'Up here it must be like the crow's nest of a whaler when there's a sou'-wester blowing,' he said to Joanna, who had joined him.

'On a clear day you can see the Welsh hills from here,' she said. 'When I was little, Gran pointed out to me what I thought she called the mountains of whales. For a long time I used to peer out of this window hoping to see them spout.'

'Funny girl!' he laughed, and kissed her on the back of her neck.

She wriggled away from him and tugging his hand led him towards the narrow, winding servants' staircase.

'It used to be my bedroom when I was little,' she said.

'Well then, you must have it. Shall we swop?'

'I might share it with you.' She glanced at him from under the corner of her eyelids with a coquettish look which was not at all what he expected from a woman doctor. It was one of the things he liked most about her: that small streak of the flirt in her seemingly so disciplined exterior. The stairs were uncarpeted and resounded beneath her high heels.

Bare feet tonight, he thought.

Tea was being served in the drawing room by Beena, who still wore her smeared apron and hadn't combed her hair. Not many guests had yet arrived but those who had were talking volubly. It shocked him a little that they all seemed to accept her service as right and proper. When she struggled through the doorway with a second loaded tray, and he leaped towards the door to hold it open, they turned their heads to look at him in mild surprise.

'Gran, this is Joss,' said Joanna.

Lucy regarded him from the depths of her winged armchair by the fire through half-closed eyes. Polite, she thought. I suppose that's a good thing. I must concentrate on this young man if Joanna's thinking of marrying him. He's handsome and looks healthy, and has a winning smile; but those steady watchful eyes do calculate. She proffered her hand, and he saw at a glance with a little shock of excitement that her fingers were literally loaded. That sapphire and diamond cluster ring alone must be worth several thousands!

A walking calculator, Lucy thought. Do Walking Calculators outlast Disappointed Romantics in the long endurance test of marriage? Joanna could certainly do without one of *them*! No Byrons, no Heathcliffs please! The romantic man searching always for the impossible-to-find ideal of his imagining, and believing himself to be unmatchable anyway, is also impossible to please. A good wife might twist herself into corkscrews trying to satisfy him, waste herself utterly in trying to do it, and then come to realise in middle life that she'd failed. No Romantic egoism in the family please! But I do hope he isn't a cold fish.

'Joanna tells me you'd be interested to see the Klimt Portrait,' she said.

'Very much so.' He bent slightly and very formally towards her and asked, 'And I wondered if perhaps you'd allow me to take some photos of the garden while I'm here? I know it's a very special place.'

'Certainly. Of course. All in good time . . .' murmured Lucy. She seemed suddenly weary of him.

Joss noted her half-closed eyes, the wrinkled hoods of her eyelids, and supposing that she was too old to maintain more than minimal conversation dismissed her from his thoughts and began to examine the room instead: high ceiling with prettily plastered cornice, big french windows opening out onto a terrace, a large iron basket-grate containing burning logs and above them a mantelpiece of wood, simply but skilfully carved, on which stood a pair of porcelain peacocks. They were probably Derby, certainly not Meissen or they would be kept behind glass. But you never could tell! People were so foolish about porcelain; so often they put their most precious and fragile pieces in an exposed position. There was an interesting carpet on the floor. He couldn't quite place it. It must be sixty or seventy years old at least, as it was rather worn in places – oriental of course. These families which had crossed and recrossed the Indian Ocean for generations inevitably accumulated antique oriental rugs. But the portrait was not in the room. He wondered where they kept it. It certainly wasn't that gleam in the dark hall; that had proved on closer inspection to be the broad beaten copper frame of a rather fine Art Nouveau mirror.

Joanna was sitting on the floor beside her grandmother's chair and talking across the hearth to two girls, a plump teenager she addressed as Ellen, and a very attractive French girl called Danielle who was Charlotte's granddaughter. It was difficult to believe such a delightful girl could be descended from the dreadful old bag they all called Charlotte, an overdressed, overpainted dyed blonde in her eighties looking like some twentieth-century Rowlandson painted by Beryl Cook! Bedizened was the word to describe her, with those heavy dangling ethnic earrings and those high-heeled scarlet shoes: a vulgar old thing; but yes, she might be funny. He couldn't hear what she was saying, but people near her were laughing. He suspected she'd probably got away with murder all her life by making people laugh. This Charlotte now tripped across the room and stood by Lucy's chair. Lucy reached out her hand.

'Dear Charlotte,' she murmured. There was a glint of tears in her eyes. Was it possible she actually loved this female clown? Time had been kinder to Lucy, who still possessed a lot of white hair worn like a halo round her face, devoid of make-up, pale and wrinkled but gathering a little fire from the deep red colour of her dress and the sparkle of a diamond star pendant hanging from her neck on a long chain. Very good it was, too – Victorian, not rare but a good, sound piece. He heard the twang of a transatlantic voice from near the window. It came from the only other male in the room apart from an adolescent boy who sat alone in a corner, glowering, and bored so stiff he couldn't move. The man must be Duncan, that Canadian Joanna had mentioned; but she had not introduced him. She had deserted him, left him stranded like one of her whales, expecting him to spout and go on spouting to all these strangers while she immersed herself in childhood reminiscences with the pretty French girl. He suddenly felt resentful and very much out of it, so to cover his feelings he helped Beena clear the cups and saucers and insisted on carrying the tray out to the kitchen, which was behind a swing-door in that dark recess of the hall.

'It's very kind of you,' she said. 'I don't mind doing it myself, you know.'

He watched her silently as she ran hot water into the sink. There was no dish washer; the kitchen, though containing a few basic labour-saving gadgets, was not what advertisers call luxury-fitted. More luxury was displayed on the old lady's fingers than in her daughter's kitchen. He suddenly remembered the occasion when as a small boy he had been taken to visit his grandmother when she worked as a housekeeper at Headstone Hall. His mother held his hand firmly when she pulled him through vast empty rooms (the gentry were all in London) towards a model of a steam engine she thought would interest him. He remembered her nervous commands. 'Don't sit down! Don't drag your feet on the parquet! Don't touch!' Above all 'Don't touch!' He hadn't really wanted to touch; he was too busy craning back his neck to stare at the painted ceilings, the carved gilded pillars and the great paintings on the walls of this palace of the gods. It was those ceilings

17

which lit the first candle to Art in his imagination. That was many years before he had any idea he might make a living out of it.

'Art is something for *Them*,' said his father. 'For Them as has money. Not for Us. So don't lose your head over all this Art you go on about.'

His mother, quietly pouring tea at the kitchen table, commented: 'There's a lot of Art in big public galleries and museums for all to see. Those pictures belong to the Nation. That means us.'

Dad admitted she had a point there. He was not an argumentative man; but he understood quickly that he and Mum lived in a different world from the one their son was peering into and would later join. It had been a hard climb for Joss into that other world, mixing with upper-class young men and women born into the twentieth-century equivalent of the purple, all living in orderly rooms, often surrounded by beautiful objects from the time their infant eyes first focused. They had been carried around in expensive cars with their nannies to parks and fields, later to school, and to and from expensive shops, never learning how the rest of the human race struggles to keep alive; but he soon found he was a great deal cleverer than most of them, and a more persevering student, so he learned to hold his own, and even to despise them as a pleasure-seeking frivolous lot. Joanna was not like that. Besides being lovely to look at she was thoughtful and serious, sometimes uncomfortably so. She seemed to carry on her young shoulders the burden of an old-fashioned need to work in order to make the world a better place to live in. Joss saw himself as rather serious too, a man to be envied since he was now an expert opinion and a valuer for the globally respected firm of Frithby's International Fine Art Dealers and Auctioneers. He believed he owed most of all this to those ceilings, though he doubtless owed something to Dad's accurate ear, inherited from a family of Welsh

18

singers, for without that he'd never have been able to alter his vowels sufficiently for the job. He smiled; he was complacent, till he suddenly remembered the end of that visit to Headstone Hall. Granny had joined Mum and him and insisted on showing them the portrait of a great queen. She wasn't a real queen, Granny said; she was a grand lady who had a special dress made to wear at a *durbar*, or reception for all the great ones of India. It must have been the last display of Imperial grandeur before the First World War brought the old order and so many fixed pillars of wisdom tumbling down. He hadn't, of course, understood any of this then; all he saw was a beautiful lady in a dress with an enormous train made entirely of peacock feathers. Afterwards he was led down to the kitchen where the servants were drinking tea at a scrubbed table. Granny, who wanted to show off his reading to the others, pointed to a big slab of slate fixed to the wall and inscribed with a text.

'Can you read that? What does it say?'

He read aloud in a piping voice: 'Waste Not Want Not!'

A murmur of soothing praise followed; but his grandmother burst into derisive laughter and got very red in the face.

'What's the matter, Granny? What are you cross about?'

'I'm not cross with you, love,' she said, patting his shoulder. 'Not with you, but with them upstairs.' He didn't understand her, because there weren't any people upstairs to get cross with, and because she'd obviously loved the picture of the bird-queen and had even rubbed a speck of dust off the corner of the frame with the edge of her apron. 'It's gold and jewels and peacock feathers for them, but waste not want not for us!'

A silence fell in the kitchen. It was broken by the cook, who said soothingly: 'He's a fine boy, that grandson of yours.' But it was a young Irish maid in a black dress who said what really mattered: 'Sure he has the face of an angel!

19

He will rise above us all.' And in that moment he knew that because of his cleverness, and most of all because of his face, he was destined for a great future. He saw himself sitting up in one of those ceilings amid the pretty cherubs and the glorious ladies wearing golden crowns. Ever since that day he had been aware of his good looks, though time and a certain development of tact had taught him to hide this awareness. Beauty is power, he thought, not only the beauty of the human body but the beauty of things. That was why people wanted to possess them, would even pay enormous sums of money to possess them.

On that fateful day he'd also learned from his grand-mother about the ambivalances of English life. You had to bow your head and swallow your pride to keep your job; but you were free to like what you liked as well as to say what you thought behind your boss's back. He supposed somebody like Joanna could be so straightforward because she had never yet had to perform this balancing act. He smiled a little grimly. She would have to do so in due course, when she came up against the barriers of prejudice against women in the old-boy network which doubtless still existed in the medical profession. He guessed there was just as much kow-towing for promotion among the bacteria as there had been among his grandmother's brooms and dusters.

'You shouldn't be a servant to all these people!' he exclaimed with an indignation which surprised himself.

'What's wrong with being a servant?' Beena asked.

He was taken aback. 'Domestic servants,' he said, drying a cup on a not-very-clean teatowel, 'were traditionally downtrodden, weren't they?'

'Jesus washed the feet of His disciples,' was her reply.

He blushed, and was immediately ashamed of the panic he felt. He knew he was trapped; she was going to start preaching, and he couldn't run away.

'If the King of Kings washed the feet of His disciples why should I feel it beneath me to serve others?' she continued.

'It was a clear signal all right,' he added cautiously.

'We just have the wrong attitudes to service. It's not something you can easily put a price on – that's why. Courtesy, dedication and altruism have no market value in our hard, materialistic times. And doing things for free is out of fashion.'

'I expect you vote for the Opposition,' he ventured.

'I don't vote.'

'That's bad you know. You should.'

'Politics are no good – a mish-mash of half truths and unproved theories.'

'But we do have to have government. Don't we?'

'If all men were virtuous there'd be no need for any government.'

'But men aren't virtuous, never have been, and probably never will be.'

'What England needs is God – not my vote.'

He decided further discussion was pointless. 'All I meant,' he said, briskly and unnecessarily polishing a teaspoon, 'was that I thought you shouldn't be doing all the work. Some of those others could lend a hand.'

She smiled at him over her shoulder.

'They're guests and I'm hostess, you see. It's *noblesse oblige*. And Lucy is too frail to do much. And little Joanna works too hard and doesn't get enough sleep in that hospital of hers. So I think she needs to be cosseted a bit when she comes home.'

'What about the French cousin?'

'She *is* rather gorgeous, isn't she?' Beena smiled again, knowingly this time. 'Do you know she has a teeny-weeny drop of Turkish blood in her? Charlotte – that's her grandmother – married a half-French, half-Turkish fig merchant in Cairo before the war. You met Charlotte? She's a real card! She's a lot older than Lucy you know, but so full of life you'd never guess her age, would you?'

He didn't want to try. 'Everybody likes Charlotte. I can see that,' he said.

'I like her coming here because she makes Lucy laugh; but Danielle, though as pretty as a china dolly, would be a nuisance in my kitchen. She wouldn't know where to put anything.'

'Nor do I,' he said; but she babbled on: 'I'm not really overworked you know. I have cleaners to do all the house-work. The Moppituppers: you saw them as you came in. Marvels! – so much better at cleaning up the messes I make than I am myself! I hate cleaning. But I rather like doing things for people.' She knew herself well enough to under-stand that doing things for other people was not often for free. It was her personal strategy for buying love: to sell her attention and her services for IOUs of gratitude and guilt. 'And anyway I actually find washing up less boring than all that talking that goes on as soon as the family gets together.'

He saw that she meant it. He supposed that conversation, exchange of ideas and news and all the modification of prejudices and beliefs that was part of the process of com-munication was boring to her because she had already made up her mind about things. She knew what she thought, and wasn't interested in other people's ideas; she was happy in the design for living she had chosen, and didn't want to change it. In spite of the appearance she gave of being humble and downtrodden there was a streak of pride in her. She was rather like his own mother, he decided, which perhaps was why he liked her.

'To be quite honest,' she said, squeezing out her old-fashioned dishmop, 'I've always preferred horses and dogs to people. I taught Joanna to ride. Did you ride when you were little?'

'No.' Not bloody likely was his silent comment. It

22

wouldn't have been too easy to keep a pony on the small strip of grass between his mother's backyard and the bank above the railway line.

'We don't have a pony now,' she chattered on. 'The fields are let; but we do have a dog. My dog, Rufus. He's not allowed in the house. Orders from on High.' She dried her hands on a piece of torn towelling. 'But I'm forgetting. You probably want to join the younger ones. And don't worry about me. Tomorrow I'm not to do any work. Orders from on High again. Caterers are doing the lunch, and I have to appear spick and span and all dressed up at the party.'

'Good!' he said. 'I shall look forward to that.' He was being a nice young man for her with very little effort. He was pretty sure he had already won her over in spite of his cageyness on religious topics. He knew Lucy would be another matter.

When Danielle left them to talk to other people in the drawing room Lucy placed her much ringed hand on Joanna's shoulder and asked: 'Is your young man a Yuppie?'

'I suppose he is. At any rate his father was a railway signalman. Joss has come a long way with hard work and brains.'

'Good for him!' said Lucy. 'And are you in love with him?'

Joanna hesitated before replying. She was getting uncomfortable in her cross-legged sitting position, so she rose to her knees. 'I'm not really sure,' she said.

'Well, if you're not sure, you probably aren't,' said Lucy. 'Do you bonk with him?'

Joanna made a face. 'Well I don't call it that. It's such an ugly word. And it sounds much worse when *you* say it!'

'All our English words for anything to do with sex are ugly,' said her grandmother. 'Like the life of man in Nature after Hobbes: nasty, brutish and short.'

'It's not like that at all!' cried Joanna indignantly.

23

Lucy fell silent, playing with the pendant at her neck and looking over Joanna's head towards Danielle standing in the far corner of the room against the long curtains of the french window where Joss had joined her. He was smiling at her as she chattered. Lucy had seen that smile before on the faces of men, on one man in particular. It was like the archaic smile carved on the stone faces of Greek statues; it was not a kind smile; it was impersonal and uncommunicative, a smile of inward-hugging pleasure, entirely self-centred, which set alarm bells ringing in her mind. She glanced back at Joanna's face, so open and honest, so outward-looking and trusting, and thought: I must not be too fanciful. I must not let my imagination run away with me. I must not be irrational; but a mild general warning might be a good thing.

'Love can enslave a woman, Joanna,' she said, 'destroy her frail hold on freedom. Byron was very nearly right when he made that aphorism: "Man's love is of man's life a thing apart. Tis woman's whole existence." That was probably true in 1820; but not any more. It need not, must not be. And marriage can be a jump into prison too, you know. Love, marriage and a professional career are often incompatible time-sharers of a woman's life.'

'Perhaps it's not so much like that now, Lucy, as it was in your day.' Joanna saw Lucy as old, her hormones withered, leaving her without desire but full of fears and caution, while she herself needed love nearly as much as food, and certainly had every intention of grabbing it whenever it came her way. 'You fell in love, Lucy, didn't you? But did you know for certain it was the real thing?'

'Yes I knew. It wasn't called bonking then. It used to be called sleeping with someone; but of course it wasn't sleeping at all!' They both laughed.

When Lucy looked around the room again she was pleased to see that the two Canadian children were laughing at something Charlotte had said, and the girl Ellen was scratching herself unashamedly underneath her voluminous pullover, which made Lucy smile. But where was Danielle? She was nowhere to be seen, nor was Joss still in the room. Could they have left together? A little niggle of anxiety gnawed at her once more. Everybody knew Danielle was a compulsive flirt, and so pretty and charming with it that few men could resist her. Lucy suspected, too, that she was probably amoral when it came to affairs of the heart. She wondered uneasily where they'd gone . . .

Beena wiped her hands on her apron, untied it and hung it up on the back of the kitchen door before going out to unlock Rufus and take him out for his evening run across the fields. Rufus lived in an old stable on the far side of the yard. He was listening for her footstep and barked a joyful greeting as she crossed the gravelled space. She paused for a moment to look down the garden. This was the time of day she loved best, when her work was finished but there was still enough light, and those lovely, long, caressing shadows cast by the going-to-bed sun lay on the lawn. She could release Rufus before she fed him, and run about madly with him, enjoying it as much as he did. From where she stood she could see right down to the copse and the statue of that female in front of it. Something was moving there. Two people were there, bending together, their heads hidden by the legs of the stone girl. They came apart as she watched, and walked away into the trees. The tall figure was that young man of Joanna's who had been so nice to her earlier in the kitchen, but the other one was not Joanna. Joanna was wearing black pants; this girl was in a white skirt. Why! It was Danielle! You couldn't mistake that provocative walk. But they could only have met an hour or so ago! What could they be doing together in the garden? Beena couldn't help envying Danielle her youth and beauty and her obvious enjoyment of sinfulness. The way she positively flaunted her body! Beena decided quite calmly that Danielle was probably damned. But you could never be sure, the Lord being so forgiving . . . No. She hadn't actually seen them kissing over the feet of that horrible old statue; but their heads had certainly been very close together.

She ran towards Rufus and released him, and was immediately reassured by his jumping up on her, and his rough lickings. She let him out into the field through the upper gate, and ran after him. She threw sticks for him to chase, called him to heel when she saw him eyeing sheep through another gate, and made him walk close to her; but all this activity did not dispel her worries. After half an hour's exercise she put him on a lead and led him down the garden to the copse. Nobody was about now, but in her mind's eye Beena still saw those two heads close together. She sat down on the stone base of the statue with her back to its back, and stared up towards the house. She had always disliked that old Victorian statue of the maiden with the cloth slipping off her hips, one hand clutching it while the other shaded her eyes as she peered through the trees down the hill to Frenester, or into the future, or whatever else you liked to imagine she was gawping at. She would get rid of her as soon as the house was hers, smash her up, or at least get her carted off to a saleroom somewhere. That statue had witnessed too many things in her family life, too many of her own humiliations to be a comfortable companion for her old age. And now she was standing up there, taller than human, cold and hostile above them all, as this Joss, this handsome Judas already, even before marriage to her little Joanna, was betraying her, was running after Danielle, was kissing her – or as near as – over the statue's feet!

Beena began to weep remembering her own frequent rejections. There was that time a schoolfriend came to tea. They must have been nine or ten years old. They had been playing in the garden when they quarrelled. She couldn't

26

remember what they quarrelled about, but she remembered the girl's name: Tracy. Tracy had called out loudly that Beena's mother was a snob, and her gran was posh.

'They're not!' Beena had defended them angrily. 'They want to build a classless society!' It was a phrase she'd picked up from conversation heard at the dinner table. 'And anyway *I'm* not a snob! I just want to be the same as you.'

'Well you can't,' Tracy had said. 'And I don't like you. You're too ugly – so there!'

'I don't want you either!' Beena had shouted. 'You're horrid! Go away! Go home!' and she had fled, leaving her teatime guest, fled to hide in the copse and weep bitterly before the silent stone girl holding her drapes politely over her private parts. It was there her grandmother Louise, dressed in her baggy corduroy gardening trousers with mud-caked knees, had found her.

'Whatever's the matter, Beena?' she had asked.

'She says I'm ugly!' Beena had blurted out.

Louise had put down her trowel and the bucket of dandelions and other noxious weeds it held, and clasping her granddaughter in her arms had said: 'You're not ugly, Beena. How could you be when you have the most beautiful blue eyes, just like forget-me-nots?' And Beena had dried her eyes and been comforted; but not for long. She had soon understood that she was not distinguished and talented like her Gran, nor clever like her mother, and never beautiful like Auntie Patsy. At meal times Louise and Lucy used to talk such a lot of stuff above her head; but she didn't listen. She let her mind wander out of the house, across the fields to her pony, a pretty little pony called Kitty, and her King Charles' Spaniel called Sukie, whose long silky ears she loved to stroke. Tracy had forgotten the quarrel, and had actually asked if she might come again to tea, this time to have a ride on Kitty. Beena had felt wanted and important then, though she knew it was the pony, not herself, Tracy wanted to play with.

The most bitter of Beena's rejections came after she left High House and went to live with Auntie Patsy in Wimbledon. She went there to attend a secretarial college and learn shorthand and typing, and remained with her when she got her first job in a London office. Everything was all right till she was swept away with that happy hippy Sixties crowd. Oh! The wicked bliss of that time! The joyful relinquishing of all those too-heavy responsibilities – the fear of the atomic bomb, of personal failure in a too-demanding society, of her own incompetence as well as the fear of never being loved by a man in spite of her often urgently felt sexual need – all brainwashed away by the smoking of a little grass and the holding of hands, anyone's hands. They threw flowers at each other and lay about in parks or on the floor of bed-sits, happy in carefree universal loving while they listened to, and sometimes sang, the Beatles' songs. Her favourite was 'Eleanor Rigby' – such a lovely song for all the lonely people . . . Young siren voices singing to the young all over the world: Make Love not War. Oh! The wicked bliss of it all! Wicked in hindsight, because she'd fallen in love with a marvellous man who loved her, or so she thought when she lay in his arms and stroked his beard, and teased him because she found a grey hair in it. It was all heavenly happiness forever till she missed her period.

'Don't worry, darling,' he told her. 'Everything will be OK.'

But after her second missed period he said he was going to Katmandu to meditate, to discover the real central kernel of all Truth. He looked deep into her forget-me-not blue eyes and promised he'd never forget her, would see her when he got back and would talk things over then. She never saw him again.

There was a girl in the office where Beena worked, a

thin, pop-eyed girl who moved jerkily and smiled quickly and toothily. She was very kind to her at that time. She belonged to a fundamentalist sect which sang rousing hymns and thumped tambourines together on Sundays. She invited Beena to come along to one of these thumps, and Beena went, and loved it. She especially loved that Sunday when a choir of black gospel singers visited the chapel to sing Negro Spirituals. There was one Beena would never forget: 'He has the whole world in His hand. He has the whole world in His hand. He has the whole wide world in His hand!'

That was the moment of revelation for her. She knew then that it was Jesus she was searching for; it was His love she needed now. She knew she was a nobody; but that didn't seem to matter to Jesus. She didn't need to be worthy; He would make her worthy of His love. He healed the sick, He loved the poor and meek, He promised them the earth. He would never reject her. Such a wonderful feeling of elation came over her when she saw this truth that she thought she'd burst with joy; and she did indeed cry out in anguish and happiness both inextricably mixed together. Then all the members of the congregation embraced her; somebody shouted suddenly 'Hallelujah!', and the singer of that particular spiritual kissed her. Everybody wanted to hold her hand. Tears were flowing freely from all the eyes watching her, and she didn't mind. She guessed these tears were washing away her sins, all her nobody-unworthiness away. Here, she suddenly knew, was where she belonged.

She left the office, she left Auntie Patsy's house in Wimbledon and went home to Frenester to have the baby, to Lucy and Louise and the little country church where there were no gospel singers but where at least the Vicar and one or two parishioners did believe. From that time on she tried to live her life for God. Her mother and grandmother welcomed her with open arms, accepting her born-again religion without scorn, though she was afraid they would have laughed if she'd told them about the thumps and hallelujahs. She supposed they thought of her as the prodigal daughter. They were absolutely delighted when the baby came; and she enjoyed their pleasure. She began to see, especially after Joanna's birth, that she had found her own place. She learned to manage High House, to take control of all the domestic chores and problems that neither Lucy nor Louise were very good at doing and solving; she felt at last that she had a family of her own, a rather peculiar family, she sometimes had to admit, consisting as it did of four generations of females without men.

She sighed. Auntie Patsy would arrive tomorrow. Auntie Patsy knew nothing of the unwanted pregnancy till after Joanna came into the world. She had been rather hurt at the time not to have been told before. She would have liked Beena to confide in her. Since then Beena had always made a point of being extra nice to her whenever they met.

'Dear God,' she prayed, as she stroked Rufus, who was panting quietly beside her. 'Please let Joanna see through him before it is too late!'

Lucy gave a sigh of relief as she sat down in the armchair in her den, which used to be the little dressing room beside her parents' bedroom in the old days. The big day, Sunday, was still to come; but thank God Saturday at least was over! She glanced up at the portrait, remembering the day her mother had moved it up here. It was during the war, when fuel was so scarce it became impossible to heat more than one room during winter. So it was decided to turn Herbert's old dressing room which was small and had a fireplace, into a sitting room for the duration. Two men dragged the painting upstairs and hung it over the *chaise-longue* opposite the window. Here it was not exposed to the damp which inevitably invaded the rooms below once the fires stopped burning in the grates.

Someone was playing the piano, far away it seemed, on the floor below; and she could hear distant sounds of voices and laughter. The young ones were still up, talking, or playing a game. It must be Robbie's son who was playing the piano, which sounded like tinkling – some sort of jazz. It gave her a strange feeling, meeting those Canadian cousins whom she'd never seen before. The fresh-faced girl and the good-looking boy with the absurd name were Robbie's grandchildren. Robbie . . . She remembered skating with him on the frozen pond on Wimbledon Common one very cold winter when she was twelve years old. Robbie who was her cousin, who was like a brother, but who was really her first love. . . . Robbie had gone to Canada after the war and married a Scottish-Canadian girl. When he died she didn't go to the funeral. It was just too far away. But here was his son, Duncan, playing Louise's piano, perfectly relaxed and at ease with himself as if he was at home.

Duncan's wife had not turned up. She'd decided instead to visit an old friend in Scotland, where her family would join her after the weekend. Lucy told herself she must make an effort to remember their names. The apple-cheeked girl in the big loose pullover was called Ellen, the silent glowering boy was Dewey.

That young man of Joanna's, who she suspected was just a go-getting philanderer, had expressed an interest in the portrait. No doubt he hoped it was a genuine Gustav Klimt. Lucy herself had very serious doubts about its authenticity. Louise used to call it 'school of Klimt', or 'painted in the Secessionist style'. Lucy suspected it had been painted by a student, perhaps in Klimt's studio, in which case, although everybody agreed it was valuable and very beautiful, it would never fetch the sort of money a genuine Klimt could command. But she would show it to Joss and ask his opinion of it; and perhaps he would be able to give her an up-to-date valuation of it. She glanced at it again, more attentively. Familiarity had not quite dulled the slight chill she felt each time she looked at it anew, a tinge of fear, a foolish superstitious dread that hands could reach out from it and pull her back towards the past. The design resembled a Japanese Satsuma vase, in the gold surface of which, among the many complex patterns are embedded heads of gods and ancestors. At the top stood Grandmama Dambresac, an empress majestic in her great beauty, with all her wonderful red hair piled high on her head in the Edwardian fashion, her long neck clasped in a boned collar of lace, and her large bold eyes looking at the artist with unmistakable sexual challenge. She was truly a *femme fatale* of her times. The gold cloak falling from her shoulders enclosed and half hid the figure of her daughter, Louise, her dark hair in a schoolgirl plait, and her eyes already sad and pleading. The girl's hands cradled the head of a sleeping baby with red hair: Lucy as yet unborn. In the flowering draperies round their feet, among the pretty field flowers (poppies, anemones, daisies and cornflowers) were scattered other baby-heads, all still sleeping in the future. Here were Beena, Joanna, and her children not yet conceived. Immediately behind the main figure stood an aged naked female, her long grey hair straggling to shoulders whose bones protruded and whose skinny arms fell loosely to a sagging belly. Even the skin was colourless. She was entirely grey, this ghost of Grandmama Dambresac; but round her neck a strong green serpent squirmed. Further back was a sombre wood full of menacing symbols, for faintly glimmering skulls hung like decaying fruit on winter branches. Lucy tried not to look at them. She saw only the glorious matrilineal tree of life inside which all the women were wrapped. That's it, she told herself as she began to undress and prepare for bed. It's that great cloak of love which holds us all together still.

A door upstairs slammed. That was Beena. Her habit of

slamming doors irritated Lucy beyond words. Beena . . .
Lucy had unfinished business there, she knew.

Beena had been studying at a Secretarial College in
London while Louise was dying, and afterwards she went
on living in Wimbledon with Patsy who had inherited the
family house near the Common when her parents died.

Beena had been caught up in all that Flower Power of
her times. Lucy conceded that it had been an important
movement. She could see that the young of that era were
trying to overcome by brotherly love an aggression which
since Hiroshima was just too dangerous to be unleashed in
the world. But what Lucy always feared was that Beena
might take too much cannabis and walk out of an upstairs
window thinking she was treading the pathway to heaven.
What Lucy didn't foresee was Beena's pregnancy. She'd
told her about the old-fashioned contraceptives in use at
the time. The Pill, which has given women greater liberation than any number of burned bras, was not then widely
used. Beena was impatient of all restraints anyway, and
when Lucy said: 'Not without a French Letter, Beena!' her
daughter replied, 'Oh Mummy! How old-fashioned you
are! Of course I won't need one!'

And then she had met this hippy twice her age, but
trying to look young and with it, bushy-bearded with his
hair in long sticky strands. He wore a loose, multi-coloured
psychedelic shirt over tight jeans. His name was Jason. He
was full of stronger than brotherly love, and so laid-back
he was oblivious of the responsibilities of fatherhood, and
ignorant or careless about preventing it. They were never
married. When Beena told him she suspected she was pregnant he was seized with an urgent need to study Hindu
mysticism, so off he went to Katmandu, where drugs could
be bought easily and cheaply, and smuggled back home
among his clothes, or tied in little tubes to the thick locks
of his messy hair. Lucy imagined him drifting away on his
flower-strewn path to India where, in a stuporous state, he

33

would doubtless have been fleeced of all his possessions by some Indians, who would have turned the tale around on this modern Jason, and laughed at him into the bargain. Lucy hoped they'd laughed their heads off. What had happened to him she neither knew nor cared. She knew she was being cruel; but she was still angry, even now, because of what he did to Beena. If she'd been on the Pill, Lucy told herself with remorse, it would never have happened.

Beena came home to High House and never again attempted to live an independent life. She regressed to childhood, to her animals and to local church activities. In winter she hunted with the hounds. The Master swore at her in the field in picturesque language on more than one occasion, but as this was quite usual, and even expected, she didn't flinch. In fact she thought it funny. She always came home from hunting flushed with exercise and radiantly happy. In summer she took her Brownies camping. Lucy looked after Joanna during her absences; and when Lucy was working Mrs Colbert took charge of the child.

Abortion had never been considered. There was no necessity for it. Beena wanted the baby; and Lucy was able to provide a home for them both. She did sometimes have misgivings about Joanna's future when she thought about what Joanna might have inherited from her father; but whatever rattling of the genetic dice took place at her conception Joanna was thrown a double-six. Beena's faith in men was broken, and her self-confidence badly shaken; but she made her own sort of life afterwards. She took over the management of High House, the ponies and dogs and, as Lucy grew older, of her as well.

TWO

Sunday Morning

'Thank you, dear,' said Charlotte as Beena carried a breakfast tray into her bedroom before rushing off to church. 'And which service is it today?' Nowadays Beena was ecumenical, and attended whichever service at whatever church or chapel suited her taste or convenience on any particular Sunday.

'Early Mass this morning,' she said. 'Then I can get back in time for the caterers. But they won't give me Communion you know. because I've not been properly received yet.'

'The caterers won't? Mean things! I think they might have included it in their menu!'

'*Charlotte!*' protested Beena. 'Don't be blasphemous! You know perfectly well what I mean.'

'Are you going to be properly received?'

'Perhaps. Perhaps not.'

'I don't like all that turning round in the middle of Mass that Romans do nowadays,' objected Charlotte, 'all that shaking hands with people in the pew behind – being matey with persons you wouldn't speak to in the street.'

'That's the idea you know – being matey.'

'Ugh!' said Charlotte. She took the lid off the coffee pot and sniffed. 'Smells good. You make coffee almost as well

35

as the French do, Beena dear. Ta-ta then! Say a prayer for the old sinner here, won't you?'

In the kitchen Joanna was serving breakfast to the other guests. Dewey, who seemed more awake than any of them, was helping her. He had tied an apron over his jeans and stood at the head of the table pouring tea out of an enormous brown earthenware teapot.

'Come on, Dad!' he said. 'You come too! You want to see this Hetty Pegler's Tump, don't you?'

Joss, who was spreading marmalade on toast, looked up at the boy with distaste. Joss was never at his best so early in the day, but to have to observe this Canadian's adolescent energy at such a time made him feel positively old.

'You go with Joanna,' said Duncan. 'Maybe I shall go to church with Beena. And who's this Hetty Pegler anyway? And what the heck's her tump?'

'Something obscene, if you ask me,' was Joss's comment.

'It's a tomb,' said Dewey. 'Joanna says it's four thousand years old. Isn't that fantastic?'

Joss was wondering how Joanna had managed to stimulate the boy's brain to so much intellectual activity after the apparently paralytic boredom he'd suffered yesterday, when she said: 'It's a bronze-age barrow further north along the Edge. Once we leave Hazelwood Farm and the new housing estate behind us it's a lovely walk with marvellous views all the way.'

'How far is it?' asked Danielle sleepily.

'Three or four miles.'

Joss watched the three girl cousins over his cup of hot tea. He saw them as a trio of modern Graces, all easy on the eye, all with some not-quite-definable family likeness, but all very different. Beside the innocent health of Ellen with her simple monosyllabic speech of 'Hi!' and 'OK!' and 'It's great!' her shining pink cheeks, and her large firm breasts obviously braless under a voluminous blue pullover,

36

Danielle looked very sophisticated. She was wearing a trouser-suit of some sort of rust-red silky material, her bare feet in sandals showed painted toe-nails, and on her wrists jangled a collection of silver bracelets. She was effortlessly seductive, he thought, like Lorelei, the siren of the Rhine when she sang to lure poor sailors on the rocks. But of course she didn't sing. It was Ellen who sang; she was studying singing at a school of music in Montreal. And there stood Joanna by the table above her seated cousins, Joanna splendid, cool, collected and intelligent, with plans for the morning's activities.

'You think we'd better clear out of the house till party-time?' he asked.

'That's the idea,' she admitted.

'And this Hetty Somebody – must we visit her too?' asked Danielle.

Joanna laughed. 'Hetty Pegler's been dead for centuries. Nobody knows who she was. A witch perhaps, who hid herself in the old burial chamber.'

'Gee! That's real creepy!' murmured Dewey, his mouth full and his eyes bright. 'You coming, Ellen?'

'Sure! Me too!'

'If we go soon we can get back in time to smarten up before lunch,' said Joanna; but Joss, glancing at Danielle, decided to spend the morning studying the garden.

'I promised to take some photos for this friend of mine who's writing a book on the gardens of Gloucestershire,' he said. 'And I think the light's right just now.'

'What about you, Danielle?'

'Oh no!' she grumbled. 'I am not very *sportive* today. And I don't wear the right clothes for this long walk. It is too far. I will 'elp your Joss take photos in the garden.'

So it was arranged; and so the party split up for the morning.

Feeling the sun on their backs as it rose higher, the walkers removed pullovers and tied the sleeves round their waists before entering a shady tunnel between hawthorn bushes. They were walking in single file, Dewey a little behind Joanna, and Ellen bringing up the rear. The dog Rufus ran ahead, occasionally stopping to wait, casting patient but slightly contemptuous glances at them.

'Say,' said Dewey, 'how come you have the same name as your Grandma Joanna? Marshall I mean? Did Beena marry a cousin or something?'

Ellen stopped and gasped. A violent blush spread from her face right down to the neckline of her pullover. 'Dewey!' she cried angrily. 'Why can't you mind your own business?'

But Joanna called over her shoulder coolly as she strode on: 'Beena never married, you see. I'm what's called a bastard. I never knew my father. He disappeared before I was born.' She stopped to allow the others to catch up with her. 'I was brought up by Beena and Lucy; and in a funny sort of way Lucy stood in for my father.'

Dewey was speechless, unable to voice his confused feelings; but Ellen said: 'It must have been sad, Joanna.'

'Not really,' said Joanna. 'I never knew anything different, you see. Of course I sometimes wished I had a more ordinary family when I was a kid. Brothers and sisters especially were what I missed.'

'Mind the thorns!' cried Dewey.

They had to push their way out of the overgrown path before emerging onto open land. Feeling she had to defend her mother's image before these cousins Joanna added: 'Beena's great, you know – rather a special person.' Walking steadily they waited to hear more. 'She's always there, you see – always there when you need her. When things are going well she may not seem so important; but when you're in trouble, that's when she comes into her own.'

Although she had outgrown what she regarded as the too-simplistic aspects of Beena's religion Joanna valued her mother beyond simple affection. She recognised her unselfishness, knew she was unworldly and, in spite of the early mishap of becoming a mother without being married, essentially pure in heart. There was reciprocal respect between them. It didn't need stating; it was just there. Joanna knew that her own arrival into Beena's life had rescued her mother. In fact Beena had once said to her: 'You saved me, darling – you and God together. Did you know that? Saved me from drugs and all sorts of disease and wickedness.' Though she was embarrassed by these words at the time Joanna treasured them.

The path along the Edge curved around a steep cliff above a valley into which a scarlet-winged machine suddenly swooped.

'Oh my God!' gasped Ellen, who had been to convent school in Montreal. 'It looks like a falling crucifix!'

The three of them stood perfectly still as the man strapped to the underside of his hang-glider, feet together, arms apart, hovered for a second before mounting on the warm air stream and turning away. Then another with striped blue and white wings hurled himself on to an incoming gust, and floated.

'Gee!' sighed Dewey. 'Wish I could do that!'

'It's rather a dangerous sport,' warned Joanna; but she was as thrilled as her young cousins to watch it.

'And they don't have any engines?' Dewey was incredulous.

'It's just gliding in the wind,' said Joanna. 'Like birds.' She was watching Dewey's rapt expression. Yes. he would do it: fling himself off the cliff simply for the thrill of it, to feel that elation of power that came with the physical mastery of his body over the air and the pull of gravity, whereas she would be cautious; she would think first and probably never do it. That was one of the essential differences between male and female, she thought. It wasn't only the stronger arm and fleeter foot, but that little element of recklessness, of the willingness to take risks which must reside in some tiny area of the Y chromosome, and which had to be what made young men drive racing cars, pilot tornado bombers, conquer peaks in the Himalayas. And was it what might make them criminals as well? In prehistoric times it made them hunters and killers to gain essential food and territory for the tribe; but now in big cities where there were no wild animals, what had once been an envied prowess might even become an antisocial nuisance. But she had to admit she envied Dewey, because she had a suspicion it was the same characteristic that helped to make a good surgeon: the skill to decide in a flash when and where to take the necessary risk, that held his hand so absolutely steady with the knife. She knew she could never be a surgeon; she just didn't have what it took. Of course what I do have, she told herself, are other gifts, more female medical skills than this boy could never possess. Women have another sort of courage. How different we are! she thought, and then: How different Joss and I are! But she remembered the delight they'd both enjoyed last night in her attic bed at the top of High House. The act of love was the miracle – no doubt about it – which dissolved all differences between them, which made them feel one in that wonderful flood of understanding of each other it brought to them both. The phallus was the metaphysical as well as the actual bridge between the sexes.

'No, I could never do that.' Joanna broke the silence. 'I just haven't got the nerve. I wish I had. You need that sort of nerve to do all those things people have to do in earthquakes or in wars, rushing in among crashed buildings or under gunfire, to rescue the injured.'

'You're thinking of *Médicins sans Frontières*?' asked Ellen. 'I know a boy in Quebec who worked for that.'

'That's what I'd like to do,' said Joanna. 'Only wish I could . . .'

Dewey looked at her with an expression of adoration.

He believed she could do anything. She seemed to him some sort of superwoman who made no attempt to push her superiority down your throat; she simply was what she was: a goddess. Rufus sat up, panting a little, his tongue hanging out in the attempt to cool himself, patiently waiting while the humans talked above his head, but anxious to pursue his interesting trail of smells, familiar to him from running this way many times before with Joanna and her mother and grandmother.

'We'd better move on,' said Joanna, 'if we're going to reach Hetty Pegler on time.'

The burial chamber was a disappointment to Dewey because they could not go inside. An iron railing and a small padlocked gate guarded it from intruders. All they could do was lean on the gate and peer into the dark entrance.

'I suppose vandals would make a mess of it if they could get inside,' said Joanna. 'It used to be open when I was little. But very dark and rather smelly.'

So she led them away from the place once inhabited by a witch and back to High House.

Joss and Danielle were strolling down the lower slopes of the garden. Its south-westerly edge was protected from the prevailing wind by a semi-circular plantation of ash, chestnut and sycamore, big trees sheltering the banks of rhododendron beneath. Some of these planted in the Thirties had grown into trees with thick rust-red trunks, but as they were not in flower and had only their coloured bark to tempt the camera Joss moved his attention to the other side of the copse, where a group of Japanese maples stood blazing in the last flamboyant energy of autumn.

'I think that's the sort of thing they want,' he said. 'Frithby's, that's the people I work for, have commissioned a landscape gardener to write a book on Gloucestershire gardens, and they want me to winkle out some of the most photogenic.'

Danielle reached the holm oaks arching above the statue. The stone figure stood in a semi-crouched position on her plinth, peering through the branches as if lost. She held a fold of moss-eroded stone drapery across her thighs. Her long stone tresses hid her breasts, and ivy was beginning to creep over her feet.

'Marvellous, isn't she?' murmured Joss, as he moved round her trying to find the best angle for his photograph. 'I must get the light on that ivy! A bit macabre, but so absolutely mid-Victorian!'

The garden here was neglected, brambles encroaching on paths, and ivy everywhere; but to Joss it was all the more romantic for being overgrown. 'How the Victorians loved to keep things covered up!' he said. 'I think they were excited by hidden things. We all are really. Don't we all love secrets?' Danielle's answer was also secret, for she gave none. 'I sometimes wonder, you know, if our frankness about sex hasn't destroyed a lot of its mystery.'

'You think so?' Danielle ran down towards a gate which separated the garden from fields sloping steeply away, where sheep were feeding in the October sunshine under a cloudless dome of pale clear blue.

'It is like your English hymn,' she said as Joss joined her. 'That song about your English green and pleasant land.' He put his arm round her, and together they stared at the quiet scene. When she turned to look at him he stooped and kissed her on the mouth. She was not reluctant; she responded eagerly, and rather to his own surprise he found himself seized by powerful erotic feeling. He knew he'd have to be careful if this thing with the French girl was going to develop. He had succeeded with bilateral love affairs before; but it was risky with a girl like Joanna who had sharp eyes. What Danielle was like he really didn't know yet. She of course already knew of his attachment to Joanna. Either she didn't care much about female loyalties, or she was a girl who put her physical desires first. Or was she one of those girls who liked snatching men from under the noses of other women as part of a power game? We are all multi-faceted beings, he thought. Joanna reflects many of my facets, but not all; Danielle responds to a vital few. He believed he could safely run two affairs at once. It was a tempting prospect; and it excited him. Each girl would add zest to his desire for the other. But what he did not want was a *ménage à trois*. He didn't want any sort of *ménage*. In his innermost sanctum, which was his tastefully decorated London flat, he liked to live alone. Women tended to disrupt his chosen patterns, to bring with them cosy conveniences or practical improvements that invariably spoiled the design. No. He didn't want any invasion of his privacy, so he must not let any of it get out of hand.

As they walked back to the house she asked: 'Will you come to see me in Paris?'

'As a matter of fact I have to go over there in a fortnight to value some paintings for a very rich client.'

'Why – that is marvellous!' she exclaimed. 'You must visit Maman. And I will be your guide. I know Paris like the back of my hand!'

It was all suddenly unexpectedly easy; and such a very satisfactory culmination to the morning's work!

In her den Lucy was making her own brew of Piccadilly Jackson's breakfast tea, strong enough to wake her up. She could hear Beena's car starting up outside, and guessed Beena was off to church. She idly wondered which service it would be today. She heard the door of the Metro slam. It was a heavy metallic noise, rather like a train door being shut. Lucy closed her eyes and listened to the distant rhythmic hum in her head of a train moving, carrying her back to thirty, forty, fifty years ago. Tickety-tack, tickety-tack . . .

Of course she always knew it was the real thing, the once-in-a-lifetime sort of love even then! It was the intensity of each and every day that made it so different from ordinary living. It wasn't only her feelings that were violent, it was the speed: time racing past, everything round you changing, literally collapsing, familiar faces disappearing and the whole world as you knew it threatening to go up in smoke. All her youth was lived through in that one summer, the summer of the Spitfires. Whenever she thought of it she remembered love, laughter and fear – in that order.

She and Nicky had had so little time together they did it anywhere whenever the opportunity offered. She remembered that time in the train . . . And how terrified she was that somebody would enter the compartment – perhaps the ticket-collector! She needn't have worried. Ticket-collectors had all been called up into the army or the Home Guard according to age and fitness.

Nicky was on duty for days at a time. Then suddenly he would have twenty-four hours Release, and if at all possible she would get out of the lab to meet him. The lab had a glass roof, and the two technicians were scared of flying glass during an air raid. She didn't worry about glass at all. Compared with the risks RAF pilots were taking all day and every day hers were negligible; and anyway she was leading – they were both leading – a charmed life; protected by the armour of love. All she worried about was working through all those blood counts (red cells normal, or mis-shapen, white cells normal or abnormal, haemoglobin estimations, blood sugars and blood ureas in their regiments of glass tubes, all those little round glass boxes filled with blood-swamped agar to feed their bacteria) in time to meet him. *Oh my darling put your arms around me and I shall be safe*. Sometimes they spent his Release in the flat on the top floor of the old Workhouse to which the hospital was evacuated from London.

The medical superintendent in charge of the Workhouse

hospital had cleared some of his wards for London patients; his own were crammed together into a smaller space 'for the duration'. The new young doctors sometimes gave him a hand with his cases: mostly old and dying, some with such advanced and horrible disease that even Lucy and her friend Brigid, hardened as they were by six years of medical training, averted their eyes, and perhaps their care as well. Lucy remembered a woman there who had secondary cancer deposits in bone. A lump was growing behind one eye, pushing it out of its socket and giving her the appearance of a cyclops, so insignificant was the other eye in comparison. The ward sister, a compassionate soul, had ordered the nurses to brush the patient's hair for her and never allow her to see herself in a mirror; but one day while Lucy was checking her record and signing for her prescriptions she took from her bedside locker a handbag, and from that a small mirror and her lipstick, and began to touch up her lips. Lucy stood transfixed, watching her. When she finished she smiled up at her doctor, 'Must do our bit to keep going, mustn't we?' she asked; and Lucy replied immediately, a sort of automation taking over: 'You do it very well, too!' She found her hands were shaking. She never knew whether that woman was showing supreme courage at a time in history when so many ordinary unknown people did so, or whether the growth was already invading her brain and destroying her critical faculties, so protecting her, as disease sometimes does, from the anguish of seeing herself as others saw her.

Brigid, who was house surgeon to Lucy's pathologist, shared the flat above the wards. When she knew Nicky was coming she used to move out into a cubbyhole with a camp-bed on the floor below; and Lucy did the same when Brigid's boyfriend arrived. They had to hide their men from the senior staff, all serious-minded women in that all-women's hospital, who in their own youth had sacrificed sex and marriage in their struggle to climb up the medical

45

ladder, almost exclusively male-dominated as it was in those days. They frowned on any flirtation with men as frivolous, and marriage was treachery to the Cause. If you became pregnant you were a hopeless case. Nowadays it's called Wastage.

It was easier for Brigid because she was in love with a young American surgical registrar, whose hospital had been moved out to Surrey on the other side of London. They both had regular duty rotas, and so were able to arrange their meetings, chiefly in his digs. But Nicky never knew when he'd get time off. He didn't mind being smuggled into the flat; he enjoyed the secrecy in the way children enjoy hidden parcels at Christmas. Anyway he usually fell asleep in Lucy's bed till she finished work. Those chaps were exhausted half the time. One pilot of his Flight, when he sat down to a meal after his third sortie of the day, promptly fell asleep at the table. His face actually hit the plate of eggs and bacon. Nicky always slept like the dead after making love; but Lucy sometimes woke in the early hours with a start hearing the call 'Scramble!' ringing through her dreams. It was then that she trembled with fear. It was the signal for each pilot sitting around on Readiness to drop his newspaper or playing cards and run across the airfield to his Spitfire (its engine already ticking over), jump in, adjust his goggles and parachute straps, pull out the throttle, and take off. Airborne in two minutes. It was nearly always the real thing. Radar installations along the south-east coast were so good at intercepting signals from enemy metal massing over in France that there were not many false alarms. Nicky was in radio contact with Operations Control on the ground all the time he was rising. He'd be talking the Group jargon: 'Vectoring 3 000. Angels 20 000', while trying to get into a good position high above the enemy and with the sun behind him. Then as he sighted them: 'Christ! Whole bloody hordes of them!' before he dived down into the centre of the German formation. As he descended the Heinkels would peel outwards one after another to avoid him; and the other Spitfires on his flight would pick them off one by one, each shouting 'Tally-ho!' as he cut radio contact and went into the attack. It was not the joyous cry of pink-coated huntsmen chasing an outnumbered little fox over fields and furrows on a bright autumn morning with no worse hazard than a hawthorn hedge to jump or a mud-filled ditch to fall into. It was the signal that a fight to the death had begun. They were all not only huntsmen but also little foxes, seeing death behind if they got ahead of the bomber's guns, and death above, below, and all round them from the Messerschmidts.

After a few minutes Lucy was able to shake off the nightmare and return to reality. It was still dark, and Nicky was not then flying at night. He was safe in her bed. It was mid-August, the time of the daylight raids, when Goering tried to smash Fighter Command's defensive ring round Britain prior to the invasion. He reckoned he could do it in four days if he made the attacks heavy and continuous. The Attack of the Eagles he called it. Those big birds came over every few hours of daylight, in great swarms of Dorniers and Heinkels escorted by their protective Messerschmidts, which far outnumbered our Spitfires and Hurricanes.

'Four to one,' Nicky told her. 'We've got to knock out four of them for every one of ours if we're to hold back the invasion.'

People delivering milk in towns and people working in the fields of Kent, and sometimes people coming out of shops would look up when they heard distant gunfire, and would watch those dogfights, see trails of white vapour criss-crossing the sky, would watch the planes wheel, somersault and dive, and hold their breath when at last one fell spiralling out of smoke and sometimes flames. They would pray it wasn't one of ours, and mutter 'Bloody

Huns!' as they resumed work with spade or milk bottle or shopping basket.

In the middle of August she realised she was pregnant. August 14th was the day the papers reported that 500 enemy planes attacked our shipping in the Channel and Thames Estuary, strafed our airfields and airbases and anything that looked like an aircraft repair or maintenance factory.

'We'd better make it legal,' Nicky said. 'The poor little blighter will probably be fatherless; we don't want him to grow up a bastard as well.'

'Don't!' she begged. 'Don't!'

'You've got to face it Lucy, honey. I might be blasted into eternity tomorrow. How soon can you get a special licence?'

She didn't see him at all for a week, nor did she hear a word from him. She had no idea whether he was alive or dead. All she knew was what she read in the papers: 100 German planes knocked out for 30 of ours, 170 Huns for 25 of ours, and so on. Even then she used to wonder if they were exaggerating. Nicky was scrambled four times every day during that terrible time. Then suddenly he was beside her, his face paler, more haggard, but he was alive, whole and uninjured, not burned, which was what everybody connected with the whole business dreaded most. 'Oh my darling, Nicky!' Tears streamed down her cheeks.

'Don't cry, Lucy. We're going to be married. It's a joyful occasion isn't it?' To live for the day, for the moment, was the only way to survive those times.

'I Nicholas Marshall do take thee Lucy Brunoye to be my wedded wife to love and to cherish till death do us part.' Only it wasn't quite like that because they were not married in a church but in a grubby Registry Office, which had been badly shaken by bomb-blast the week before, and would probably have benefited from a direct hit. Its windows were broken and its walls flaking paint of a faecal colour, though with not such a bad smell. The language used by the Registrar was humdrum and banal. He was a little black beetle of a man, crouching his shiny, black-coated shoulders over his desk, and fussing over papers in between scribbling and peering at them through thick spectacles. They had two witnesses: Nicky's friend Alan, who was his Number Two in Flight, and Lucy's friend Brigid. When they'd all signed their names in the proper places they stood up straight and smiled. The black beetle smiled too and took off his glasses to polish them. He looked naked somehow without them. Brigid threw a handful of confetti over them as they emerged into the sunlit street. Strangers stopped to stare and smile, and two of them shook hands and wished them luck. They were bathed in kindness like sunshine. It wasn't only their youth and marriage which brought out the smiles; it was the RAF uniform and Nicky's Squadron Leader's stripes on his cuffs, and of course the Pilot's Wings he wore over his left breast pocket. People knew even then what they owed him.

Afterwards at the Anvil, where they celebrated, he raised his glass. 'To Mrs Marshall!' He meant Lucy! She couldn't help laughing. It seemed so strange to have acquired this new name. 'To Mrs Marshall who looks stunning in her mother's silver foxes!' It was true about the furs. Lucy's telegram gave Louise no time to arrange transport from Frenester and a visit to London for the wedding; but she sent her furs with a friend who was travelling up by train and who delivered them the day before. Lucy wore them slung over an emerald green linen suit. Luckily the day was not too hot. Over her red hair she wore a black velvet pill-box hat at a rakish angle, with what used to be called an eye-veil. Louise never saw her furs again. They disap-peared, burned to ashes by an incendiary bomb dropped a fortnight later on the house to which they had been returned. Her friend was fortunate to escape with a frac-tured collar-bone. They were beautiful furs; they would have made any woman look glamorous. In later years whenever some button in memory was pressed accidentally and threw up on the screen of her mind the picture of those furs she thought of their destruction as providential. You couldn't in the face of Animal Rights protestors, wear them easily today, could you? But on the day she was married she carried them proudly.

The radio in the pub was playing a popular French tune of the times. '*J'attendrai* . . .' I shall wait for you day and night. I shall wait forever. I shall wait . . . It was a haunting tune full of the sadness of separation and longing of all lovers in wartime.

'You'd better keep it dark at the hospital,' warned Brigid. 'The old Battleaxes wouldn't like it at all. There'll be no promotion for married women when it comes to a choice of candidate.'

Nicky was delighted to be able to continue the plotting and the secrecy. 'It's so wonderfully wicked to be married!' he declared.

Lucy grinned at him over the glass of bubbly. Yes, they drank champagne, thanks to Louise's cheque, which arrived with the furs. 'It'll be funny, won't it,' Lucy laughed, 'when *you're* promoted!'

'What do you mean – funny? It'll be bloody serious. I might be moved to another part of England.'

'I mean, when you're Air Vice-Marshal Marshall.'

'I shan't live long enough to reach those heights! Here today gone tomorrow is more likely.' Positively jaunty. It was all part of the ethos: live for the day and don't care a bugger for the morrow; but her stomach used to give a nasty squeeze when he talked like that. 'I'll never be an Air Marshal, but meanwhile I'd like a bit of the Vice!'

They had booked into a London hotel for the night, paid for by Louise's cheque: 'Don't stint yourselves, darling. Enjoy a little luxury for once.' The room was quiet, although the bed creaked a bit; and they had a bathroom attached. That was a great luxury in those days. They weren't afraid of the bombing; the first real night attacks on London were still a fortnight away. When they undressed he took all the pins out of the coil she wore on the back of her neck and let her hair fall down over her shoulders.

'Such a wonderful dark red,' he said. 'And hiding those lovelies underneath.' He pushed her hair away from her breasts before he kissed them. 'It's rather like that fine seaweed floating in a calm sea.' He kept lifting strands of hair as if to make sure it was real. 'And you're the little mermaid. No other in the swimming. You're my one and only. I'm glad you haven't got a tail though, instead of legs. I wouldn't know what to look for if you had a tail.'

'It's called a cloaca in fishes,' she said.

'Well that's not what I call it.'

'Fishes are not really intimate.'

'No. I didn't think they were. But to be serious – we'll have to be a bit careful, won't we? We don't want to wake the little fellow up.'

It never occurred to Lucy that she might miscarry. She thought, then, that it might be the best thing to happen, for she couldn't see how she was going to work with an infant on her back; but Nicky wanted this baby. She could see that. She supposed it was his stake in the future, a certain frail hold on immortality.

It was the week after they were married that the Battle of Britain reached its fiercest. During that week the Luftwaffe made a last push to break Fighter Command's defences, which they knew were so badly weakened they thought it impossible for the British to hold out any longer. Our Fighters had learned by experience that a few highly manoeuvrable Spitfires and Hurricanes, although outnumbered, could inflict great damage by diving down very fast through the centre of an enemy formation, firing in all directions. They couldn't stop the bombers, nor stop them dropping bombs; but they killed a few pilots and destroyed a few planes each time. It was this relentless erosion of the Luftwaffe's men and machines that was holding back Hitler's threatened invasion. Our own losses were crippling. Nicky's squadron was reduced to six usable planes that week; they had lost seventeen out of their twenty-four pilots and had to borrow officers from Bomber Command and the Navy to keep going. These were all experienced flyers; but the new young recruits, who were rushed in to fill the gaps, had only done a few hours flying training. They were boys of eighteen or nineteen who saw themselves on a Hollywood set swaggering across the runways to their cockpits. To them it was all beer, women and the thrills of high-speed zooming up into a blue sky to shoot down the enemy while Nazi bullets whizzed harmlessly past. They didn't understand a thing till they came face to face with the rear-gunner of a Dornier taking aim. If they came out of that fix by turning away in time, ducking and falling, and letting off smoke to pretend they'd been hit, they learned to be fighter-pilots instead of film-clip heroes. But many of them didn't come down alive from their first sorties. The loss of young lives was terrible. That really was Wastage. Lucy didn't know any of this at the time. All she knew was that she hadn't seen Nicky, had no news of him, not even a phone call since they'd been married. Then one day a strange voice called her up at the hospital. 'I'm Bill,' it said, 'Is that Mrs Marshall? I'm going to call you up every day or two to give you news. He's safe and well. Needing sleep but OK.'

'Oh! Thank God! And thank you for phoning. And by the way you mustn't call me Mrs Marshall. I'm not supposed to be married. I'm Dr Brunoye here. How did you get through to me?'

'I asked for the Pathology doctor. Top Secret, is it? It's secret for your hubby too. They don't like them being married. Gives them the jitters, marriage does.' He laughed. 'But your old man's OK. No jitters either.'

'Thanks!' She gasped and giggled. 'Who are you by the way?'

But he rang off.

She learned later that he was a mechanic who visited that station daily to deliver spare parts and remove damaged bits, which the RAF fitters, though working more or less without a break to get the planes airborne again, couldn't mend on the spot. He worked in a depot removed from the airfield; and from time to time he was able to use an intact telephone line. The RAF ground crews, fitters, riggers, armourers who pulled out spent ammunition and replaced it with new, and the Bowser-tanker drivers who refuelled the engines, went on working right through air-raids. The Bowser crews were arguably the most courageous of all. They were driving high-octane petrol tankers which, if hit, would explode, sending their drivers instantaneously to kingdom come; those handling the stuff, doing the refuelling, wore petrol-soaked overalls which would, if a stray spark landed on them, turn them into living torches. Even their skins were impregnated with the greenish fuel, so that when they sweated their faces dripped green drops.

That week the raids were unremitting all day long, until it was too dark for the Germans to see their targets.

'It was the ground crews who kept us flying,' Nicky told her.

Bill phoned her daily for several days. It was always the same message. 'He's OK. Alive and kicking. All parts intact and functioning.' At last one evening he added: 'You'll be seeing him tomorrow. Hopefully wool-gathering.' That was their private word for Shepherds in Shepherd Market behind Piccadilly Circus. That pub was always filled with fighter pilots on Release from all over the south-east. They were on call there, connected by a telephone which rested on the seat of an antique sedan-chair in the corner of the bar. The floor was a chequer-board of black and white squares on which they played draughts with pints of beer

53

as pawns. In between drinking, playing draughts and telling jokes they exchanged news, and discussed the tactics they'd had to learn by trial and error during the battle.

That evening Nicky looked ill when she met him in Shepherds. He obviously hadn't slept for days. The alcohol he drank didn't make him happy as it usually did; it made him look wild. He cracked a joke but didn't smile. His eyes darted around the room continually, and when the phone rang he jumped.

'I don't see how we can go on much longer,' he said when Lucy got him back to her hospital bed. 'Till yesterday Jerry kept coming over, swooping low over us, bombing and machine-gunning so that we had to run for trenches. The place is in a shambles, the runways botched up with craters and full of unexploded bombs. There's a girl, a WAAF, who clambers out of a trench whenever the Huns disappear, and rushes out to stick flags on craters and unexploded bombs, so that aircraft landing can weave a way in safety. She's a heroine really. Airmen are defusing bombs as fast as they can. They're paid threepence a day extra for it.' He laughed. 'Then suddenly yesterday – nothing. All quiet. It's a bit uncanny. We're all wondering what they're up to. Perhaps it's the invasion now.'

She cradled his head on her breasts. It was a relief for him to talk.

'God! Am I glad of this day of rest! I needed it. I have a feeling my lucky streak has petered out.'

'I don't believe it,' she declared. 'You always said it was the young recruits who copped it, and the old experienced pilots who survived.' Nicky old? He was twenty-four. That was considered old for fighter-pilots. Age made them too cautious, while the extreme youth and lack of experience of the new trainees made them risk too much. Twenty-one was reckoned the perfect age.

'Everybody's getting shot down now,' he said. 'There's this character called Bruce. He's an Ace who's bagged at least a dozen Huns. A few days ago he was in a dog-fight when he must have got a bit too close to the plane he was firing at. It was going up in smoke and flames, and the pilot was bailing out. Before he knew what was happening this Hun landed on Bruce's airscrew and got sucked in. Of course his engine stalled and he had to fall and glide his way down as best he could. Luckily he wasn't too far off base, and being a very skilled type was able to crash-land in a field. The German was plastered all over the Spitfire: bits of flesh and pieces of his uniform stuck inside and outside of it. The fire-service had to hose it down. Miraculously Bruce got away with no more damage than a sprained ankle; but he looked like a ghost when he reached the station. He was given a swig of brandy and the usual hot tea; but he couldn't lift the cup without spilling it – his hands were shaking so much. Immediate sick leave for him. He'll be posted. Fact is his nerve's broken.'

'I'm not surprised,' she said.

'And he's an Ace!' He paused to kiss her and then threw himself back on the pillow and took a deep breath. 'You can cope with it if you think of it as some sort of dangerous sport. You can zoom up there into the sky and play this deadly game knowing it's either you or him; but you can't think of him as human. If you did you couldn't handle it. This thing that's happened to Bruce has shaken us all. It's brought it home to us that – God help us! – the Hun is horribly human just like us.' He laughed again, inappropriately Lucy thought, but it was because his mind was racing ahead of his speech. 'There's always a funny side.'

'Tell me, tell me,' she urged. She wanted to share the joke, to make laughter push back the horror, to build a dyke in her mind against the floods of fear.

'There's this Polish character who was shot down in flames. When he bailed out one of his boots was jammed in the cockpit, and he had to jump without it.' He parachuted smoothly down and landed literally in a bed of roses in a suburban garden. The irate rose-grower, who met him shouting: 'Do you know this is private property, sir?' must have noticed the state of the pilot's trousers and perhaps his parachute, because he ended: 'Come in and have a cup of tea.' The poor young Pole didn't dare speak for fear of being mistaken for a German and summarily hit on the head; but when he was sipping his tea he explained: 'I am Polish.' The woman of the house patted him sympathetically on his shoulder, whether because she felt sorry for his crash or because he had the misfortune of not being born British, who knows? As he was rather a stickler for formal dress he was dreadfully embarrassed by his missing boot, especially as there was a hole in the toe of his sock. 'Excuse, please!' he said, pointing to his toe. His host immediately went upstairs to fetch a pair of knee-length golf socks. They were knitted in large coloured diamonds, the sort that were made fashionable in the Twenties by Edward VIII, when Prince of Wales, with those baggy knicker-bockers known as plus-fours. The Pole was a small man with small feet, and his host's shoes were too big for him; but the wife offered him a pair of her slippers. They were bright blue.

'And that was what he was wearing when he got back to base. The poor chap was more upset by the cheers and jeers that greeted his jazzy garb than by being shot down!' They both laughed; and then he relaxed. The pinched look of battle fatigue began to melt away from his face as he fell asleep in her arms.

She was still awake when her phone rang. Nicky leaped out of bed before he woke. He thought it was the call to Scramble; but it was for Lucy. A male patient had been admitted with a ruptured stomach ulcer, and they were going to operate. He needed a blood transfusion, and she was needed to give him that. Nicky was fast asleep when she got back a couple of hours later. They didn't make love that time till the early hours of the morning.

'How could I help loving him?' Lucy asked herself as she sipped her Jackson's breakfast tea. He was one of the Few to whom so many owed so much, lent to her temporarily by history.

The real bombing of London began on 7 September. 'Sorry, Londoners!' said one of the pilots in Nicky's squadron. 'But they're giving us a breathing space, and time to tidy up the runways.' Lucy could hear the distant drone of bombers going over. Pretty continuous it was. She and Brigid went round wards saying: 'It's not for us this time! It's London that's getting it.' It was impossible to move all those terminally ill patients into shelters anyway. 'There are no military targets around here. We're not attractive to Germans.' One or two of them laughed. They were amazingly brave; perhaps they no longer cared much for life. The London Docks were the first target. A massive load of incendiary bombs lit such a big bonfire that its glow could be seen, when night fell, for twenty miles around. Brigid and Lucy stood at their bedroom window and stared at the colours of it for quite a while. Then they pulled their beds close together for comfort and lay awake in the dark, listening. It was too far away to hear gunfire, but now and again they heard a thump. It was a clear warm evening, and the window was open behind the blackout blind.

'Nicky thinks it may be the invasion now,' Lucy said.

Brigid was smoking an American cigarette. She liked smoking in bed. Lucy didn't object; in those days everybody smoked. The only reason Lucy didn't was because the smoke made her eyes water, and her tears made the mascara on her eyelashes run in black streaks down her face.

'Andy says Britain is not an island any more,' Brigid reported. 'It's a sinking ship.'

Lucy made no comment. She had had such thoughts herself, especially during the Blitzkrieg earlier that summer when Hitler's panzer tanks, outflanking the Maginot line and the waiting French and British armies, had cut through Belgium and Holland like the proverbial hot knife through butter, scattering all resistance before them. But the escape of the British Expeditionary Force from Dunkirk, which seemed like a miracle at the time, had given her hope.

'He thinks the French, being more intelligent than us, saw the writing on the wall and read it pretty quickly. They realised it was futile getting killed for nothing.' She puffed strongly, inhaled and blew out a stream of smoke. 'Bloody Frogs! He thinks the British will fight to the end, but that won't stop us sinking.' Lucy was feeling sick and thought it must be due to pregnancy. They lay on their backs staring at the dark ceiling across which a lighter shade of darkness spread whenever the blackout blind lifted a little in a draught. Streetlights had not shone for a year, but there was moonlight.

'Andy's going back to the States,' she announced suddenly. 'End of the month. Leaving hospital. Leaving me too.' She was quite calm.

Lucy leaned across and squeezed her arm.

'I'm sorry,' she said. 'So very, very sorry.'

'So am I.' Brigid turned away and stubbed out her cigarette rather noisily in the ashtray that was always beside her bed.

'Supposing they get over here – the Huns –' Lucy suggested.

'Life will be very different.'

'But whatever kind of life – however ghastly – we do have a trade, you and I, don't we?'

'We shall certainly be needed, if that's what you mean.'

'We can always work,' they told each other. 'In a caravan if need be – or a garden shed.'

It was then they decided to go to London as soon as possible, to that shop in Charing Cross Road where they'd bought their student stethoscopes, and buy all they needed to equip a basic surgery: scalpels, needles in various sizes for various purposes, catgut and horsehair for stitching (nylon had not been invented), bandages, splints, midwifery forceps, and syringes in metal containers (disposables belonged to the future). They already possessed instruments for examining eyes, ears and blood pressures. A few essential drugs they could get from the hospital pharmacy. They never used all this, of course. Things turned out differently.

When her term as a pathologist ended Lucy did not apply for another resident job. Brigid was the only one at the hospital who knew of Lucy's pregnancy but Lucy knew she couldn't hide it much longer. Since she was fairly tall it didn't show much at twenty weeks. She wore loose clothes, and of course the hide-all overall in the wards. Luckily she hadn't suffered from vomiting, though she felt sick all the time. Nicky had been posted north to learn to fly Beaufighters, the new radar-equipped night-fighter planes coming into use. They decided the best thing for her was to go back to Mother, at least till the baby was born. So there she was back in her childhood home, Christmas 1940, and very cold; but there was plenty of wood from copses and hedges to keep a fire burning in the snuggery Louise made in Herbert's old dressing room. Here was Louise's own comfortable living space. It was here they retired in the evenings to listen to ITMA – It's That Man Again, the radio comic who kept everybody laughing after they'd settled down to the long-drawn-out resistance to bombing and the enduring of small privations which followed the Battle of Britain.

Louise was still in her fifties and very fit; she was doing all the gardening, sawing up wood and stacking it for fuel, and a good deal of the cooking and cleaning as well. An old woman cycled up the hill from Frenester once a week to do the washing and what used to be called 'rough' work: mostly scrubbing the kitchen floor on her hands and knees.

Lucy remembered a certain evening because it was then, after the ITMA programme, that Louise gave her the little silver cigarette case enamelled with a blue butterfly which, she said, belonged to a girl called Rose, a pretty Irish-American dancer who taught Lucy to dance the Charleston to the music of a squeaky gramophone in her cabin on the ship which carried them to Calcutta after the First World War. Lucy didn't remember much about her. It was all too long ago. She must have been about six years old at the time. And then, as she held the little silver box in her hand and looked at the blue butterfly on its lid she suddenly recalled the image of a shambling old man with no sense of timing trying to do the Charleston. She used to laugh at him, and so did Rose. Rose called the Charleston – Lucy remembered in a flash – 'shakin' out da feet': something he was utterly unable to do!

'Oh yes!' Lucy laughed. 'I can remember Groggy-legs!'

'That made us laugh too,' said Louise, 'because he was known to be a heavy drinker. His real name was Greg. You were only little. The captain became quite fond of you because you said such funny things, mostly at meal times in the dining saloon. The cigarette case belonged to Rose; but she must have given it to Greg. He wanted you to have it.'

'Why me?'

'He was fond of you. They all were. Perhaps there weren't many children on board that trip. He used to call you Miss Twenties. He used to say the future belonged to you. And anyway you were quite a charmer as a child.' She smiled at Lucy; and then looked away quickly. 'Don't you remember going into Rose's cabin, and finding all the blood and broken glass everywhere?'

'No. I don't.' Then Lucy suddenly remembered a string of green beads on a girl's neck, and a trumpet-like horn attached to a gramophone in the cabin. 'Why? What happened?'

'Oh, I think she cut her finger on a broken glass jug or something. But you were rather frightened at the time.' Louise was gazing out of the window as she spoke.

Lucy examined the cigarette case. It was beautifully made, delicately enamelled, really an exquisite thing. She opened the lid with the edge of her thumbnail and saw inside another little circular lid, over a tiny well in which to collect the ash. Rose must have been a tidy smoker, not like Charlotte, who scattered ash all over the place.

Louise said no more about it then; but twenty years later, in this same room which Lucy now called her private den, Louise told her the rest of the story. Lucy often wondered why she did. But she didn't tell her on that day. Something must have interrupted the flow of her confiding; and Lucy never asked about that secret of hers. She was soon too caught up by the events of her own life to be interested in anyone else's past.

That Christmas before Beena was born, although so long ago, still felt like yesterday. They were hoping that Nicky might be able to get leave and join them, travelling down all the way from Northumberland in his old banger. Semi-derelict cars were all that those heroes could afford on the pay they got; but Nicky was a good mechanic and could make an old engine work if anyone could. As it turned out his leave was postponed, so Lucy kept the Christmas cake she'd made for him till the New Year: Lord Woolton's War-time Christmas cake. You used strong cold tea to darken it, and a mixture of dried egg and bicarbonate of soda to make it rise. There was a ration of sugar and a bit of dried fruit in it too. It was a surprisingly edible cake; but Nicky didn't eat it.

He phoned early on New Year's Eve to say he'd arrive late that afternoon. After dark . . . and in imagination, as she listened to his voice still so far away from her, Lucy saw the car's headlamps heavily shaded because of blackout restrictions. Late tea, he said. So she and Louise prepared a festive table in their snuggery, with scarlet ribbons on a white cloth, a few red apples, and sprigs of holly bright with berries from the garden, and Lucy's iced Christmas cake in the middle, and they waited. Tea became later and later as they waited for him. Louise went to bed just after midnight; but Lucy sat up huddled over the dying fire. It was two o'clock on the first day of the New Year when the phone rang in the hall and Lucy hurtled down the stairs to lift the receiver. A soft voice spoke from a hospital somewhere in the Midlands, hushed because it belonged to a night sister on duty with grave news to impart. Lucy found it difficult to understand what was said and what she refused to believe: road accident . . . fractured skull . . . head injuries . . . dead on arrival in casualty. Nothing they could do. *Nicky was dead. Dead.*

It was ironic, wasn't it, that Lucky Marshall, as he was known by the rest of his squadron because he'd won so many contests of speed and daring in the air, should die in a car crash. Driving south to join Lucy he drove too fast round a corner, and the tyres, worn too smooth, which he couldn't afford to replace, didn't hold the road. He who had so often looped the loop and dived over the Channel to get out of a Messerschmidt's firing line skidded and turned over, killing himself against the trunk of a tree. There was a short paragraph in *The Times*, Lucy received a war widow's pension and was presented with his medals; but a pension does not compensate for a life taken, nor medals for the loss of love. She was desolate, desolate.

In her mother's house she was surrounded by familiar things: Louise's hovering hands, her father's books, the tactful silences of friends, and a place of her own to hide in; but everything seemed foreign to her because it bore no relation to her inner world, which was uniformly grey and meaningless. She was an alien in her own country.

Even her dreams were colourless apart from the images of Nicky crumpled upside down in a car, his air-force blue jacket streaked with bright red blood. She thought she had lost everything. *My darling Nicky, light of my eyes and breath of my body, why wasn't I with you in that wrecked car?*

Louise was worried about the baby she carried. She thought Lucy's sadness would shadow the child through life; she believed it should be exposed to beautiful, joyful things even *in utero*, and that Lucy, by visual green grazing could achieve a certain bovine peace. So she made her walk with her every evening in her garden. By April her camellias were blooming, and even Lucy in the colour-blindness of her mourning was forced to recognise their beauty. Gradually her female body and hormones, which cared nothing for her, but were all concentrated on the nurture and transit of this new life she carried, did work a healing process in her. She began to notice the bright stars of blackthorn and the first primroses. She began to think about Nicky's baby: a boy whom she would call after him. She never really thought about a girl till she was born.

It was rather a long labour of eighteen hours. She was left to get on with it in the Frenester Cottage Hospital. She walked about the room, and in between the pains she stared out of the window into the car park below to watch the comings and goings. She drank tea and orange juice and exchanged desultory conversation with the midwife, who had, she remembered, a certain down-to-earth sense of humour. When the contractions became so violent that Lucy felt she was being blown off the face of the earth by a hurricane, the midwife made her lie down and flex her knees, and told her to pull on the end of a towel tied to the bedhead.

'Pull like hell!' she said. 'And yell as much as you like! Nobody can hear you, as the room next door is empty. Doctor's on his way.'

The exhaustion and the feeling of peace that came with

it when it was all over was wonderful; but Lucy very soon stood up on the bed and demanded to hold her baby. The midwife fussed; she didn't want Lucy on her feet. 'Lying-in' was necessary for ten days, standing up too soon was a danger to the pelvic organs, and mothers and babies were separated except for the correctly time-tabled feeds. But the doctor, who was an old, experienced GP, brought the child to her. She was a tiny, sweet creature, all mouth, an avid feeder and an excellent burper, and at the expected times she produced appropriate yellow messes with an expression of heavenly bliss on her little red face. Lucy could see it now: red and demanding before feeds, pink and angelic afterwards. She was such a lovely baby! Poor Beena! She should have been Milton's naiad of Severn, Sabrina with her amber-dropping hair, for that was the name Lucy saddled her with. She must have been mad, she thought, looking back at herself over her shoulder, unhinged perhaps after Nicky's death, and snatching at shreds of romanticism to comfort herself. It was ridiculous to think of Beena now as Sabrina, with her hair of straw streaked with grey, so like a scarecrow's, or like the fringe of an old, dog-chewed rug; it would have been laughable even in her childhood. She would have been nicknamed Sabby, which is only one consonant away from Scabby, and 'Scabby! Scabby!' would have been yelled at her with happy ferocity across the playground. Fortunately she avoided these torments by calling herself Beena in baby-hood; and Beena she remained. It was not her fault, poor child, that she left her babyhood beauty behind her so quickly. The charm of childhood made others love her; but she emerged into adolescence stocky, clumsy, demanding and doglike. It was inevitable that she found her level among horses and dogs, and loved them more than her fellows, it was inevitable that she never found a lover till her late twenties, and then it was an unsuitable man who soon deserted her, inevitable that she came home with her darling baby Joanna, to Lucy at High House, and of course to her animals. If this house belonged to her, Lucy thought, it would be full of unruly dogs rushing through the rooms, scratching deep runnels on the mahogany doors, invading human privacy and jumping into the best chairs; and the fields would be crowded with dying donkeys longing for a more comfortable plot underground.

Lucy clicked her tongue, reprimanding herself for wasting time. She must really stop thinking about the past and get dressed, or she would be too tired to cope with the day's junketings. She opened a small packet carefully and drew out a new pair of dark blue tights, which she put on, pulling up and smoothing out the calves. If she were honest she had to admit that she had somewhere at the bottom of her psyche a bit of a grudge against Beena. Perhaps it was because Beena arrived into her life at a time of bitterness after Nicky's death; but it was more probably, she reflected, to do with Steve. She walked to the window and looked out beyond the garden to the fields where once they kept ponies, and further off still to the woods behind which, though she couldn't see it, Hazelwood Farm hid in its hollow. She wondered what had happened to Angie, the schoolfriend of her teens, whom her father had called his Gloucestershire lass. Was she still alive?

Angie came to say goodbye after the end of the War. She had just married a French Canadian Air Force Pilot.

'Never thought I'd marry a foreigner, did you?' They sat in the drawing room sipping tea. 'He says my French is terrible; but it can't be worse than his English. Dad can't understand him at all; and Mum was horrified at first. You remember that time she said all foreigners were evil, and you laughed at her? But when he said her pastry was fit for the angels to eat in paradise she forgave him for being a Frog.' Lucy remembered that they both laughed then.

'Lovely to see you again, Angie,' she said. 'You look so happy.'

'And you look well, Lucy.' Angie put down her cup as if preparing herself for action. 'Dreadful news it was about – about your being widowed Lucy. We were all so sorry. But now you have the baby things will be better.'

'I suppose so.' Lucy sipped, and smiled over her cup encouragingly at Angie, who always looked on the bright side of things.

'You heard about my brother Teddy?' Angie went on. 'He was drowned, you know – on his way out to India. One of the U-boats torpedoed his troopship in convoy. He jumped as it was keeling over; and as he went over the side a WREN in uniform stuck her head out of a porthole, shrieking. He caught her by the hair as he fell, and his weight pulled her out. She wrote to us afterwards. Seems she made friends with him on board ship. She was picked up in the water. Funny she survived when he didn't.'

Lucy flinched at her sudden vision of Teddy's bare arms, their golden hairs glistening above the water as they rose in supplication. She too put her cup down and faced Angie. Without a word they hugged each other fiercely, and wept. Even for Angie the bright side was shaded then.

Lucy sighed as she thought about Hazelwood Farm. She'd met the new people there, but didn't care to visit them. It was too painful to be reminded of what the place used to be like. The old house, marooned now on its tiny island of green like an ancient Jacobean lion couchant in a cradle, was cowed by the surrounding development. The cider orchard had disappeared. On the hilly field where once she had tobogganed with Teddy and Angie one January long ago, screaming with delight at their speed over crisp snow, small houses stood in red brick ranks, one above the other; and the fluttering armies of chalk-blue butterflies that used to feed upon the wild vetches growing there in June had fled.

Lucy slipped on her new midnight-blue shoes, hoping the toes wouldn't pinch her too much by the end of the day. No, it was Steve, she thought, whom Beena was so fond of, Steve, so good with horses, who taught Beena to jump. He lent her a tent and showed her how to put it up in the copse at the bottom of the garden as a rehearsal for the real thing: the camp which Beena and her two Brownie friends would make with their Brown Owl leader by the sea.

Lucy liked listening to Steve. He was a schoolmaster with a good voice, gentle and persuasive, perhaps a little donnish in his speech and manners; but his stories were so often full of drama and magic that she guessed he held his pupils spellbound.

'I don't have much trouble with them,' he admitted. 'Boys will always listen to tales of blood and murder. And history is mostly that.'

For the greater part of the year he lived in his house-master's rooms in the boys' boarding school where he taught history; but during the holidays and at occasional weekends he occupied a cottage he owned near Frenester. Steve knew about horses. He kept a hunter in a field near High House; and in winter whenever he was living in the district he followed the local hunt. It was on the hunting field that Beena made his aquaintance. She fell at a jump. He was just behind her, and after she fell he reined in his horse and trotted back to her as she lay moaning in the mud. She had broken her collar-bone. When he brought her home to High House he was immediately overwhelmed with garlands of gratitude and glasses of sherry. After that he called several times to see how the bone was mending, and then his visits became a habit.

On the evening he helped to put up Beena's tent at the bottom of the garden he sat with Lucy in the kitchen over a glass of Tio Pepe while the kids settled in for the night.

After dark he and Lucy walked down towards the tent, and prowled around to make sure the girls were all right. From the tucked-up safety of sleeping-bags inside came sounds of giggles and a low voice, often interrupted, trying to tell a story. Outside the tent lay the scattered remains of supper. There was an open tin of Nestlé's sweetened condensed milk with at least half a dozen flies trapped in its sticky surface. Lucy found a spoon to scoop them out, and then covered the tin with a saucer.

'Coo-ee!' she called. 'Everything all right?'

'OK!' came the answer. 'Smashing!'

'Well, goodnight then!' Sounds of giggling pursued the grown-ups back to the house.

Beena must have told Steve the secret of her real name because he said: 'Sabrina was a river goddess before the Romans came.' He then told Lucy how, according to Geoffrey of Monmouth's History of Britain, Locrin, a Celtic king, put aside his wife Gwendoline and took a concubine by whom he had a love-child, Sabra. The angry queen gathered together an army and challenged him to a battle, in which he was killed. She then drowned the offending woman and her little daughter in the river Severn; but Sabra rose again to become the spirit-ruler of its waters.

Steve helped the girls to clear up their camp. They threw all the hardware into the bottom of Louise's wheelbarrow, while he folded the tent neatly before placing it on top. Then, taking one of the guy ropes he harnessed himself with it. 'I'm a lazy old nag,' he said, 'and I won't budge.' Beena and her friend needed no persuasion to pick up twigs and switch the barrow shouting: 'Gee up! Gee up!' When he began to move they followed him, hitting him as they ran, till, breathless and laughing they all reached the house. Here he released himself and, threatening to beat the living daylights out of them, he chased them, but they ran shrieking in mock terror, zig-zagging about the garden and hiding behind bushes till he gave up.

Beena fell in love with Steve. He was a replacement for her missing father, and they were so obviously happy together that both Louise and Lucy liked him. He used to talk about horses with Beena and history with her mother. Things might have gone on like that for years if Beena hadn't spoken out one Saturday afternoon in the kitchen. Steve and she were sitting near the Aga with saddles on their knees. They were busily rubbing in saddle-soap; Lucy was buttering slices of bread at the table, and Louise was pouring milk into a jug.

'I wish Steve was my daddy,' Beena suddenly said, and turning to her mother: 'Why can't you make him my real daddy?'

Lucy dropped the breadknife in her confusion, and laughed: 'I'm sure Steve wouldn't like that at all!' But to her surprise he said: 'Oh! But I would! I would!'

Perhaps he was only being polite; perhaps he was as embarrassed by Beena's wish as Lucy was. He was a bachelor of forty, she was thirty-eight. In her naivety, and truth to tell her lack of interest in his personal affairs, she had never asked herself why he was still unmarried. It was 1951. Beena was ten years old. Such a short time ago it seemed in Lucy's memory; but what a world away! Post-war rationing had not long been discarded, the austere military cut in clothes was abandoned and the New Look (full, flared, swirling skirts made of extravagantly abundant yards of material) had arrived, along with a new femininity. A Socialist Government had fallen, but there was still a certain innocent altruism around, a clinging to the idea that society might yet be arranged somehow for the collective good. Did all this excuse her blindness, which in hindsight, she admitted, amounted to stupidity?

Lucy asked Louise what she thought of Beena's proposition. Louise was shovelling some of her excellent garden compost into a barrow. It was November and already cold, and she thought it time to give her old bush roses a protective mulching around the roots.

'It's up to you, Lucy darling,' she said, vaguely pushing a loose strand of white hair behind one ear. She was slowing down a bit in her movements, but she still struggled with heavy loads and digging. 'He's good for Beena. And perhaps you both need a man about the house. Do you like him enough?'

'I like him a lot.'

It seemed an extraordinary thing to Lucy in retrospect to have to admit that that was true. The fact was that when Steve was in the house the atmosphere was warmer, more relaxed. His presence in some way completed their contentment. He seemed to bring out the best in all of them; they were all more companionable, more united, laughing more when he was there. And so Lucy was gradually pushed into her second marriage by Beena's wish, her mother's approval and Steve's caressing voice, which she had to confess had an erotic effect on her. There was never any mention of love. Lucy supposed the Fate had already allowed her more than her fair share of that before they snatched it away. But Steve was always nice to her, and she appreciated that. When he put his hand on her shoulder in an appealing but also protective way, and spoke to her with that beautiful voice of his she did feel weak at the knees. It must have been the sort of emotion felt by strictly corseted Victorian ladies attending the opera: a sort of delightful swoon due to the permissible musical eroticism aroused by an Italian tenor.

Steve used to give her cousinly kisses at greetings and goodbyes. 'I'm a Christian, you see, so I believe in chastity before marriage,' he once told her. It was almost an apology.

They were married in Frenester church in September 1952 towards the end of the summer holidays, and it was really more Beena's wedding than Lucy's. She wanted all the customary rites. Lucy refused to be a white bride, but she did carry a bridal bouquet of roses. Beena would probably have liked a Brownie Guard armed with tent-poles forming an arch over them as they left the church porch. She was persuaded to settle for being a bridesmaid with her three best friends, all dressed up in blue flounces with crowns of artificial forget-me-nots on their heads. At this stage of her life Beena was undergoing orthodontic treatment, so her smile in the wedding photographs was mercilessly reflected by her steel dental brace. But she was radiantly happy. She was an only child who hankered after a family life.

Steve never talked about his own family but he managed to dig out a half-brother to attend the wedding, and Charlotte came over from Paris to 'look him over' as she put it. She didn't say what she thought after looking. Lucy wondered if perhaps foreboding silenced her. Nothing dampened the high spirits of the bridesmaids. They giggled their way through large slices of wedding cake to the shame of their parents who were invited to a small reception at High House; and they gave three cheers for the happy couple after Steve presented each with a gold horseshoe brooch with names and date engraved. To Lucy he gave as a present on their wedding day all his mother's jewellery in a red leather box lined with deep blue velvet. There was so much of it, and it was so beautiful it took Lucy's breath away. That at least had lasted, Lucy thought; and Beena would have it all after her death.

Steve put on a pair of hideous striped pyjamas before climbing into her big double bed, so she put on a nightdress. She remembered noticing the firmness with which he tied the pyjama-trouser cords. That night he held her in his arms and kissed her eyelids, murmuring: 'You're a lovely woman, Lucy! So lovely!' Then he turned over and fell asleep. It was not what she'd expected on her wedding night, nor what, a little wistfully, she'd hoped for in her secret fantasies. She lay awake for a long time staring at the ceiling. Stunned.

In the morning he explained he had to go to his cottage for some necessary business.

'All right, Stevie dear. I'll wait for you here.' They had arranged to drive up to the Lake District for the last week of the summer holidays, but later that morning he telephoned to tell her he'd received a telegram from the headmaster to call him back urgently to school where some unexpected crisis had blown up. Naturally he was disappointed. So was Lucy. He was vague about the nature of the crisis. Whatever it was it had blown over by the time she saw him again, which was in the Christmas holidays. In the interim she visited a medical library and read up on some of the literature on the art of love-making. Nicky had never needed any teaching; there was never any stopping him. But Lucy guessed Steve was inexperienced and shy, so she made up her mind to be the more active partner next time.

She gave him rather a lot to drink for dinner hoping to thaw him out, relax his fears, overcome his inhibitions, or whatever it was that was blocking his sex drive. By the time they went to bed they were both slightly drunk. As soon as the door was closed she rushed at him and began to take off his clothes. He didn't resist; he seemed to like it. When he was stripped to his underpants he said: 'Take your things off too, Lucy.'

'You do it,' she said. He began to undress her gingerly, but when he reached her lace-trimmed pink slip he stopped.

'I like you in that,' he said. 'So please stay like that.' They stood for a moment embracing. 'Will you do something for me, Lucy darling?' She heard his special caressing voice.

'Of course I will, Steve.'

He stooped down to the floor where his trousers lay and took a pair of leather luggage-straps from a pocket.

'It's a sort of game, Lucy. Will you strap my wrists to the

end of the bed?' It was a wooden end, the uprights too far apart, so she tied both of his wrists to one post. He fell on his knees and burying his face in her petticoat be begged piteously: 'Now hit me, Lucy! Hit me!'

She recoiled first in horror, and then with increasing anger she cuffed the side of his face sharply with her left hand.

'No! No!' he said testily. 'That's no good. You've got to use a weapon – something hard!'

Panic seized her. She wanted to please him, but was bewildered and outraged by his strange demands. She ran to her dressing-table, picked up her hairbrush, and with the wooden back of it she struck him several smart thwacks on his shoulders. He lifted his head and looked beyond her. On his face was the secret archaic smile that can be seen on antique Greek statues.

'Now untie me!' he ordered. And when she did so he embraced her hips, pressing his head into her silk-covered belly. Then with a gentle moan he ejaculated all over her bare feet, while she stooped over him, ruffling his hair, and her tears poured unchecked on to her hands in an unholy baptism.

He didn't try it again that Christmas. During term times they separated. He went back to his teaching, she to assisting Dr Gillow, a GP in the district for whom she worked part-time doing surgeries and visits. This job suited her well, as it fitted in with running High House and looking after Beena, who attended the local Primary C of E school and was working hard for her eleven-plus, and cooking for Louise, who took very little interest in housekeeping because all her energies were used up by the garden. Her mind ran continually on the care of her small woodland, which needed a lot of weeding (it was a long-standing battle against invading bramble and nettles) or the pruning of her roses and the tying-in of herbaceous clumps. She had bought a motor-mower at great expense, which she drove triumphantly around the lawns during the summer months, leaving a trail of wilting grass in her wake.

By Easter Steve seemed to have come to the conclusion that his form of marriage was acceptable to Lucy. 'It's a game, you see,' he used to say. 'We usually make a game of serious things, don't we?' And she, not wishing to hurt his feelings nor to judge, complied. She began to look upon him as a medical case, a rare one, of course, since she'd never come across it before. Nothing in her medical training had prepared her for it. She didn't know what to do. She thought of discussing it with Dr Gillow; but she knew he'd be terribly embarrassed, and feared their pleasantly jokey working relationship might be destroyed. She couldn't talk it over with Louise, who would be shocked and distressed but unable to advise her. And she still naively hoped that with patience and affection she might bring Steve round to loving her way. So she kept silent and began to hate it all. She began to hate him sometimes too, and once or twice, when she wielded the little riding whip Steve now wanted her to use, rage seized her and she hit him as hard as she could. And that made her tremble with fear and shame, because she could see a time coming when she might actually enjoy being cruel to him. This charade was releasing in her some primitive desire for cruelty long smothered by her upbringing, but now surfacing. She was disgusted by him, and yes, frightened by herself.

At the beginning of that summer term, when Steve returned to his teaching and Beena went back to school Lucy decided she needed a holiday, so she made arrangements with Dr Gillow, asked Louise to look after Beena and the house, and sent a telegram to Charlotte in Paris, whose wire in reply read: 'The Turk will meet Flight Le Bourget. Love Charlotte.' A milder man you couldn't find, but that was how Charlotte chose to refer to her husband, whose father had been Turkish, his mother French. His name was Anatole.

Inside the new turboprop aircraft Lucy found herself unexpectedly agitated: her heart raced, her mouth was dry. She waved aside the lunch neatly packed like a children's game into its plastic tray, but took the tiny salt and pepper pots to give to Beena.

'For my little daughter,' she explained. 'I'm too nervous to eat.' The air hostess, amused, asked if it was her first flight.

'No – as a matter of fact,' said Lucy. 'And yes, I'll have the coffee.' She was remembering the time when at eighteen, and a Fresher at University, she was taken out one Saturday afternoon by a student from the Engineering Faculty. They drove to Croydon Aerodrome in a ramshackle banger, said to be a car, and went for a five-shilling spin in the open cockpit of an old biplane. She hadn't been at all frightened then. She remembered squealing with pleasurable excitement as the wind screeched past her head, loosening the hairpins in her bun, pulling out her long hair into streamers so that she must have looked like a witch on a broomstick. Flip Collins was that young man's name. He was crazy about aeroplanes, an amateur pilot who belonged to a weekend flying club, and must have been swallowed by the RAF during the Battle of Britain, when they used up all the pilots they could get. Flip Collins . . . almost certainly he was killed in that war. . . . She looked out of the round window beside her on to a thick bank of creamy-coloured cloud. It looked solid enough to walk on. With a sudden pang she thought of Nicky, and was almost overwhelmed by feelings of tenderness and longing. What an idiot she'd been to marry again!

Charlotte's Parisian house was full of marvellous oriental rugs collected by Anatole. When he saw Lucy examining a small pale blue one hanging on the drawing room wall he lovingly stroked the silk pile and said: 'It's a Nain. Flat like a mirror.'

The rug at their feet was even more beautiful.

'Is it Persian?' she asked.

'You have chosen my favourite,' he said. 'It's a Kashan prayer rug – entirely woven of silk.' The ground colour was a subdued rose broken by a spray of fine black lines which opened into a shower of delicate cream flowers. 'But let me show you something older.' He took her across the room, and pointing to a Turkish prayer rug on the floor explained: 'This is woven in wool. And here you see in the middle of a field of flowers the *mihrab*, or niche, where you kneel down to pray. You must touch the ground with your forehead there. It points always to the east, to Mecca.'

After dinner he retired early to bed leaving the women to talk; but before he did so he lifted the blue rug from the wall and rolled up from the floor the Kashan as well as the Turkish prayer rugs. Heaving them into his armpits he said: 'The house next door was burgled last week; but no burglar will steal these.'

Charlotte, blowing out her cigarette smoke, said: 'He keeps them under the bed at night. They are his concubines.' And Lucy laughed, thinking that after all hers was not the only marriage to hide obsessions in the bedroom.

She sipped her strong, black, sugary Turkish coffee thoughtfully and tried, haltingly at first, to describe her plight. Charlotte listened quietly till she heard about the hairbrush. This sent her into peals of laughter. Stubbing out her cigarette she jumped up from the sofa, threw off her high-heeled gold sandals, and began to prance about the room seeking some hard object she could use. She found an ivory fan on the side table.

'Does he grow hairs on his chest?' she demanded. 'Oh! I do love a man who grows hair on his chest!' She hurled a bolster-shaped cushion into an armchair, and using the fan began to make little curving movements down its silk shirt-front. 'And what about a shampoo and set?' she cried. 'Or even an old-fashioned marcel wave with very hot tongs? Your hand might slip with the tongs, Lucy,' she suggested. 'He'd like that!' Then she pounced on the cushion and belaboured it furiously with the fan, until, breathless with exertion and laughter she fell back on the sofa to embrace Lucy. 'Oh, my poor Lucy!' she gasped at last. 'What a mess you've got yourself into!' But she didn't have any remedies to suggest; and although Lucy joined in the fun she didn't really consider the mess a laughing matter.

Charlotte must have confided in Anatole that night, because next morning over breakfast of coffee and croissants he addressed Lucy as tenderly and solicitously as if speaking to a sick child.

'Today I want to pamper you,' he said. 'I'm going to take you girls to the races. You can watch the beautiful horses, and in between races you can turn round and watch the elegant women dressed in their French best.' He put on a jaunty flat cap for the occasion, and wore a tie of yellow silk emblazoned with foxes' heads. 'We can also have a brandy between races if you like.' And then he kissed them both solemnly on their foreheads.

Lucy greatly enjoyed the thrill of going to Longchamps for all the pleasures the Turk had promised; but in the middle of the afternoon she became aware through the warm glow of her mild inebriation that something hot and wet was sliding down between her thighs, and thought: My God! It's the curse! The emotional turbulence she had been enduring must have upset the delicate timing mechanism of her hormone clock. This bleeding was out of phase and unexpected. She rushed into the nearest ladies lavatory and looked around for a slot machine selling the necessary pads, but could see nothing of the kind. A fat woman sat at a table guarding a saucer full of tips; but Lucy's French was not adequate to describing her needs. She rushed out again, found Charlotte, whispered in her ear, and Charlotte whispered to the Turk who gallantly put a hand on his racing tie.

'She can have this!' he offered.

'Thank you, Anatole,' said Lucy. 'You are very kind; but I'm afraid of foxes.'

Charlotte then seized her by the arm and hurried her back to the *Dames*, where her excellent French and a few coins moved the fat caretaker to produce from a locked cupboard what was needed.

Before Lucy boarded her return flight from Le Bourget they both kissed her. Charlotte murmured: 'I'll keep my fingers crossed for you. You must survive, my darling.' And Anatole, tapping the side of his nose with a forefinger conspiratorially hissed: 'He is *grosse merde* – the big shit – king size!'

By the time Lucy got home she recognised that her brief visit to Paris had been therapeutic, because her mind seemed to have changed gear. She was determined no longer to play Steve's game, determined to tell him so when he turned up at High House during the half-term break.

'This game isn't much fun for me you know,' she said, when he put his arms round her.

'What do you mean, Lucy?'

'I seem to please you, Steve, but you never try to satisfy my sexual feelings, do you?'

There was a long silence. He withdrew his arms from her and sat down on the bed.

'Do you think you could try making love to me some-times in the – ordinary way?'

'The fact is, Lucy – though I know you're a lovely woman – and a kind, sweet person as well – the fact is I can't bring myself to – the idea of it simply turns me off. I thought being a doctor you might understand.'

'Nothing I learned in medical school taught me about this,' she said, too bitterly. That was true in her young day. (She wondered, bringing her thoughts back to the present, if Joanna learned more about these things now. Indeed she hoped so).

'I'm sorry, old thing,' he said. He had never called her 'old thing' before. Was she being dumped in the wastepaper basket already? Then after a thoughtful pause he said, 'My way of it doesn't do any harm to anybody – nor could it, except to myself.'

Lucy wasn't so sure. 'I'm still young enough to have another child,' she said.

'Do you want another child?' He was genuinely surprised.

'Yes, I'd love another baby. And so would Beena.'

'Ah, Beena!' He said no more for a while, and then burst out, his honeyed voice suddenly bitter with mockery: 'Well! How I have been deceived!'

She persisted in sweet reasonableness, which must have infuriated him. 'I think not, Steve. I think it was I who was deceived.'

'I'm disappointed in you, Lucy – just when I thought you were beginning to improve.' After a pause he added: 'It's the rescuer I love, you know.'

'Does it make any difference whether the rescuer is a man or a woman?' she asked; but he didn't answer. In the long silence that ensued her mind was filled with other unanswerable questions. Were there other partners, men and women, perhaps boys, in this peculiar game he played? And was he playing it somewhere during his long absences from High House? She realised she knew very little about him and what he did for what was after all most of the year. She suddenly felt lost in his strange emotional world, and she asked herself, was she just a diversion for his school holidays? Worse still, was it High House with its pastures and stabling for his horse that he had really married? Was the security and comfort of the family life that went with it more important to him than she was? Or was it – could it be Beena whom he loved?

'Have you ever thought of seeing a psychiatrist about it?'

After all you must admit it's not the – well, a biologically natural form of sexual activity, is it?'

'What could a psychiatrist do for me?' His voice was quick, hostile.

'De-conditioning, they call it. They give you unpleasant feelings by showing you unpleasant pictures linked with your type of sexual behaviour, till you lose the pleasure from it.'

'But that wouldn't guarantee my having pleasure from other ways of making love, would it?'

'I don't know. Perhaps they use pleasant stimuli with images of normal loving.'

'*Normal* loving!' He shouted angrily. 'I don't want *normal* loving!' After a minute he stroked her arm. 'I'm sorry, Lucy darling. I thought you went along with my – eccentricities.'

By this time she understood them only too well. He didn't want the comfort of her body and loving arms to cradle him; nor could he comfort and cradle her. What he wanted was an image of a woman in a silk slip (that was important, more she believed, to cover up than to reveal her female body) an image, inflicting pain or at least pretending to. She was not a lover, nor a wife, but simply an erotic symbol. She was just a piece of porn.

It was at the end of the summer term that she received his letter.

'Dear Lucy, I've been doing some hard thinking since I last saw you, and have come to the conclusion that it's best we part. Impossible situation for both. I can see that. No blame attached either way. I shall never forget you and all that. I know it's a cliché, but it's true. Love Steve.' When she dropped the letter into her pocket she was thinking: I shall never forget him either. How could I? The past lives inside us. It is part of our souls; it is what we are made of.

She never heard from him again. His cottage was sold and his horse removed from the field where it was feeding. They were never legally divorced. They were never really

80

married; non-consummation is the old-fashioned term for it. Divorce was impossible anyway, because she had no idea where he was. He simply left High House and its inhabitants behind him. The last they heard of him was a rumour that he was teaching in an Arab country. Lucy resumed her former married name. She couldn't truthfully say she was heartbroken. His desertion was rather a relief; but she felt she had somehow failed. She also wondered if she'd been made a fool of.

Nor was Louise unduly upset. She liked Steve around the place. He was useful when she couldn't start the motor-mower and stood swearing at it in Anglo Saxon monosyllables, which he described as uncanny coming from her lips, and moreover quite inappropriate to the functions of a lawn-mower. Then he calmly took over, corrected whatever fault of petrol mix or spark failure was responsible, and got the thing going again before handing it back to her with a sweet smile. But he did not appreciate her camellias, nor understand the transcendent beauty of peonies and all the reasons why they figure mystically in Chinese paintings and on antique Chinese plates. So she had never given him the special affection she felt for the elect: those who shared in some degree her worship of the shapes of natural things and how they fitted together into the design of the Whole. She never even asked Lucy what had happened, guessing there was some mutual sexual disappointment – or else she would have been told more.

It was Beena who missed him. Her question 'When is Steve coming back?' became in a few months 'Why isn't Steve coming back?' Later still Lucy caught her watching her sometimes with an unspoken interrogation on her lips: 'What did you do to drive him away?'

For a long time after he disappeared from their lives his shadow fell between Beena and her mother. Perhaps she still wondered why they parted. At the unruly, irrational levels of thinking Lucy and Beena still blamed each other a little. Lucy because she married him, Beena because she lost him. But the whole episode did teach Lucy how ignorant she was about the human psyche. She thought she might be able to learn something from psychiatrists. So it was her experience with Steve which pushed her towards studying psychiatry and pursuing a new career, while Beena was growing up and Louise was growing old.

Louise found it increasingly difficult to cope with all the garden chores. It was then that Bailey came to High House. He cycled up from Frenester two or three times a week. He could read and write; but he was not what you'd call a scholar. Having endured in childhood some terrifying experiences, and then spending several years in a Corporation Children's Home (where, as he told Louise, he got all he needed except love), his temperament was subdued if not bleak; but he loved working in the garden, and he loved Louise. And because he grew succulent vegetables for the house, and respected plants, never digging up anything without the most careful thought, and because he found a pleasure almost as acute as hers in the shapes and colours of plants, she returned his affection. His recreation on Sundays lay in reading all the world's horrors in the *News of the World*. He revelled in gloomy predictions, and a really gruesome murder filled him with satisfaction. There never was a greater pessimist; but in Louise's eyes he was one of the elect, because he was able to grasp through his gloom a little of the meaning tangled up in the mesh of her all-enveloping universal net. Lucy supposed being a gardener could sour your outlook a bit when you considered all the enemies gardeners have to face: black spot, aphids, birds, slugs and snails, carrot fly, weevils, red spider, wire-worm, and not least the weather and untimely frosts. Once on a perfect spring day as Lucy passed him on his knees weeding and greeted him with 'Well, Bailey, you can't complain of the weather today, can you?' his reply was: 'Ah, but 'tain't out yet!' Poor Bailey! The sadness of his early childhood and garden pests blotted out his sunshine.

Louise was altogether more optimistic. 'Orpheus, you know,' Lucy heard her say to him, 'was such a good musician that he made trees bow themselves down when he played the lute.' Bailey's silence was scornful. 'I'm not as musical as that, of course; but I can with spade and trowel and quite a lot of thought, make my plants obey me. Though some are obstinate of course.'

Louise brought back from India some less tangible things than the brass-topped occasional tables resting on camels carved in wood, one of which Lucy used for her breakfast tray, and the big carpet in the drawing room which she remembered being woven in the penitentiary in Patna. She could see, even now, the small boy of about her own age, six or seven, sitting on a shelf above the loom, perhaps a warder's son, perhaps a criminal's child, possibly belonging to the family of a political prisoner (for it was the time of Gandhi's non violent protest) whom Daddy was visiting on that day when she was taken along for the ride in his big open Overlander car. She could see the ball of red wool held in that little boy's brown hands, the same red now subdued a bit by time, which still burst out in sudden flourishes to hit your eye when you walked across the carpet. Louise used to say that India left her fingerprint on all who lived there. The special mark that she brought back was the Hindu concept of reincarnation, which she modified to suit herself. She didn't believe in any personal migration of souls up and down a scale of animal life, but she did accept that she was made of the same elements as all organic matter, and that when she disintegrated she, like the plants she loved so much, would be reduced to the same basic earth. *Dust to dust, ashes to ashes*. That didn't horrify her. She found comfort in the thought that she belonged to, was one with, in a true physical sense, the whole natural world. Her own body would recreate, by feeding them, new life forms.

She was suddenly with Lucy, almost in the flesh sitting up on the day-bed below the Klimt portrait. She stared at Lucy with those large, sad eyes, abnormally large in her wasted face; begging eyes Lucy used to think they were. She knew she was dying. The cancer she had struggled with for two years was invading her liver, and her skin was just beginning to show a tinge of jaundice. She was not in any pain, but her appetite for food was poor, and her appetite for life, which had always been so strong, was waning. Dr Gillow came daily to see her. He must have told her the truth. Lucy almost loved him then. He who would have floundered hopelessly if faced with the problems of deviant sexuality was calm and kind and knew what he was about when dealing with death. He was a staunch ally to Lucy and a veritable ministering angel to Louise in those last weeks.

'There's something you ought to know,' Louise said. 'I've kept it secret all these years. I never told your father – Herbert I mean – but I think you ought to know . . .'

Lucy supposed she was compelled by a desire to confess, to wipe the slate clean before the end of the class so to speak. What she wanted was her daughter's forgiveness; but if she hadn't known about it Lucy wouldn't have had anything to forgive. Louise leant over and pulled from under the day-bed a battered and rather dusty old cardboard box.

'There,' she said. 'It's all in there. You must read it. I intended burning it; but as you see I didn't. I don't know why. Perhaps I thought you should know the truth one day.'

It was a journal of a sort, a record of that voyage they made to India in 1919, a time which Lucy regarded as belonging to an *ancien régime* before the motor car and votes for women. It was a loose file of yellowed papers written in now faded ink with Louise's old Waterman fountain pen, and tied together with pale pink tapes which were once the red tapes of colonial bureaucracy. Lucy took it to bed with her and sat up nearly all that night reading it.

THREE

Louise's Journal

December 7th

Port Out Starboard Home was the way you always travelled, and that's what I'm doing too. Poor Herbert, when suddenly recalled from leave, had to go starboard. The German U-boats had sunk so much of our shipping he had to take what berth he could get. It was the beginning of the hot weather and he must have suffered horribly from the heat. No accommodation was available for Lucy and me, as we were not essential personnel. As a matter of fact, Herbert didn't want us to travel with him because of the danger; and I must confess that after the sinking of the *Lusitania* and the drowning of all those women and children, I was rather scared myself. Anyway, since you were so ill at the time I was glad to be able to stay with you in London, dearest Mother.

Now everything is different. The War – thank God! – is over at last; and since I am now quite rich, with my own bank account in the Chartered Bank I can afford a little luxury for Lucy and me on our journey. Although it is at present very cold at sea, and we are thankful for our serge skirts and jackets, I know I shall want to throw them all overboard as soon as we reach Suez. I know, too, from previous experience, how grateful we shall be for any available shade the portside can give us in the Red Sea.

I first conceived the idea of writing you this letter on our third day out. It is well known by seasoned travellers (isn't it?) that as soon as the steamer leaves the fog and rumble and all the familiar landmarks of dear old dirty London, and noses out of Tilbury Docks on the ebb tide to join its shipping lane in the Channel, the traveller's mind also slips its moorings and enters a new, small but independent world: the ship and its passengers, all suddenly separated from their proper environment, and in a sense freed. Certainly that is the nearest I have ever come to feeling free.

With this new-found freedom I intend writing to you things I have never been able to say to you. There are, I suppose, more reasons in our family life than in most for our extreme reserve. The presence of ayahs and nannies between you and us when we were very young, and later the separation when we were dumped in English boarding schools so far away, left to sink or swim in that cold, rough sea, with only our Sunday letters to link us, inevitably caused estrangement. Of course I understand your very good reasons for all that. I am not in any way putting the blame on you. Ayahs were necessary – and mine much loved – to leave you leisure to pursue those important social duties of an Indian Civil Servant's wife. Moreover, Father needed you so much. Perhaps you were his only solace in an alien, hostile world. And then there was that myth that white children somehow wilted and died in that germ-laden dust of India, or, if they survived, grew up to be pallid, lanky, pleasure-loving ne'er-do-wells. It was believed that India somehow undermined the moral fibre of the young. So we had to grow up more sturdily, healthier and certainly more lonely in a northern climate. I can understand well your fears when I think of all those gravestones of little children buried in English cemeteries from Simla to Madras, and when I remember that your mother

88

lost her first three children in as many weeks during one hot summer in Bombay. It was not, I think you told me, the cholera; but it was bad enough to kill them all.

Will it surprise you that I intend keeping my little Lucy with us? She will not be sent home to school. She will attend the local convent school. You may be sure we will see to it that any mumbo-jumbo of a religious nature she picks up there will be quickly corrected by ourselves. She will learn a great deal from Herbert, as I have. No one could be a better influence educationally than he with his large learning, his liberal mind, his love of the Persian poets, and indeed of all the arts. Lucy shall have her mosquito-net around her bed at night to prevent malaria, and quinine to treat it if she contracts it. (Which God forbid!) She will never drink water that has not been chlorinated, nor milk that has not been boiled. She will never have to suffer the desolation of being left alone with strangers which I endured, and I hope she will grow up without feeling the psychological gulf which divides you and me, and which I am now trying to bridge.

Inability to talk to each other was increased by your ambivalence towards the truth. I remember once, ages ago, during the year of long leave which you and Father spent with us in the Kensington house, I quarrelled with a neighbour's daughter who was having tea with us in the nursery. I told her she had buck teeth like a rabbit and should nibble carrots instead of so many slices of our sponge cake. You scolded me severely for my bad manners.

'But it's the truth!' I burst out. 'She ate half of it before we had time to finish our bread and butter!'

'My dear Louise,' you explained more kindly to me later, when my rage and my guest had departed, 'if we all told each other the truth the world would come to a grinding halt. It's good manners which oil the wheels of society and make the world go round.'

'Is good manners just lies then?' I demanded indignantly.

'White lies, if you like,' you said. 'And if white lies mean being kind to people, avoiding hurting their feelings and making them happy, – why then, they're worth telling.'

I didn't understand till much later how deeply your white lies were embedded in our lives. I tried to grow up a well-mannered, quietly spoken, self-controlled little girl. I learned with difficulty all those proprieties which are now being unceremoniously heaved overboard by the younger generation. With increasing age and subtlety I accepted the deceptions, learned how to climb over and through them; but they divided us.

When I was little in India, before I was sent home to school, you and Father spoke Hindustani together when you didn't want me to understand what you were talking about; but as, by the time I was five, I spoke better Hindustani than you, you were forced to break into schoolroom French whenever, as it seemed to me, the conversation took an interesting turn. I used to feel locked out. Years later, when you were both home on leave and we spent that lovely hot summer all together in the long low farmhouse in the middle of a field of wheat in Kent, you and Father spoke a kind of code language full of understatements, of little jokes I didn't understand, of silences barbed with criticism and ironies which made you both laugh but which were meaningless to me. It stated plainly that there was no admission for me into your private garden. It was a summer gilded in memory by your presence, by weeks of steady sunshine, by joyous bicycle rides with Tom down country lanes, by ecstatic plunges into the sea with little Victoria, but shadowed at the end because of what happened to Tom.

My Lucy, whom you loved so much because you thought she had inherited your good looks and style, and most of all your red-gold hair (you used to call it your pre-Raphaelite heirloom from Grandmama Dambresac), has also inherited my passion for truth. I don't intend curbing it. Of course, it leads her, and me, into fearful embarrassments. Already she has made several *faux pas* and has been dubbed an *enfant terrible* by Mrs Vexham, who sits next to me at the captain's table.

'An *enfant terrible*,' repeated Mrs Vexham. 'Whatever will she come out with next? But charming, I assure you.'

Mrs V.'s assurance was not given with a smile. She is the wife of the head of the Engineering Faculty in the new Hindu College of Sunderband. He hasn't yet shown up in the dining-room. I understand he is a very bad sailor.

When we were steaming in the Channel, Mrs Vexham sat up on deck, her chair pulled up against a funnel for warmth and a rug tucked about her knees. The brisk breeze carried away the smoke, so she was not covered with sooty particles. She wore an old-fashioned black straw hat tied under her chin with a scarf which made it look like a bonnet. She peered at us over her spectacles as we approached, and then rummaged in the depths of her shabby black bag for a toffee wrapped in paper. Lucy dropped Peter Pushkin, her battered, dog-eared cloth rabbit, in order to unwrap the toffee. She sucked it slowly, examining Mrs V. with that stare which you have called implacably, unnervingly truthful.

'You look like a wolf,' she said.

I confess I gasped. For a moment I felt a fearful sinking of the heart as I fished wildly about in my imagination trying to find something suitable to say. How could I possibly assuage the insult?

'It's your black straw hat,' I explained. 'And your reading glasses. There's a picture in her Red Riding Hood book. And as you no doubt remember, the wolf put on grandma-ma's hat and spectacles, after – after – '

'Quite,' she said. She took it with a very good grace, and even laughed a little. 'I only hope I won't have to eat you, Lucy,' she added, 'because I can see you would not be a tender morsel to chew.'

Lucy was unmoved at the prospect of being chewed by Mrs V.

'The toffee's nice to chew,' was her comment before she ran off, leaving me very little time to pick up her rabbit and make my apologies before I chased after her. As you know, Lucy is so dreadfully energetic and inquisitive she keeps one on the go all the time.

People are being especially kind to us, probably because I am in deepest black. I have refused to dress Lucy in black; but she does wear a black armband out of respect. She seems inordinately proud of it and shows it off to strangers with the explanation: 'My Grandmother died, you know.'

I was rather surprised when I learned that you'd left me so much money as well as the Kensington house. I always believed Victoria was your favourite. But of course I did become the eldest after poor Tom's death.

He wanted to make his pony jump a five-barred gate – an exploit forbidden by Father. He wanted to show off in front of Victoria and me. I think he must have heard Father describe it as one of the tests young ICS candidates had to go through during their probationary period: jumping a five-barred gate with arms folded and stirrups crossed. Tom took the gate at a gallop and actually cleared it, but on the far side he suddenly slid off the saddle in mid-air and fell, and to our consternation simply folded up on the grass and never stirred again. I was surprised to see how easily a neck can be broken. I remember how silent Father was afterwards. He just stopped talking for days on end. I remember, too, how absent-minded he seemed when he parted with us girls at the end of his long leave, sad and distant. We didn't know, then, that it was to be his last leave and his last leave-taking. He had always been a distant figure, only to be seen on special occasions when I was carried to his knee from the nursery, and later far away in India working in the heat of the plains when I was at school in England, and further away than ever when he fell from a rock while climbing in Nepal and never regained consciousness.

Our third day out was rough and blustery, as was to be expected in the Bay of Biscay. Even Mrs Vexham was driven below decks. Very few passengers appeared in the dining room for lunch; but Lucy was indefatigable as ever. So Lucy and I were alone with the captain at his table.

He treats me with great respect and courtesy. I sometimes wonder if he regards me as a piece of fragile porcelain. I think he is also a little afraid of me, and I guess he has placed Lucy next to him as a buffer between us. On the other side of him is Mr Vexham's empty chair. He is the only other man at the table. Laid low by sea-sickness he has not yet appeared. The boat, you see, is crowded with women and children rejoining husbands and fathers after the long separation enforced on us by wartime shortage of shipping. There is also a sprinkling of single ladies past their first bloom who are part of the fishing fleet journeying to find romance and a husband in the outposts of the Empire. And a very wise journey to make it is too, in 1919, when, I'm told, there are half a million surplus women doomed to remain spinsters if they stay at home, since their might-have-been lovers and husbands lie dead in the mud of Belgium.

The captain calls me 'Mrs Brunoye' with a gentle, nostalgic inflexion in his rather beautiful voice. When Lucy finds someone to play with I am often left alone reading, writing or simply sitting staring out to sea. Then if the captain catches sight of me on his way to the Bridge, or taking a turn on deck with one of his officers, he bends slightly towards me as he passes by, and solicitously but without slackening his pace he invariably asks: 'Are we all right, Mrs Brunoye?' to which I always reply: 'Quite all right, Captain. Thank you.'

I guess that he has strong feelings of his own which he would like to share. He is aware of my grief, but afraid to show too much sympathy. His face is far from beautiful. It is deeply furrowed. He has a short, bristly beard, and above his big nose thick, iron-grey eyebrows sprawl over his eye-lids. His eyes are not really kind, though they sparkle when he screws them up to laugh, chiefly at Lucy, who seems to amuse him greatly. He knows all about your family, of course, and tells me he once travelled when a very young officer with your grandfather Dambresac, the judge. I think he regards you, and perhaps me as well, as part of a classical and now fast-disappearing landscape: the great days of the Raj and all that. It's possible that his deference towards me is on account of my mourning. I laugh inwardly when I imagine how his voice would sharpen, even squeak with alarm, did he but know that Mrs Brunoye, for all her ancestors, is an unhinged, hysterical woman who lies awake at night in her bunk as she is swung relentlessly on Biscay billows while Lucy, rocked in oblivion like a baby in a cradle, lies in the bunk opposite. 'Poor Mrs Brunoye! Are we all right, Mrs Brunoye? The shock has been too much for her. These old British Raj families are so intermar-ried. They become delicate with in-breedi..g. She is writing a long and absolutely truthful last letter to a woman who is dead.'

On the fourth day, after we had rounded the northern coast of Spain, the others appeared at lunch. I saw Mr Vexham for the first time. He is not a man of many words. There is also another lady at our table, a widow, Mrs Chinkwell, who is going out to keep house for her bachelor brother. He is a tea planter, and I wish him luck. She is one of those people who enjoy poor health, very often into their nineties. She talks incessantly about her ailments, which are numerous, sometimes bizarre, and treasures them like interesting pets whose progress and eccentricities she describes with relish. She has few other topics of con-versation and would probably die of boredom were she suddenly cured. She confided to me that she has invented a form of medical record for use in every home. She wants to patent it. It is to be called Chinkwell's Clinical Chart, on which is to be written morning and evening temperatures, daily pulse rates, speed of breathing as well as more indelicate matters. I asked her its purpose, and she replied that it would provide instant access to a scientific record for her doctor.

'But,' I objected, 'he already knows everything is normal on most days of the year.'

She looked offended, and has not, I'm glad to say, brought me a copy of her chart as promised. She must have filed away the subject for another listener, and meanwhile she has returned to her borborygmi which by the fifth day reached her scalp. Her scalp had been undulating during the night. She declared she felt as if she was carrying a plate of spaghetti on her head.

I was not quite quick enough to intercept Lucy's question: 'What's spaghetti?'

'Sticky white worms, my dear!' barked the captain abruptly. 'A whole plateful of them!' And everybody laughed with relief in such a way as to keep Mrs Chinkwell guessing whether we were laughing at the captain or her.

Lucy kept gazing at the top of Mrs Chinkwell's head, making me twitter with nervousness lest she say something unforgivable; but fortunately she held her tongue till next day, and then it was the captain, not Mrs Chinkwell, who was the subject of her implacable scrutiny.

'Why,' she asked during a conversational lull, 'do you grow hairs in your nose?'

Even Mrs Chinkwell was silenced for at least five minutes. The captain, who had been observing through a distant porthole the turbulent seas, reluctantly pulled back his gaze to regard Lucy gravely.

'They are very useful to me,' he explained. 'They tell me the strength and direction of the wind. They are invaluable in a gale. I can even smell one coming.'

Lucy nodded solemnly.

'How,' she asked, 'do other people tell which way the wind blows, when they don't grow hairs there?'

'Ah!' he sighed. 'They probably can't tell. But you see,' he continued, bending confidentially towards her, 'it's very important for *me* to understand winds. When they blow against me they slow down the ship.'

'And might even make us late in Calcutta, which would keep Daddy waiting on the quay,' I added with a laugh compounded of embarrassment and relief.

'Daddy's got a new car,' announced Lucy. 'It's called an Overlander.'

'That's a very fine car,' said Mr Vexham.

'I wish he'd bought an elephant instead,' she grumbled. 'I like riding in a howdah better.' While we were all smiling at this she continued thoughtfully: 'Elephants walk like a fat man, you know.'

The captain burst out laughing.

'It's so true!' he exclaimed. 'Young Lucy is a very shrewd observer.'

I caught his eye across the table, and to my surprise he blushed. It was then I guessed that this bluff man, this seasoned sailor is afraid of women, perhaps doesn't like women very much, although he obviously likes my little daughter.

I began to wonder as we munched through the rather tasteless, stringy meat what it was about women he didn't like. Was it their wiles and their ambivalence which he found so refreshingly missing in Lucy's transparent honesty? If so, he was being hardly fair to us, was he? Men like him exclude women from their lives. They catch us and keep us in a box called home-sweet-home for display on special occasions in a social net like so many butterflies, which can only fold their wings in protest of camouflage and wait to be released. To what? All they can hope for is release into another male hand, which may or may not be kind. That's what we ladies have been offered hitherto, isn't it? Release from childhood imprisonment into the parole of wifely duties.

For a few days I felt rather resentful towards him, till I began to wonder if perhaps I might even be a trifle jealous of my own small daughter. I realise that because I am at present not quite myself, I have been churning up my feelings over an entirely imaginary situation. In any case I can play the accepted sex-role game pretty well if need be, having learned from you how to use the rules to my advantage. This does, of course, as we can both agree, create a certain ambivalence towards the truth.

Truth, the whole truth, and nothing but! I laugh inwardly. Who can tell it, and who can even know it? When their feelings are involved, people see events not as they are but as they wish them to be. Then there's the truth about ourselves. Do we ever know that? We can see ourselves in a mirror prepared, as it were, for viewing. We never see ourselves as we move away from the mirror, move about the room busy with other thoughts – which probably explains our frequent surprise at seeing our own photographs. Sometimes we may catch a glimpse of ourselves through an unguarded expression on another face; but the man who makes it his business to tell others the truth about themselves we never believe. We think he has an axe to grind, a chip on his shoulder, is spoiling for a fight, or simply that he enjoys being nasty.

Herbert, of course, believes in Truth. The Law, he says, depends on establishing it. Democracy depends on government by law accepted by the majority. That's what we're hoping to hand on to India, isn't it?

I think of the Law as a sort of net we have thrown over the jungle; and Truth is the bamboo peg holding it down.

In the days when he was Magistrate as well as Land Settlement Officer up-country he used to have great difficulty in arriving at the truth. Sometimes, he admits, he probably never did. Perjury and paid witnesses abounded everywhere. To ferret out the facts, patience combined with a shrewd eye and an unbiased ear were needed, and these Herbert possessed. He also had the ability to reduce a long-winded witness to brevity without giving too much offence. The experience of those early days has taught him, he tells me, that there is no freedom without justice, no justice without law, and no law without truth.

Akbar the Great united warring India for two hundred years under the Moghul Empire. He achieved religious tolerance at a time when in England the Tudors were putting people on the rack and cutting them up in pieces for differences in belief. Herbert hopes we will not leave India to a condition less than Indians enjoyed then.

I can hear you laughing derisively. You say that as soon as we leave India Moslems and Hindus will begin slitting each other's throats. Lots of people are afraid of that; but Herbert is not afraid. He says that after the carnage India will emerge into her own new democracy.

Herbert would certainly be frightened though, if I were with him and he knew what I am doing. He would wrap me up in Cashmere shawls (your mother's by the way), and make me sit for hours in enforced idleness in a cane chair on the verandah when cool enough, and during the heat of the day he would insist that I lie down on my bed. All this resting would be to prevent – though in my opinion it positively cultures – madness. There was never any lunacy in his family, though they were all excessively endowed with missionary zeal, which peppered his family tree with early Christian names. It was the merest chance that his mother, during the last days of her pregnancy, read and liked a poem of George Herbert's so much that she decided to call him after the poet instead of christening him Theodoric, which was his father's choice.

There were, however, one or two strange figures in our family, weren't there? There was Aunt Josephine who gave all she had to the poor and entered a nunnery, though she did have the consideration to choose an Anglican convent, so avoiding the ultimate solecism of turning to Rome. And what about Great-uncle Louie from Bristol who fell off Brunel's Suspension Bridge into the Avon Gorge not altogether accidentally? They were never talked about. Madness, like tuberculosis, was a blot on any family escutcheon. These misfortunes somehow lowered a family's social value, and if known would certainly reduce a girl's chance of making a good marriage.

Well I'm not at all mad. I am, in spite of my bereavement and the heaving of the boat, quite steadily sane. I did have a shock yesterday, it's true, which caused me to turn pale as I walked on deck with Lucy. Indeed it made me tremble so much that I had to sit down for a few minutes on a spare deck-chair for fear of falling in a foolish, ungainly heap.

It was during the very rough weather. It was while I was bending to face and steady myself against the wind that I saw Greg coming towards me from the opposite direction, his coat tails billowing before him and his plus-fours so full of air he looked as if he was being puffed forwards against his will on a couple of balloons. A trifle absurd, in fact. Lucy, who was impersonating a fairy queen, was making an attempt to fly, which finished abruptly as they bumped together and he caught her to stop her fall.

I didn't at first recognise him because of the great mane of hair and beard which the wind was blowing about his face; but I smiled and thanked him.

'It's a pleasure, Mrs Brunoye,' he bellowed, 'to do the smallest thing!'

'I beg your pardon?' I shouted, for the wind was snatching our courtesies and scattering them over the waves like ashes from an urn burial.

'A pleasure!' he shrieked. 'Mrs Brunoye – Louise – a pleasure!'

So he knew my name.

As soon as I had passed him, his voice plucked a deep, familiar string in my memory, and the bright blue eyes that had glittered into mine dragged reluctant pictures from the past to the surface of my mind suddenly and so vividly that my heart began to beat uncomfortably fast and my throat felt tight. Could this be that Greg, that young subaltern you looked upon with such favour when I was an awkward, fat schoolgirl, when he stood beside your piano in the big, cold drawing room of the Kensington house and sang to your accompaniment:

> *I know she likes me*
> *Because she says so.*
> *She is my lily of Laguna,*
> *She is my lily and my rose.*

Most of the time he was leaning over you, smiling at you, speaking to you in such sweet, caressing tones that I suspected he was flirting with a widow still beautiful but twice his age. But once he smiled across at me over your head, causing such a turmoil in my adolescent heart I couldn't sleep all night afterwards.

Well Greg has certainly changed. He is no longer that young Adonis with luxuriant red-gold curls, who flirted with us both one Christmas long before the War and so many European deaths ago.

I could look back on the affair as at a Victorian sentimental painting, charming in the supposedly realistic every-picture-tells-a-story school of art, but just as romantic, as unrealistic and false as it could be. But to be truthful I must look back at myself as at another person: a fifteen-year-old, over-plump (puppy fat, you used to call it), not-too-pretty girl with straight brown hair still in a pigtail, and her armpits a bit smelly from running madly up and down stairs with too much adolescent energy and too little lavender water, while he in his officer's uniform was the most devastatingly handsome young man I'd ever seen.

Why, good heavens! It was the time of the Boer War and Queen Victoria was still on the throne, though very old, and seldom seen abroad in her open carriage in which she sat in her frumpy black clothes, crowned with that awful black straw bonnet above her drooping cheeks, and her round eyes so like a spaniel's pleading for love!

I remember what you said when pop-eyed Victoria died at last.

'Well, of course, she was *good*. The Bible says of the virtuous woman that her price is beyond rubies. She was a great queen too. Of that there is no doubt; but it will be rather nice to have Alexandra on the throne. She at least knows how to dress.'

I daydreamed about Greg for several years, imagining him wounded by the Boers, or by mutinous Indian sepoys, and I saw myself nursing him back to health, leaning over him. I held a lamp in one hand and a bandage in the other, and I murmured words of hope and encouragement into his curl-covered ears. His features became increasingly indistinct as the years passed, till he assumed at last the shape of one of those naked young gods carved in marble we were hurried past when we were taken to the British Museum on days too wet for walking in the open air.

Am I really that same introspective, mooning-about, sulky girl? A feeling of unreality settles on me when I think of her. It is like the nightmare I used to have in childhood of seeing myself walking down a long, straight road further and further away from me, until I grew so small I became frantic with fear that I would vanish, and woke up crying. It is an image of life, of looking back in the middle of it at one's disappearing past self, once so real but gradually becoming a stranger; and it is an image of death, too, when all oneself and one's days will disappear.

Did Greg disappoint you? Did you hope to see him again

during his next leave from the army in India, when you were still young enough, perhaps, to fall in love, certainly to indulge in a not-too-serious affair? Or did you look upon him as a prospective son-in-law? A few years after that Christmas I was a marriageable daughter. But he never called again.

I didn't tell you that I met him many years later. It was on my voyage out to marry dear Herbert, who had waited for me for eight months after our courtship and engagement in London. That was in 1912. I was twenty-eight and you were getting understandably fidgety and anxious that I might be left on the shelf, especially as Victoria, who was younger and of course prettier than me, was married and already the mother of two babies.

Greg was a captain by then, still very handsome with a dashing, beautifully groomed moustache. The luxuriant curls of his early youth were cropped into a copper helmet becoming to his brisk, soldierly walk. He was travelling starboard then, as I have discovered he is now. I had long recovered from my girlish crush on him but I was pleased to see him and to receive the attentions of so handsome an escort, especially at dances because, although I was engaged and eagerly awaiting reunion with dear Herbert, I was desperately shy and literally at sea, and had a horror of being left a wallflower. Greg saw to it that I never was.

So he remembered me, after a lapse of – what – seven years, which was gratifying; but I did not at first know him. The reason is he is greatly changed. The War, which he has so obviously survived in India instead of having to fight in that blood-soaked mud pit in Belgium, has altered him almost out of recognition. He is thicker, a little paunchy above his plus-fours, coarser, the skin of his cheeks stained by tiny bluish veins, and his lower lip, which was once so tremulously, so divinely full, now hangs purple and a trifle loose. Perhaps his appearance could be blamed on the cold winds to which he had turned his back, but more probably

102

I think it is seven Indian years of shouting stentorian abuse at terrified and uncomprehending underlings, both black and white, and of too many double whisky-chota-pegs which have changed him. It is sad, although I no longer care for him of course, that my young Adonis has grown into this prematurely middle-aged Bacchus.

I made up my mind next time I came face to face with him I would certainly greet him with pleasure and affection suitable from a lady, now seven years married, to an acquaintance of former, happy childhood days. Nevertheless the confrontation did for some reason unnerve me. I felt rather shaky as I descended the brass-tipped stairs to the dining room, which I was relieved to see almost empty. At our table there were only Lucy and me and the captain himself. He glanced at me quickly from under the thicket of his eyebrows.

'Are we all right, Mrs Brunoye?'

'Yes,' I smiled back at him. 'I'm beginning to get my sea legs. Lucy seems to have been born with them.'

'Well, that's not surprising, is it?' he said. 'Must be in the blood. So many generations of travellers back and forth to India.'

After lunch Lucy and I took coffee in the card room, and here Greg joined us. As he was not in uniform I couldn't tell his rank; but he informed us he is a major now.

'I see Lucy's drinking her coffee black like a grown-up young lady,' he commented. His voice, I noticed, was still mellifluous.

Lucy sat under his attention as complacent as a cat with a stomach full of cream.

'She hates the tinned milk,' I explained. 'And I don't blame her. It's really horrible. She won't even have milk on her porridge at breakfast.'

'I like golden syrup instead,' said Lucy. 'I like pouring it from my spoon, high up. And I write a big L with syrup before I eat it.

'It's the best way,' he agreed pleasantly. 'And the best way to drink coffee is the Turkish way.'

'What's the Turkish way?' she asked.

'Sweet as an angel, black as the devil, and hot as hell!' he replied, at which we all laughed and felt very companionable.

'Do you like syrup with porridge?' asked Lucy.

'I stick to my chota-peg,' he replied.

'Is that instead of milk?' she pursued.

'Yes,' he said. 'I don't like milk, and I don't like porridge.'

'There's one thing I do enjoy at breakfast,' I said, 'and that's the marmalade. You couldn't get good marmalade in London by the end of the War. I do believe it was made mostly of mashed swede!'

Greg nodded, and then went on: 'D'you know, Louise, I thought at first you hadn't recognised me. In fact for a moment I thought you'd cut me dead.'

'Oh no, Greg! Of course not!' And then my little white lie came out. 'It was the wind in my eyes, and a lick of salt spray blinded me for a moment!' To call him Greg came back to me as naturally as if I'd seen him only yesterday.

'Well, I'm glad to hear that,' he said. 'I'd begun to think you were behaving like the Governor's daughter in the old story.'

'I don't think I've heard that one.'

'The Provincial Governor's daughter who cut a Junior Officer dead as she passed by him on deck, to everybody's surprise, since she had danced all night with him at the ship's fancy-dress ball and had been seen leaving his cabin the morning after. Her explanation was that she had not been introduced, sleeping with a man not qualifying as an introduction.'

To my intense chagrin I blushed, which made Greg laugh all the more at his own story. It was certainly an indelicate one, to put it mildly, to tell in front of Lucy. Luckily her attention had been distracted by another little girl, Sophie, who was playing on the floor nearby with a large French doll. To Lucy's amazement the doll squeaked 'Mama!' when she sat up, and when she lay down her blue eyes were closed by eyelids fringed with long black lashes. Lucy was entranced, and it was not long before the two little girls were playing together.

I was then able to tell Greg of your death, and also something about dear Herbert to whom I am so very happily married. Greg was a kind and sympathetic listener, and I began to feel that in spite of his rather rakish appearance and his risqué talk, he is a true friend.

December 11th
at sea

Mr Vexham has proved to be less taciturn than I'd feared. I found I was able to draw him out on the subject of steamships. It's quite a hobby of his, his wife explained. This was a piece of luck because the others joined in the conversation with gusto, telling stories of how their ancestors had travelled on earlier, and of course much slower, boats. The captain as a child travelled on the *Ravenna*. It was the biggest at that date, the first with a steel hull, and was considered the height of luxury not only because of its double staircase of oak leading from a drawing-room, whose ceiling was painted in white and gold, to a dining room panelled in oak throughout, but also because in the recesses of each stairway there was an array of potted plants. Here gentlemen going up hurriedly extinguished cigars if they met a charming lady coming down.

'Speed thirteen knots,' said Mr Vexham.

Then Mrs Chinkwell, suddenly emerging from her hypochondria, began to tell us about her own great-grandfather who had travelled to Bombay long before the Suez Canal was thought of, in the days when for the long journey round the Cape cows were kept on board to provide fresh milk, and also poultry for eggs and the occasional *coq au vin* for the chef. He and another lad recruited as writers for the old East India Company set up a cockpit on deck and opened a betting shop to take wagers on the fighting quality of two very fierce cocks. This greatly relieved the tedium of the long voyage, especially as one of the cocks in an access of fury flew at a seated lady in the audience and attacked a bright red cherry on her bonnet.

'Six months and more in the days of sail,' said Mr V.

'I wish we had a cow on board now,' said Lucy. 'Then I would have proper milk for my porridge, not the nasty tinned stuff.'

Everybody laughed. So by the time we entered the Mediterranean we were all getting along famously, feeling ourselves bound together by the trade routes that our ancestors have taken for generations, and recognising that, in more ways than one, we are all in the same boat.

Greg (the others call him the Major) sits at another table behind me, which is why I didn't see him at first. He sits with the ship's surgeon, a slim young man with calculating eyes and a body like tempered steel. His whole appearance reminds me with some apprehension of the surgeon's knife. With them sits a Miss Kelly, and beside her is an empty chair, which I believe was meant for the aunt who has failed to accompany her. Miss Kelly is an Irish-American girl of quite uncommon beauty, probably not more than twenty and dressed in the latest fashion. The waist, it seems, is disappearing. It is sliding down towards the thighs. Miss Kelly's waistline grips her hips to reveal the swing of a neat bottom. Her skirt is much shorter than any other woman's on board, and shows a great deal of her legs. But such legs she has! Slim and shapely with delicately turned ankles. Her black bobbed hair is cut straight into a fringe across her forehead. Her large blue eyes are expressive and gentle. She is one of those girls who draw stares from strangers. I think she must have what the Yanks call star quality, though she is no film star. She is a small New York hotelier's daughter on her first trip out to marry her fiancé, who is a police officer in Calcutta.

'Well, she's not one of *us*!' Mrs V. confided to me in an undertone when we were sitting together up on deck and Miss Kelly passed by on the arm of the Major.

'He's nearly old enough to be her father!' was what I said.

We met them together again in the Alameda Gardens when we stopped at the Rock. We took on board fresh water and some delicious oranges which have since appeared in the dining room. Lucy was dying to see the famous Gibraltar Apes. When she tired of watching these we strolled into the gardens where it was very pleasant and quite warm. Arum lilies were in lush bloom, and fragrant mimosa drooped from a dainty tree on which Lucy caught a glimpse of a black bird with a scarlet tail which I couldn't give a name to.

We chatted with Greg and Miss Kelly who, I must say, was charming. In spite of the fact that she wore make-up on her face by day, which I know you would consider common, I found her rather unspoilt and unsophisticated. She seems to be travelling alone, which is perhaps surprising for such a young, unmarried girl. She won Lucy's affection immediately with a gift of 'candies'.

'Why don't you paint your nails pink like Rose?' Lucy asked me when she saw me giving myself a manicure later in our cabin. I was polishing my nails with a chamois leather buffer.

'Grandmama would think it common,' I said, hastening to add for fear of Lucy's outspokenness: 'Rose isn't English. They have different customs and different tastes in America.'

I can't prevent Lucy attaching herself to Rose, and to the Major too, since he is constantly at her side. They seem pleased to have her and to be honest, although I realise she is being spoilt by all their petting, I am glad to be rid of her now and then. I need a little solitude.

Lucy repeats at mealtimes bits of their conversation, which is received, I notice, with avid attention. In fact the whole ship's company and passengers are agog with the affair of Rose and the major. Every voyage has its *affaires* and flirtations. I can't help reminding myself wryly of one of your favourite French aphorisms: *De deux amants il y a toujours un qui aime et un qui se laisse aimer*. It is certainly true on board this ship. The captain has fallen in love with your granddaughter Lucy, and she with Rose. The Major is fast falling in love with Rose while she, presumably, is pining for her policeman in Calcutta.

It used to be said in the old days that no Indian voyage came to an end without a marriage or a duel, sometimes both. Well we shall see. Though there are plenty of very young children on board there are few of Lucy's age for her to play with apart from Sophie. Older children have, I suppose, been left at home and at school or with grandmothers, aunts, nannies and so forth. Mr Vexham, seeing Lucy and Sophie playing with their dolls today, asked how the dolls were behaving themselves.

'Belinda has been naughty,' said Sophie; but Lucy, who was sitting on the floor brushing her own doll's hair remarked:

'Mavis has real hair.'

'Is she called Mavis then?' he enquired kindly. 'That's a nice name. It means a thrush, you know, a singing bird.'

'I saw a black bird with a red tail in the Alamma Gardens,' said Lucy.

'Alameda,' I corrected her.

Mr Vexham turned to me.

'It must have been a redstart. They winter in the Mediterranean regions.' He seemed delighted. He told Lucy she had sharp eyes which she must keep on the lookout for the albatross, in case that bird of doom began to follow the ship; and when he rose to leave us he stroked Lucy's hair. Lucy, it seems, is getting almost as much attention from the men as Rose, though I suspect the ladies regard her as too forward for a little girl and rather a show-off. They certainly voice their disapproval of Rose, who is described as fast, a flapper, a vamp even, and much too flirtatious for an engaged girl. They also carp about her short skirts, her excessive make-up and her 'free' talk.

And so we steam across the Mediterranean, the sea calm, the breeze light, the sky blue, the air comfortably warm and the passengers settling into new friendships and enmities. I myself feel my heart lifting, the anxieties and sorrows, and yes, the oppressions of the past year dissolving as we move, and I am able to observe with amusement and some detachment (since my mourning prevents my taking too active a part in them), the shipboard dramas to come.

'Did you know,' asked Lucy one morning at breakfast, putting down her cup of tea with an expression of distaste for the milk the steward had added, 'that Rose *smokes*?'

Even the early morning lethargy was dispelled for a moment as we listened to this new evidence of Miss Kelly's emancipation.

'In her cabin,' Lucy went on. 'She has a lovely blue butterfly-box to put the ash in. And she keeps her cigarettes in it too.'

'Cigarettes?' echoes Mrs Chinkwell, recalled from hypochondriacal concentration by memories of past pleasure. 'I used to allow myself one from time to time. In privacy, of course. Till I found smoking made my heart flutter so alarmingly I had to give it up.'

'She keeps them in her handbag,' Lucy continued as if Mrs Chinkwell hadn't spoken. 'The ashbin is ever so pretty.'

'She means the ashtray for her handbag.'

'Yes. It's silver with a blue butterfly on the lid.'

Today, when the captain spied me sitting on the deck,

alone in my mourning, he bent his 'How are we today, Mrs Brunoye?' towards me as he passed; and I replied with my usual 'Quite all right, Captain. Thank you.' I held an open book in my hand for the sake of appearances, but I hardly read at all. I was too busy considering all those matters which for many years I have not allowed to surface in my rational mind. Some of these thoughts I will try to write to you.

The Japanese, I have heard, make an annual pilgrimage to the tombs of their ancestors, and there, having made libations of sake and water, they talk to the dead, telling them of the events of the past year, confiding its successes and also confessing its errors and failures. I, too, suddenly feel this need.

Dear Herbert, for instance – why did I marry him? Well, you wanted me to, and he wanted me to. I was nearly twenty-eight and suitors were not falling at my feet thick and fast as the autumn leaves in Kensington Gardens. I couldn't wait much longer for Mr Right. I had to marry somebody. That was inevitable. I must marry someone suitable, which Herbert was, as well as kind, courteous and not bad-looking. He was in a good position, with a promising, perhaps a dazzling future, since his intelligence, integrity and devotion to duty had already, so we were told, marked him for promotion to the highest ranks of the Indian Civil Service. Why did he marry me? He said I had large, serious eyes and a graceful walk (by which, I learned later, he meant I had well-shaped breasts and small, neat buttocks). He said I was the only girl he'd met who seemed to understand what he was talking about. He said there was a certain something French in me which derived, he thought, from the distant ancestor of yours who fought so bravely at Pondicherry and which, he declared, vibrated harmoniously with the Gallic instincts he had inherited from Huguenot forbears. He also liked my independence of thought and speech.

At the time he was still a Deputy District Commissioner working in the wilds of Chota Nagpur, with very little money, which was why he travelled home on leave portside, and I believe second-class. When, in 1911, he returned to India engaged, he was promoted to a more civilised part of Bihar, where he was given the use of a much larger, cooler bungalow. He prepared it for me as well as he could during the eight months of our separation. I found when I arrived that it was surrounded by a compound containing a walled garden on one side of which grew peaches, and a drive which terminated in handsome wrought-iron gates opening on to a fairly good road. This led to the sprawling city of Patna a few miles away, and also to the village and markets of Bankipore and the banks of the Ganges. I loved going down to the great river, where there was always something for me to watch: a cremation with wailing women, a festival with effigies of many-handed, garlanded gods, or simply people bathing themselves and their children.

It is really a spacious house with considerable dignity acquired by time and history, as well as a pleasing architecture, with pillared verandahs. It was built more than a hundred years ago by the East India Company for their resident Rice Collector. It stands not far from the Gola, a rice storage-container, which looks like a gigantic, mud-coloured gourd, a strange edifice, built on the orders of Warren Hastings himself. This must have been some security against a bad harvest and the famines which were more or less endemic in those days.

You had promised me a glittering social life, to which you in your day before your grey widowhood in that tall, grey and horribly cold Kensington house, had devoted an almost professional degree of skill. We had to buy, if you remember, a lot of pretty clothes to fit me out for all this before I left London, as nothing would be available in Patna. As a matter of fact I soon discovered in Bankipore a railway signalman's daughter who was an expert dress-maker with an unerring eye for elegance and an original flair for design. She rather looked down on my English clothes, preferring to copy models from French fashion magazines. She always knew what would suit me better than I did myself, and soon persuaded me to use some of the gorgeous Indian silks woven for saris, often with gold threaded borders, especially striking for evening wear. Sadly, these glamorous clothes were not worn as often as perhaps I – and certainly you – would have liked. I soon found out Herbert has very little interest in social life. He finds it boring and tiresome, and will only attend a minimum of functions.

When we give dinner parties he leaves all the arrangements to me. He laughs at my worries over who should sit where, and who should take precedence over whom, on going in to dine. It is even worse at official receptions. The sheer tedium of having to observe protocol wears him out. He never did suffer fools gladly, least of all in high places, and resents giving precedence to position rather than personal merit or charm. He recognises, of course, that governors of provinces must walk below the Viceroy and the Governor General (whom we never catch a glimpse of anyway), but when it comes to some important visiting dignitary, whether I put the senior Chaplain of the Church before or after the Commissioner of the Central Salt Bureau he doesn't care a fig. He did once assure me with laughter that he was quite, quite certain that the Assistant Director of Public Health joined hands in lowliest places with the Senior Income Tax officer in Bombay. Whether he was right or simply teasing me I never knew, because 'The Book', the Warrant of Precedence, had been borrowed from the library by another memsahib on the occasion when I needed it, so I was unable to refer to it in time. Fortunately the man from Bombay never turned up, so my anxieties were needless.

I have pointed out to him more than once that giving offence to colleagues and even juniors could create enmities, which in turn might block his promotion and so slow down the achievement of his aims. He nods reluctant agreement to this argument, but continues to dislike public entertainments, functions and the intrigues which so often begin at them, and all that busy business of top administration he calls Hustle-fussabad.

Sometimes he wishes he could return to his former life of a young DC. Then he worked virtually alone in a vast area where he was expected to be Magistrate, Collector of Taxes, Inspector of Industries Land and Prisons, and to take an interest in village agriculture as well. His integrity was expected to be unassailable. No gifts could be accepted other than fruit and flowers, lest they be seen as bribes. In those days he had only God and his own conscience to answer to, whereas now he must mind his ps and qs, speak only when politic, oiling the wheels of British snobbery as well as being careful not to throw grit into the Hindu caste machine, and pander to the foibles not only of ICS colleagues but of their memsahibs as well.

In all this he is grateful to me, because I 'know the ropes'. I am, he says, a born diplomat.

'You can tell what people are thinking better than I can,' he once told me. 'I sometimes wonder if you have second sight. Or is it just woman's intuition? You seem able to delve into other people's thoughts and fish out their motives.'

I kept to myself my own opinion that woman's intuition is a skill developed by our family system, which pushes girls to the periphery of life, expecting us to 'be good, Sweet Maid, and let who can be clever'. This makes us stand on the edge and consider, but can't stop us developing an acute watchfulness of the more active contestants in the ring. Girls grow up watching their brothers as they rush hot-headed into the fight; and if we are born with any

113

natural intelligence we learn to understand the human mind and heart, their motives and likely actions, quite well.

I left London with delight and hope. I couldn't say I was in love, because at that time I had no idea what love is. But I was certainly looking forward to seeing Herbert again, and more than that to my new changed existence. I was relieved to quit your house, which had become a prison I feared I might never escape. It was on that voyage out, alone and separated from my accustomed environment that I first tasted freedom. It was surprisingly exhilarating. I became almost drunk with joy in all the new sights and sensations and the knowledge that I was at last no longer subservient to you and your massive array of family traditions and what was *comme il faut*. I was in charge of my own destiny. Or so I thought.

I have already told you of my stroke of luck in finding Greg on the boat that first time. He was a marvellous dancer. It was, of course, 1912, and the dreadful War had not yet fallen upon us, sweeping away so many of our familiar ways of living; but Ragtime from America had already hit us, and as we had on board a gifted pianist and an inspired drummer we danced and danced, and went on dancing half the night. I found the new ragtimes terribly exciting, but we also danced the old-fashioned waltz. Greg literally whirled me out of the safe nursery I'd been brought up in and into his own strange and dangerous world.

I look back on that brief episode now with amazement. Was that intoxicated girl really me? Well, it wasn't anybody else, so I have to take responsibility for what happened. And yet, and yet – Perhaps the young soldier facing bombardment for the first time, shells exploding like bright fireworks all round him, was caught surprised, as I was (though not for him the safe way out which, being a woman, I still had). Experienced officers tell you that it was the young, inexperienced soldiers who were so often caught unawares by death in their first shelling, while those who had survived before knew when and where to fall and to find cover. I found myself bombarded by bodily sensations which I'd never felt before, by such a violent longing for Greg's hand on my waist and for his hair to brush my skin that all ordinary, accustomed thoughts were simply pushed out of my head. I walked about in a daze. I found myself down in my cabin not knowing how I'd come down the gangway. I ate my meals without remembering what I ate. I dressed and pinned up my hair seeing only Greg's eyes in the mirror. I didn't know how to protect myself; I never thought about it. I was like one drugged.

By the time I reached Calcutta and caught sight of Herbert in his white ducks, his white Topee with its green underbrim shading his light blue eyes, it was too late to retreat. I simply let myself be enfolded in his arms, tenderly and delicately as if I had been a fragile lily to be wrapped in tissue paper and protected from coarse fingers and the frost, or the wilting heat, as the case might be. He didn't know, nor did he ever guess, that not a fortnight earlier I had been seized, pushed down on a lower bunk, my dress torn, my body explored, caressed, yes, and roughly but unresistingly entered. I was, in fact, no virgin bride.

So I entered marriage with deceit. Moreover, I soon discovered Herbert was a stranger I had to get acquainted with. He was often silent, tired after his day's work, wanting only to sit on the verandah in the cool of the evening as he sipped his chota-peg and smoked to keep away mosquitoes. I sat, too, within the aroma of his smoke, which I liked; and sometimes he would reach out from the depths of his wicker armchair and touch my hand and tell me I was a lily, a marvellous, cool, undemanding quiet girl; and I would gulp in the near darkness and shrivel with shame remembering that lower bunk. I didn't object to his silences too much because as my pregnancy advanced, I lost all my unsettled longings and much of my tendency to agitated movement and acquired a bovine calm. When he touched me gently and lingeringly, love and forgiveness seemed to flow over me, so that I gradually forgot those last few tumultuous and terrifying days on board ship. I don't believe the memory of them would have been heaved into the present had it not been for the chance encounter with Greg on this boat a few days ago.

December 12th
In the Mediterranean

Herbert was working for the Land Reform Department in 1912. He wanted to get rid of bonded labour: that traditional Indian form of slavery in which a poor man buys a plot of land from a *zemindar* in exchange for his own and his son's labour, but at such a price that neither he nor his descendants will ever be able to pay it back.

I can hear you laugh.

'How can we get rid of bonded labour?' I hear you ask. 'This sort of thing has prevailed in India for centuries. India will never change.'

But the Raj got rid of suttee. Widows no longer step onto their dead husband's funeral fires. And the secret society of Thugs who worshipped Kali, she who spat blood, was stamped out by energetic police work very many years ago. Travellers are no longer strangled on the roads for money. So why should we not stamp out this form of slavery too?

I suppose it will come as a shock to you, who so firmly believe in the Empire and its God-given guardianship over a whole subcontinent and millions of Indians as beneficial to them (and indeed, Herbert himself admits that the Pax Britannica has brought to the warring races and religions of India not only lasting peace but increasing prosperity with the trade encouraged by the railways, as well as the reduction of disease and famines and an increased life expectancy) to learn that Herbert was a committed Fabian socialist when I married him. In spite of his old-fashioned manners and impeccable family background Herbert had new-fangled ideas, which you would consider dangerous, even subversive. He believes in a time-limited stewardship for the British in India. He hopes we can pass on our constitutional, legal and educational theories, and that as soon as there are enough Indian administrators to run the show we should get out.

I know what you would say to all this: 'If we lose India it will be due to bad manners. Indians understand our class system. They have one of their own. Their caste system is much more rigid than ours. And they respect our reserve. What they don't like is to be despised. An old Hindu proverb puts it thus: "The sting of contempt penetrates even the skin of the tortoise." It is something you should never show towards another person if you have any respect for human dignity. Quite simply it's bad manners.'

There are, I know, louts in every rank and every race. Sadly there are Britons who have been worse than bad-mannered in India.

You would say that as soon as we leave India there will be an ecstasy of blood-letting, and that after their civil war they will prove ungovernable, because those clever inhabitants of the Ganges plain who might seek to rule have been rendered by their climate effete, garrulous and indecisive, and altogether incapable of the rigours of governing. Herbert thinks you underestimate Bengalis.

Then there is this man Gandhi, who returned from East Africa a few years ago. He is a completely new phenomenon in history. He is spreading a new idea: revolution through non-violent non-cooperation. As a way of dealing with conflicts of interest the gun has always seemed to me a stupid, wasteful and unprofitable way to settle arguments. Differences are not overcome, but only lie low for a while, gathering strength to renew themselves.

Such ideas would have been regarded by Grandmama

Dambresac as due to that softening of the brain and spinal cord which was sometimes seen in the most upright and intelligent of civil servants when they had lived in India too long. It was due, she thought, to the enervating climate and particularly to the action of the sun on the European spine. It was against this danger that she made Grandpapa wear, not only a pith topee on his head but a padded felt spinal support under his jacket as well. We have discarded the spinal protection with other cherished myths; but many more of them will have to go.

What I do believe is that something of the Indian fatalism, of their long view of human existence stretching back into history and forward into future reincarnations, something too, of their contempt for the material things as mere comforts and consolations which distract us from reality has rubbed off on us. Certainly when I'd lived a few years in India and had become familiar with the needs of the people, had seen with my own eyes the frequent infant funerals, I became ashamed of the waste and luxury indulged in by some English families.

You, I know, never allowed yourself excessive luxury, since in any case you considered this bad form.

Herbert would hate the handover to be a disorderly mess of rioting and bloodshed. He hopes it will be gradual, civilised, and finally a parting of friends. Perhaps with Gandhi leading the Congress it may be so; but another Amritsar and it won't ever be possible.

I am returning to India after that horrible affair earlier this year, which happened when you were too ill to appreciate its significance. If you had been able to you would have been among the many who support General Dyer's order to fire on the crowd, even though they were unarmed and, it seems, peacefully demonstrating. And your reactions would not be surprising when I remember your father was wounded at Agra during the Mutiny, and your Aunt Fanny treacherously slaughtered at Cawnpore.

Herbert writes that some civilians are saying that the danger was minimal and could have been handled by a schoolmaster with a cane, others that General Dyer was a sick man and his judgement was impaired, while others simply say he lost his nerve and that it was a damned silly thing to do; but the Army has closed ranks behind him and is supporting him loyally. We must await the outcome of the official enquiry before we can know the full facts; but Herbert writes that it is a horror, a stain on British Indian History that will not be forgiven or forgotten. So, you see, I am returning to Patna at a time of apprehension and political unrest.

Our very first leave was delayed owing to the War and scarcity of shipping for non-essential, i.e. non-military personnel. When at last we did get home early in 1918 it was to find you sadly frail in the first stage of your illness; but since you had thoughtfully provided us with a nanny, too old for War Service but not too old to cope with Lucy's exuberance, I was able to enjoy with Herbert some of our days in London. Food was monotonous of course, and I greatly missed the bananas, custard-apples and mangoes of India, and most of all the delicious peaches we grew in our own garden in Bankipore.

Coming back to England last year after such a long absence Herbert and I were struck by the changes in people's attitudes to life, particularly in young women. Everybody was so frivolous. Gravity seemed to have exploded with the shells, and everywhere an epidemic of dancing raged. Whenever we went out to a friend's house, whether for lunch, tea or dinner, after the meal the carpet was rolled back, the gramophone wound up, and everybody danced. The whole nation seemed to have been seized by a hilarity of the legs. Was this because for the first time in centuries women were admitting that they had such things?

Herbert and I were infected by the frenzy too. We joined some of the dance clubs springing up all over the place. The first one we joined was the Gilt Edge, but in spite of it's name it soon went bust, and when we arrived hoping to dance there one evening we found the blinds drawn, doors barred and no lights visible. The next one we joined had a more plebian name, the Ham Bone, but it lasted longer. Once or twice we went dancing at the very select Embassy in Bond Street, where on the crowded floor we caught a glimpse of the Prince of Wales doing the turkey-trot with Adele Astaire. The turkey-trot was considered fast, and was, I believe, condemned by the Pope as likely to incite immorality; but the Prince of Wales and his lovely ladies did it, so following his example, and the advice of the still popular song 'Everybody's Doing It Now', Herbert and I did it too.

I looked up my old school chum, Alice Pillinger, who, you remember, daubed the slogan VOTES FOR WOMEN in white paint across a pavement in Piccadilly in the early hours of one Sunday morning in 1912, and got away without being caught. She was in the army by the time her hopes were fulfilled and the Act, 'Woman's Disability. Removal of,' was passed, giving us both, since we were over thirty, the long-demanded vote.

I know you always disapproved of my links with the suffragettes, whom you regarded as at best foolish, and the most militant among them as mad. I know you took the view that women didn't need the vote, since they were in any case the stronger sex, more intelligent in their own sphere, which is the more important one, involving the passing on to the young of acquired culture. Women live longer and possess a tougher moral fibre. This last quality is due to the physically more powerful male's weakness and unpredictability in matters of *l'amour fou*. Passionate love tends to make a fool of him, you thought.

'Man may be the pioneer,' you used to say, 'but woman is

the civiliser.' You cited as evidence your belief that women civilised the prairie plains of America far more effectively than the gun-toting sheriffs, and it was women who tamed into home-owners and family men, the mad, bad and dangerous, the whisky-slugging, sharp-shooting, the feckless, footloose and hitherto rootless cowboys of the Wild West.

'Each mother is a cultural link between the generations,' I have heard you say, and heard you quote: 'The hand that rocks the cradle rules the world.' Any woman worth her salt can rule her family and her man. She has only to learn the rules of the game of life and play her cards correctly. Woman, in your view, is the *eminence grise* controlling society from the wings while cocky little man struts about on the public stage.

You did believe in women's education though, because you thought literate mothers with organised minds can better manage their family resources and so increase the health, well-being and learning of coming generations.

Herbert once quoted to me some words of that old sage Samuel Johnson to the effect that the Law gives women little power because Nature has given them so much. It seems to me that only some women have this great power. What about the majority who stumble as best they can through a world in which they are, or were before the War, locked up in bedrooms, kitchens and nurseries at home?

Here I should interpolate in all fairness Herbert's comment that men are also for much of their time imprisoned in offices or factories, and have very little freedom of movement even when they think they rule. Even in a democracy freedom is limited, he says. In a civilised society you are only as free as the freedom of others permits, and so forth. Moreover, he corrects me (and Herbert as you well know can sometimes be a little pedantic), the vote does not confer freedom, but only a somewhat limited political choice.

I have come to the conclusion that it is money which

confers freedom. Women at home do not earn. That is the difference. I have some measure of freedom because, due to what you have so generously left me, I am, or could be, financially independent.

You despised the suffragettes, because you thought they were making a dreadful fuss for the sake of irrelevance.

'A domestic servant gives a woman more freedom than the vote,' you said. There is much truth in that. But only the wealthy could afford domestic servants before the War, and now nobody can find them let alone afford them (except in India of course). The domestic servant is a character who is leaving Life's stage. In any case the interventions of electrical engineers will gradually make her services unnecessary by substituting domestic machines. Every motor car, too, replaces a driver as well as his cart. Perhaps a day will come when every working-class woman will have her own floor cleaner and washerwoman at the touch of a button, and every working-class man will employ his own car to take him to work. It is even possible that in this way all women will achieve some measure of freedom.

As soon as Herbert and I heard the gospel of Marie Stopes we realised that she was offering a much more practical freedom to women of all classes than anybody else, for it was obvious to us that both in India and at home the bearing of innumerable and often unwanted children exhausts impoverished women physically and mentally, consumes their meagre resources and perpetuates the production of inadequately fed, improperly cared for and poorly disciplined generations of young.

You never mentioned birth control, did you? Perhaps you never practised any. At home there was always a conspiracy of silence about sex. Did you believe that if women obtained some degree of sexual liberty they might, like men, indulge in *l'amour fou*, and so might lose their strength?

I would never have read *Married Love* at all, had it not been for a visit we paid (another event I never discussed with you) to that eminent Harley Street specialist. Herbert wanted a son, you see, and since I had not conceived again since Lucy's birth we agreed I should seek advice while we were home on leave.

I was nervous, so Herbert came with me. He sat on a leather armchair in the heavily curtained waiting room, the only relief in whose darkness was a brilliant expanse of red Turkey carpet on which, as I glanced back over my shoulder, his black shoes winked up to comfort me. I was ushered into the consulting room by a starched nurse with aged cheeks. I suppose all the young nurses were working in France or in military hospitals at home. Women's ailments were of secondary importance then.

Mr Probert rose from behind a massive mahogany desk to shake my hand and to signal Nurse to retire. I told him our problem. Yes, Lucy's had been a normal birth in Ranchi, India, in 1913. Yes. I had been attended by a European doctor. No. There had been no lying-in fever, no white-leg, no complications of any sort. I told him my age, thirty-four. Had I used any birth control methods since?

'I'm afraid I don't know what you mean,' I replied.

'No douches? No spermicidal pessaries?'

'No.'

'Ah! You haven't read Marie Stopes' book then? Perhaps you were still in India when it was published. It created quite a furore over here you know, attracted a lot of hostility, but much publicity as well.'

He punched a bell to summon Nurse, who led me to the examination couch behind floral chintz screens. Mr Probert was so courteous, ceremonious and pompous, and so very delicate in his movements that he made my undignified position on the couch seem almost natural. He pronounced me normal in every way.

123

'Do you think my husband should also be examined?' I asked as I emerged and sat down again opposite him.

'Your husband? Well, I don't see – He has begotten one child already, so there should be no reason – '

'So, of course have I,' I pointed out.

'Yes. Quite so. But that's rather different, isn't it?'

'Is it?'

'Yes. It is.' I could see him scribbling his notes.

'A woman's pelvic organs,' he explained, 'may be exposed to infection and obstruction, such as puerperal sepsis, which can cause secondary sterility. In your case, not. Or from her partner in sex.' He looked at me steadily for a moment across the desk and repeated. 'No. Not.'

After scribbling some more he said: 'I see no reason why you shouldn't have a son, Mrs Brunoye. You are still young and in blooming health. I'm sure you will. All in good time to be sure. Perhaps a little more understanding of the conjugal act? There is an optimum timing for it, a best time in the month, you know'

We stood up. We shook hands. Nurse ushered me out to Herbert and the red Turkey carpet.

'He says everything is all right,' I said as we emerged from the glossy black Georgian door. 'He says it's only a matter of time.'

Herbert squeezed my arm. I could tell how pleased he was. He suggested a little celebration. So he took me out to lunch at the Savoy where we sat among potted palms and listened to a trio playing sentimental music. When they played that old favourite from the Byng Boys we clinked glasses and hummed the tune together.

> *If you were the only girl in the world*
> *And I were the only boy . . .*

We felt happy and full of hope.

'Mr Probert mentioned a book, *Married Love*, by someone called Marie Stopes,' I said.

I ordered the book and discovered it was notorious when the bookseller handed it to me over his counter with the book jacket turned inside out so that his other customers couldn't read the title, as if married love were somehow improper. Such hypocrisy! On turning the fly-leaf I found the book had already been reprinted a good many times, so obviously a great many people were buying it and reading it.

To me it's not immoral at all. On the contrary the author's dedication, 'to all who wish to see our race grow in strength and beauty' seems to me an honourable, if not noble ideal. She seems to be a serious, high-minded person, rather lacking in a sense of the comic perhaps, who would approach the act of sex in solemn, Wagnerian mood, and would disapprove greatly of the frolicking of Rabelais' two-backed beast. I wonder what she would think of the occasion when Herbert, having locked the bedroom door, removed the key and hung it by its string over his erect member before we fell upon each other in fits of laughter?

What I can't understand is why that eminent Harley Street gynaecologist wanted me to read the book, Did he think that Herbert and I didn't make love often enough? Did he think I was suffering from poor Grandmama's post-honeymoon horror of sex (which I discovered accidentally and read about furtively when I came across her diary at the back of a drawer in Father's library) and was refusing Herbert altogether? If he suspected these things why didn't he ask me outright? The plain question and straight answer do save such a lot of trouble and uncertainty.

Alice Pillinger, whose brother is a doctor, told me later that such was the disapproval by the medical establishment of Marie Stopes that any doctor recommending birth control, or even the reading of her book, might be in danger of losing his hospital appointment. So that was why Mr

Probert trod so delicately! That I do find shocking. How is it that a body of highly educated men dedicated to the relief of pain and betterment of the human condition seem to have missed altogether the importance of this invention to the human race, especially the female half? Perhaps therein lies the reason. It is the female half whose interests they are unable to imagine.

The only shocking paragraph in the book to my mind is a quotation from an eminent German professor of gynaecology. 'In the normal woman, especially of the higher classes, the sexual instinct is acquired, not inborn. When it is inborn, or awakens by itself, there is abnormality. Since women do not know this instinct before marriage they do not miss it when they have no occasion to learn it.'

Of course this is repudiated by the author. And what she advocates is 'the sacramental rhythmic performance of the marriage rite of physical union through the whole of married life as an act of supreme value in itself, separate and distinct from its values as a basis for the procreation of children.' Is that so wicked? What she regards as immoral is the forcing of sickly and unwanted babies on an exhausted woman, 'on an unwilling woman and an overburdened world.' And I agree with her.

Curbing fertility became a possibility for all, you see, in the very same year in which women got the vote. I suppose it's arguable which gave them the greater freedom. Personally, since I seem not to conceive easily, I value the vote more; but I daresay all those women who are preposterously fertile would find birth control of more immediate practical help in reducing their slavery.

Herbert and I didn't feel too guilty about chasing after amusement while in London because at the beginning of our leave you were still well enough to pursue your normal life; but after he was recalled in September of 1918 to become secretary of the new Land Reforms Department you were no longer able to manage your household. I was glad to be able to give more time to you.

I didn't miss Herbert at first. Perhaps I was too busy running your house and taking you out for those painfully slow walks in the Gardens, later reading to you, sitting by you, letting you talk about the past. But after a while I began to feel imprisoned. I began to long for Herbert. Mostly I missed his kindness and his little quirky jokes, the way he calls me madam when we are alone. It is one of his erotic fantasies – to think of me as a grand lady and himself as a small boy. Sometimes he even calls me *Madamji*, adding a small Indian irony.

It was fortunate that you had dear faithful Dolly to supervise the kitchen, and that new little tweeny whose face wore a permanent expression of indignation while brushing down the stairs or washing up in the scullery, so that I was able to act as your companion and nurse.

By the spring you were needing a lot of help. Although you made such a gallant effort every afternoon to dress and come down to the drawing room for tea, and even received callers, who, you said, kept you in touch with the outside world, you were visibly fading before our eyes.

I believe it was Lucy who kept you going for so long. You seemed to suck a little vitality from her exuberant youth every teatime when she returned fresh and glowing from her walk with Nanny. After your chat with her, at the end of which you gave her one of your special chocolates and watched with triumph her pleasure in eating it, you used to retire smiling to your bedroom. It was almost as if you were allowing your life to ebb into hers.

Perhaps it was really Lucy to whom you left your property, and I am merely its trustee until she grows up. You can rest content it will not be squandered. Lucy will come into it all in due time. Herbert, being a very honourable man, would never ask for any of it. As he is neither interested in money nor very good at managing it, and would probably give most of it away if it were his own, I shall keep control, with the help of your stockbroker, of your investments. Meanwhile I have let the Kensington house on a long lease, and put aside a fund for Dolly so that she can draw a pension from it till she dies. Poor Dolly! She misses you dreadfully. She is now living with a widowed sister in Camberwell, so she is not alone, which is something to be thankful for.

We picked up the Mail in Marseilles, and there was a letter for me from Alice Pillinger. It was Alice, whose feminist views you so much disliked, who helped me most after your death. She had just been demobbed and had nowhere to live, so she was glad to shelter under my roof for a few months. She was wonderfully practical and sensible about all sorts of legal matters, about letting the house and visiting shipping agents to badger them into finding me and Lucy berths on this slow old mail boat to Calcutta.

One night in October we went together to listen to a concert at the Queen's Hall at which a new work by Elgar was being performed for the first time. It was a cello concerto, and very different from his other music which you so loved. Gone was all the imperial bombast of his pre-war marches. This was sad, plaintive music with desperation in it as well as more than a little pride. While listening to it I knew it expressed not only my personal grief for the loss of you and with you of my childhood, but was a lament for a whole generation of young men killed in Flanders, and with them for the passing of a way of life that was yours, of all that self-confident, flamboyant, and yes, frivolous pre-war world that, it now seems to us, you enjoyed so much. It was an expression of our *Zeitgeist* so true and touching that my tears fell unchecked on my hands clasped over the programme in my lap.

Alice understood my thoughts and feelings too well to question me about them; but as we left the auditorium she remarked: 'The new world we're going to build will be a better one. You'll see.'

I blessed her silently for her kindness and her optimism. It is a sad commentary on the human condition that the great divide between male and female makes it difficult to communicate our thoughts and feelings across it, so that men and women, though bound to live together by biology and social decree are often strangers, whereas women can be true companions to each other. As of course can men.

I was surprised to read in the papers a few days later how badly the critics had received this work of Elgar's, which to Alice and me had seemed the supreme expression in musical terms of the post-war soul.

Alice cheerfully declares that she is the New Woman, post-war model, i.e. spinster. She doesn't seem to mind this in the least, perhaps because she has learned to look after herself in this modern world of ours. She knows the ropes, the new ropes, as well as you did the old ones.

We are really living in a new world, you see. It's an attitude of mind, Mother. There's the change. The war and all those deaths have given us the Shakes, have shaken us loose, have freed us from a lot of our stiff habits, presumptions, snobberies, yes, even our ideas of right and wrong, have turned your world upside down. But Alice does prophesy that it will take several generations more to get rid of entrenched prejudices and oh-so-many shibboleths in the minds of people about women's status and capabilities.

Well, we shall see!

Sunday December 14th
Malta

We arrived in Malta this morning, and in spite of its being a Sunday we had to refuel, which is a dirty business. The coal barges came alongside and a crowd of busy blackened figures swarmed up into the ship tipping sacks from their backs into the coal-hole. They all look alike, made anonymous by their equal coating of coal dust. Afterwards our own Laskar deckhands soon washed down the decks and made our ship clean and sweet once more.

It amazes me how spruce and elegant they manage to look in their blue cotton coats and white trousers and their neat red turbans when they have to do such dirty work. And I'm told their quarters are very cramped.

Our stewards, by the way, who are Goanese and according to Mr Vexham very religious, have their own RC Chapel on board complete with statues of the Virgin and the Saints, although candles can only be lit before the altar during service in port because of the danger of fire. Today, Sunday, while we were coaling, an RC Padre, a Maltese, came aboard to say Mass for them.

Soon after leaving Malta we sighted dolphins, so much loved and so often depicted by the ancient Greeks in their statuary and by the Romans in their mosaics.

'Look! Porpoises!' Someone cried.

There was a general rush to the boatrail to see a school of them, five arched backs leaping from the sea's surface. Lucy, who had pushed her head between my waist and my neighbour's to get a better view, counted them gleefully as they emerged one after the other.

December 16th

We arrived in Port Said at breakfast time, when we were informed that there would be no time for us to go ashore. We were soon surrounded by an armada of bumboats filled with traders gesticulating and shouting their wares. Mrs Chinkwell was so alarmed by the noise that she looked like an agitated hen. She described to me her 'flutterings' with such a wealth of fidgets and jerks, ruffling of her table napkin and shaking of her loose pink cheeks while she cracked her boiled egg, that I half expected her to spread herself over it and settle down to brood. I was thankful to escape on deck.

Outside the air was as warm as midsummer in England. As I stood by the boatrail on the after-deck in order to get as much of the breeze as possible I watched a troupe of 'tricky men' swarm on board. All the children, Lucy sitting cross-legged in the forefront, were allowed to watch their performance, and other passengers stood by, amused as much by the children's reactions as by the conjurors, whom many of us grown-ups had of course seen before.

Lucy was astonished by the sword-swallower, alarmed by the fire-eater, but delighted when, with a flurry of tricky movements, one of the men suddenly produced a baby chick from under one of Mrs Chinkwell's armpits. She squeaked more loudly than the chick: 'Dear me! Dear me!' and blushing furiously tried to brush herself down as if covered with feathers.

Lucy clapped her hands and cried out: 'Do it again! Do it again!'

He then walked in front of the crowd with one palm open demanding: 'I say! I say! Gold watch please – please, sir – or madam. I say! I say! Want magic? Gold watch please, sir . . . .'

Reluctantly Mr Vexham allowed the conjuror to remove his own from the chain across his waistcoat. The watch was then subjected to all manner of insults. It was thrown on the deck, jumped on, beaten with a wooden mallet and finally smashed into pieces which were thrown overboard. In the ensuing horrified silence the tricky-man shouted: 'No good now!'

He stopped before Lucy and pulled her to her feet. 'Now look here, Missy,' he said. 'Put hand here.' He indicated the pocket of his besmeared and frayed jacket. Rather gingerly she dipped her fingers in and extricated Mr Vexham's watch, undamaged, which the conjuror seized and waved about in the air for all to see before returning it to its relieved owner.

Other passengers were meanwhile leaning over boatrails bargaining with traders in boats below. When the price was agreed a rope was thrown up and wound over the rail which acted as a pulley for delivering the goods. It appeared there was some delay in our ship's entry into the Canal owing to the number of queuing ships; French, Norwegian and Japanese, as well as British. So, after all, some of us were able to board small boats in which we were rowed ashore.

Lucy and I descended the gangway preceded by the major and Rose, which was just as well as we were besieged and jostled by bumboat men offering their wares and shouting: 'I say! I say! How much? How much?' I even heard one of them offering the use of his sister for a small sum to a ship's officer just above me. It was not a practical proposition, since our stay on land was to be so brief.

It was pleasant to walk about on terra firma once more, and to move among the bright colours and strange smells of the market stalls. I bought a beautiful amber necklace for £5, and for Lucy a pretty turquoise and silver bracelet. I noticed that Greg bought for Rose a silver bangle, and she herself purchased an ostrich feather dyed a startling emerald green which exactly matches the colour of a rather elegant green glass ceinture which she sometimes wears twined around her waist and sometimes dangling from her neck.

This trip ashore and the laughter and excitement it generated seemed to break down remaining barriers between us all. After this day we were all more friendly. Mrs Chinkwell spoke less about her ailments, conversation became livelier and more frank, and Greg cracked more jokes over coffee after dinner when Lucy was safely tucked away and fast asleep. I began to feel I understood Rose better, who for all her assumed sophistication seemed to me in some ways as much a child as Lucy.

She asked me: 'What's it going to be like, truly? India I mean?'

I looked at her lovely face and wondered if she would learn to avert those eager eyes from the sight of poverty. What could she know of the numberless, voiceless, the passive and fatalistic poor of India? Poverty on such a scale would be difficult for any white girl from a wealthy city to imagine, let alone the possible methods for mitigating it; but even the most frivolous of flappers could not pass through villages and city bazaars without seeing little naked boys with matchstick legs and swollen bellies, and the occasional leper with nose or fingers missing; and Miss Kelly had, in spite of her flirtatious manner, some desire, some instinct in her for doing good. So in time she would perhaps learn the facts as well as the obstacles to progress, and would perhaps add her little efforts to help fill the rice bowls, save the water, purify the drinking-water, prevent malaria and vaccinate against smallpox. It suddenly occurred to me that one of the best ways to help the women of India preserve what health and wealth they possessed would be to spread the message of Marie Stopes. I guessed Miss Kelly's religion would not allow that, quite apart from the indelicacy of discussing the matter with her. So I answered her shortly: 'Dust and heat. You'll see. And smells too. Not all of them bad. There's the night-scented jasmine . . . .'

'Maybe I could do something useful?' she suggested, her voice irritatingly naive, her great, innocent eyes shadowed by uncertainty. 'I mean, my generation being more liberated than yours . . . .'

What *could* she mean? She was not much more than ten years younger than I and yet she spoke as if I was already put aside by age, on the shelf and useless, not only in the amusing pastimes of youth (I accept that on account of my mourning) but also in the work of trying to improve the lot of the Indian masses! Did she know that although some of America's Western states have granted women the vote the Eastern states have not, whereas I have acquired one in Britain, and will use it when the first opportunity presents itself?

'Do you think you'll get the vote soon?' I asked tartly.

'I don't know much about politics,' she confessed. 'But in other ways we're more free.' She went on to explain. 'The War has broken down a whole lot of rusty conventions, hasn't it? So I guess I'll be able to move about and mix with people of all sorts and races, don't you think?'

The girl's a fool, I thought. She simply has no idea what she's going out to. In any case what liberation will she have as soon as there are two or three small children clinging to her knees? Yes, knees – clinging precariously too, since her skirts are always worn so short they would certainly be out of reach of grasping baby fingers!

'Your husband will show you the ropes,' I said. 'And of course you'll have an ayah when the time comes.'

'Yes. Jimmy will be there of course,' she agreed. And she blushed.

Immediately I felt ashamed of my irritation. I was glad I hadn't mentioned Marie Stopes. In spite of her brashness and naiveté I couldn't help liking her, so I added more gently:

'You should persuade him to take you to see some of the native dancing. You would like that. Such complicated rhythms, and so many strange and difficult movements! It is strange, but beautiful too.'

She looked up gratefully.

'Do you think – do you think I'll be accepted – welcomed, being a foreigner really?'

'With a name like Kelly you'll be quite at home,' I said. We both laughed. Did she know, I asked, that half of the tombstones of the men who fell defending the British

134

during the Mutiny had Irish names inscribed on them? Murphys and Dalys, Keegans, Regans, and Rileys and many more.

'Is that so?'

I did not explain that these Irish names represented the common soldiery, and that the Irish had infiltrated into the higher echelons of army and government to a much lesser extent; but I added: 'The General who defended Cawnpore was Irish. His name was Wheeler.'

'Wheeler? Was he killed?'

'Oh yes. They were all killed. My Great-aunt Fanny was murdered at Cawnpore. After the siege was lifted to let the women and children pass, she was dragged out of a rowing-boat and pushed into prison with the others. The sepoys refused to slaughter them, saying they were soldiers who didn't kill women and children. So four butchers from the market were paid to do the job. They hacked down all the prisoners with butchers' knives. Great-aunt Fanny's body was pushed down a well.'

'Oh my!' she cried. 'I can't believe it!' But she obviously did believe it because she turned pale and clutched the knot of necklace at her throat and twirled the loop of green beads about in her agitation.

'We didn't behave nicely either,' I continued relentlessly. 'After the Mutiny some of the rebels were tied to the mouths of cannon which were then fired.' She popped some of the green beads into her mouth which made me think she was still a baby really.

'It was a long time ago,' I said.

As we had not eaten lunch that day, owing to our shore excursion, I allowed Lucy to stay up for dinner. It was then she let slip the news that Rose was teaching her to dance.

'She has a gramophone in her cabin.'

'In her cabin?' echoed Mrs V.

We knew Rose had a cabin to herself because her English aunt, who was to have accompanied her on the voyage, fell downstairs a few days before they were due to sail and broke a leg. Encased in plaster and from her sickbed she had kissed Rose goodbye, declaring that not even a broken leg must interfere with the course of true love, and that Rose must travel without her. This we had already learned from Lucy. By the bye, the fact that Rose has lived quite a lot of her life with an English aunt explains why her accent is soft and lacks a marked Yankee twang. Her gramophone, it seems, is placed on top of a chest of drawers.

'She let's me wind it up sometimes,' Lucy explained. 'It's lovely. She's teaching us the Shakes.'

'*Us*?' Mrs Vexham pounced.

'Yes. The two of us. Groggy-legs and me.'

There was a short silence till even Mrs Chinkwell sniffed scandal.

'Who is Groggy-legs?' she asked.

'Why, the Major of course!' cried Lucy impatiently, as if we were all being very stupid. 'She calls him Gregory Groggy-legs because he can't do it as well as I can.'

'Rather an apt name, what?' interjected Mr V. Everybody laughed, because we had all noticed how much time the major spent filling, and emptying and refilling his glass; but Lucy, not understanding the reference to grog, went on:

'She calls it the Shakes because she shakes all over all the time, shakes, shakes, like the ship does near the engines.'

The captain gave her a long, penetrating stare. 'You mean she does the Shimmy?'

Lucy frowned. 'No. It's not called that.'

'Could it be the Turkey-trot?' suggested the captain.

'Oh no!' exclaimed Lucy scornfully. 'That went out with the Ark!'

'Well, that was quite some time ago,' he agreed.

'But it's a sort of dancing,' Lucy said. 'What she does with her legs.'

There was a long, scared silence.

The captain broke it with: 'I expect it's a new sort of Shimmy.'

'Her old black nanny called it "shakin' out ya' feet," ' said Lucy, and burst out laughing with sheer pleasure at the thought of it. 'Her green necklace flies about too. And she's teaching us to do it!' She was triumphant.

'Perhaps she's only just discovered that she *has* legs,' I commented. 'Most of our mothers after all weren't allowed to admit they had such things!'

'Oh come now, Mrs Brunoye, that is really an exaggeration,' Mr Vexham objected.

'It isn't their legs they didn't admit to,' remarked Mrs Chinkwell with sudden surprising logic, 'it's the uses they can be put to. We were always brought up to take healthy exercise. And just look at Suzanne Lenglen! Nobody disapproves of her.'

'No indeed!' echoed Mr V. 'She leaps about the tennis court in her white silk dress and stockings like an inspired cat after a bird!'

'She uses her legs for movement,' said his wife severely, 'not for decoration.'

'Not to say enticement!' added Mrs Chinkwell.

'Is enticement dancing?' asked Lucy.

'Why yes,' said the captain. 'In a way it is. They're both rather nice, like birthday cake.' He smiled at her. Lucy nodded. I was afraid that for years to come she would confuse enticement with icing sugar; but I did not intervene.

Mrs Chinkwell made the final judgement: 'She's just a young flibbertigibbet! All this shaking her legs will steady down when she gets married!'

Rose laughed when I reported some of this conversation to her.

'Well, I guess I do shake,' she admitted. 'It's a dance our old nigger cook taught me when I was a kid. She used to put me up on the cookhouse table and make me do it

137

while she clapped her hands in time. She came from Charlestown in the South. She called it a happiness dance. "When you's happy, Miss Rose," she used to say, "just you get movin' to that ragtime rhythm!" But when my English auntie saw me do it she was disgusted. She said it was abandoned.'

She laughed, and then her childish face assumed a serious expression.

'Do you know what I believe, Mrs Brunoye? Music's a language that speaks to all people everywhere, whatever their mother tongue. And the new jazz rhythm speaks even more clearly, especially to us younger ones. It's going to bring us all together.' She laughed again, lightly and carelessly; but I was impressed by her underlying seriousness.

'It's an interesting idea,' I said, wondering what jazz was.

Of course Lucy was being used by Rose, perhaps as a chaperon, but also as a camouflage behind which she and the Major could enjoy more fun than they could without her. Mrs Vexham took the first opportunity to draw me aside and warn me, pointing out my responsibilities in the affair.

'I wonder if you should allow Lucy to be in their company quite so much?' she began. 'She's picking up some rather questionable expressions; and don't you think there's a certain – well, a certain looseness in Miss Kelly's behaviour, considering she's an engaged girl?'

'Perhaps she's just young and flighty?' I suggested. 'And I've known Greg quite a long time, you know. That is – ' I hurried on, catching sight of Mrs V.'s sudden avid curiosity – 'that is, we used to know him years ago when he was a young subaltern. At one time he used to call at my mother's house.'

'Really? I had no idea you were previously acquainted. That does make a difference, of course,' she conceded. 'Is he married by the way?'

'That I don't know,' I replied. 'The fact is that I haven't

138

seen him for so many years I don't like to ask; but he travels alone and never speaks of wife and family.'

'Quite,' was Mrs V.'s comment. The single word jabbed and pinned him down like a specimen for scrutiny: a single man of forty-plus with a past which no one knew.

'He has changed a lot since those days,' I said. 'He has aged so much I hardly recognised him.'

'And he drinks too much,' she added sharply.

Monday December 22nd

Lucy was disappointed by the Red Sea. She pushed her head through the bars of the boatrail and peered down angrily.

'Why is it called the Red Sea when it's green?' she demanded.

'It's got a lot of red seaweed floating on it,' I pointed out. 'Perhaps that's how it got its name.'

'It's not fair,' she decided after another minute's staring. 'I thought it would be really red – like blood.'

'What a horrible idea,' I objected; but she had already lost interest and was running along the deck to catch up with Sophie, who was taking a sedate morning consti- tutional with her mother round and round the ship.

We arrived at Aden on the 21st. It was a short stop so we didn't go ashore, but were greatly entertained by the Somali diving boys who swarmed round us in their dugout canoes. They were naked except for white loincloths. Their woolly heads were reddened with a solid paste of henna and lime which was obviously impervious to water. Lucy threw in a four-anna piece and as it fell down through the clear green water one of the boys dived after it. He emerged after what seemed to us a very long time with the coin held in his startlingly white teeth. We were anxious because there were sharks about. Indeed in the same canoe was another black boy with only one arm. He stood up and, pointing at his stump, shouted with a grin: 'Shark took arm!'

The night after we left Aden a piano was hauled on deck to provide music with the help of a violin and a cello for dancing after dinner. It was very pleasant in the cool air of the evening. Even I danced a little. Greg is still a wonderful dancer, and Mr Vexham, rather to my surprise, can do the foxtrot. I also danced the waltz with the Third Officer who is in charge of Mails. He is the one who handed me Alice's letter at Marseilles.

It has, of course, been rather warm since we reached the Gulf of Aden. Electric fans hanging from the ceilings of the public rooms have begun to turn, but there are none in the cabins, which are becoming uncomfortable at noon. I am sorry for Rose. It must be a lot worse on the sunny starboard side.

I insist on a bedtime bath for Lucy at least twice a week. This, as you doubtless remember, owing to the shortage of fresh water is quite a complicated ritual to perform, what with the booking in advance and the carrying of soap, towel and sponge as well as nightclothes all to the communal bathrooms. Lucy enjoys sitting in the warm salt water but has to be helped when she stands up to soap herself, and squeals loudly when I rinse the lather off with the rather cool fresh water provided by the Bath Stewardess. She also makes a great noise when she gets out by drumming her heels on the wooden slats of the bath mat.

'Groggy-legs calls his bath King Tub,' she informed me.

I couldn't help laughing. It really is such dated military slang it puts him well and truly in the Victorian era.

The warm bath has the effect of calming her when she is excited, so she usually falls asleep in her bunk very quickly after it, which gives me ample time to dress for dinner. After I close our cabin door and tell our steward that Lucy is asleep, I can climb the companionway.

I feel calm and confident as I walk into the brightly lit

dining room. I feel less dowdy then, because my evening dresses, though necessarily black, are made of lace cut low on the shoulders. I think it is not improper to wear your pearls, and since Port Said I have sometimes worn the amber beads I bought there. The great, golden semi-translucent drops look fine against the black. I enjoy the cool draught on my neck as I pass under the fans between the pillars, and I know that under the softly shaded lamps of the dining tables black is less cruel to my complexion than in harsh daylight. I have been thinking of your last journey home in the hot weather after Father's death. You were in mourning then, and in those days there were no electric fans, only drowsy *punkah-wallahs* sitting cross-legged on the floors of the public rooms and pulling their flapping curtains to and fro to stir the air. You looked beautiful, without a doubt, the diamond brooches which you gave to Victoria sparkling against your black lace; but the heat must have been almost insufferable.

The tedium of the next long spell at sea without sight of land was relieved when we began to overhaul a ship of the British India line steaming about half a mile off from us, which signalled, challenging our passengers to a game of ninepins. Immediately the foredeck was prepared with canvasses spread out along the boatrails to check and prevent balls from rolling overboard, skittles were set up in the prow, and a team of passengers, led by the major, rapidly volunteered for the game. It was really quite amusing to watch. The slight upward curve of the foredeck as the ship moved forwards allowed the balls to roll back to the players' hands along the gunwales. The score was telegraphed between the rival ships. In this case we were the losers; and at the end of the game we signalled by three hoots on the ship's siren our congratulations before parting company with the victors. After that, to console ourselves, all players and many onlookers moved to the bar.

It is a place that is obviously second if not first place to Greg.

'Grandmother is dead,' announced Lucy this morning, 'but we shall see her again one day. Perhaps when we come home again on leave. Or perhaps in heaven.'

Mrs Vexham was visibly touched by Lucy's sentiments. She smiled across the table.

'Did you love your granny very much, my dear?' she asked.

'Yes,' said Lucy. 'She was nice. She used to give me special chocolates. But she was ill too. She was ill all the time.'

Mrs V.'s smile went sour. I realised she had never had children, never listened to the disjointed way they talk. She thinks little girls are, or should be, fully house-trained and schooled young ladies. Children to her are merely smaller, sweeter, purer adults not, as they seem to me, young human creatures with new eyes and with imaginations as yet untrammelled by conscience and dissimulation.

Lucy's remarks at table often disconcert her; but as time goes on she realises that it is Lucy who brings to her many tit-bits of ship's news. Mrs V. is one of those people who live chiefly in other people's lives. The actions, conversation and eccentricities of others, especially when these deviate from her own conception of what is right and proper, seize her greedy attention. By the time we were sailing across the hot, wide expanse of the Arabian Sea she was actually questioning Lucy at mealtimes.

'How was the Major this morning?'

'Cross.'

'Cross? And why was that?'

'He wouldn't let me play tricky-men with his watch.'

142

'I should hope not!'

'Well, it's not gold, Rose says.'

'Indeed?'

'He stamped off in a rage.'

'Did that upset Rose?' asked Mrs V.

'We just laughed.'

'We?'

'Rose and me. And the doctor.'

'The Ship's Surgeon?' enquired Mrs Chinkwell.

'He's called Morton,' said Lucy. 'He stares.'

That I too had noticed. He is a tall, thin, ascetic looking young man not long out of his teaching hospital house surgeon's white coat, but with a formidable presence in spite of his youth. I foresee he will be a distinguished London surgeon one day. At present he is gathering experience of travel and of the illnesses and ways of travellers. He is handsome in his uniform. His voice is quiet; but sometimes he laughs suddenly, not a genial laugh but a short, derisive snort. His light blue eyes are watchful and penetrating. They don't miss much.

Perhaps it was his staring and not the matter of the watch that made Greg stamp off in a rage. I had noticed, during the skittles match with SS *Manitoba* he had been at Rose's side, and afterwards they wandered off together while the Major led the round of consolation drinking in the bar.

A third man is now paying court to Rose. He does not sit at her table but has taken to joining our widening circle in the saloon for coffee. This third devotee is a shy, middle-aged bachelor. He plays the piano remarkably well. He accompanied Rose the other night after dinner when she sang *Little Dolly Daydream* for us, and then made us all join in singing the chorus. It was then, when Rose was unashamedly letting herself go with obvious enjoyment, that I caught sight of the doctor staring. He was not singing but standing quite still watching her with such a peculiar, devouring intensity that I felt quite disconcerted, and stopped singing too.

It has become clear to me that the Major now has at least two rivals for Rose's favours, and indeed may be feeling put out; but these observations I am keeping to myself, leaving Mrs Vexham to ferret things out as best she can.

It was after the ship's concert that Greg began to express his feelings of jealousy. Lucy, whom I had allowed to stay up, sat between us. The pianist began with an excellent rendering of Sibelius' *Valse Triste*. He was quickly followed by a plump Scottish soprano who sang very touchingly Dvorak's 'Songs My Mother Taught Me', which I confess made me cry a little as it brought to mind evenings spent around the piano at home with Tom and Victoria singing to your accompaniment. Then there came three not-so-little maids from school dressed in Japanese kimonos who chirped and bobbed and fluttered their fans in an authentic *Mikado* manner. When Rose appeared there was a half-suppressed murmur from the audience, partly of admiration for her beauty but also of shock at her daring costume. She was dressed in a very short white dress with three tiers of white silk fringes which shimmered when she moved. Her arms and shoulders were bare, as seemed her legs in their thin silk stockings. The long green necklace was knotted at her breast and with one hand she fingered the knot and flung the loop around as she sang. With the other she fanned herself with the emerald ostrich feather from Port Said. A bright green bandeau held her glossy black hair in place and green satin shoes with the fashionable curved heels encased her feet.

Her devoted musician could play ragtimes as well as sombre waltzes. They must have rehearsed well, for they now raced off together into what seemed to me a mad whirl of new rhythms and movements. It was all terribly exciting, and really so well done that I began to wonder if Rose could be a professional.

144

Her act began with pure burlesque. Three sailors followed her round the stage, each begging to be her partner for the dance. Their song was an amusing one originating, I suppose, in the tea dance craze. They all joined in the chorus of 'You can't make your Shimmy shake on Tea!' One of her suitors pulled a brandy flask out of his pocket and offered her a swig, upon which she grasped a Seltzer bottle handed to her from the wings, and as they knelt to ask her for favour she knocked them down one after the other with a squirt of soda water.

After they had crawled off stage she broke into a song in a clear, harsh voice quite unlike the lilting soprano, and interspersed her singing with dancing in which all her limbs did, in Lucy's words, fly about. Her song was *Movin' On!* and she sang it with such sincerity and energy that it began to mean to her audience not just moving to a new, fast rhythm but moving into the new decade so soon to come –

> 'We're going to break the bad old world,
> We're breakin' out!
> We're gonna shake it all to bits,
> We're shakin' out!
> We're movin' on, movin' on, movin' on
> To the bright new day around the corner!'

was what she promised us. We were all entranced, and when she made her bow everybody was shouting for more.

I leaned over to Greg and cried out enthusiastically: 'She's really wonderful, isn't she? Such *élan!*'

The look he gave me was not a pleasant one. The suppressed rage, even hatred in his eyes alarmed me so much that my pleasure was momentarily banished. All this was forgotten, however, as soon as she reappeared for her encore. For this she threw away her feather and grasped instead a cane. Over her hair she had clamped a white peaked cap. This time she did a lot of marching up and down the improvised stage to the tune of 'Alexander's Ragtime Band', which the pianist was vamping away with remarkable speed and vigour. When she ended up with a sudden bout of tap dancing the applause was thunderous.

I was aware that a number of the ship's officers were standing at the back of the room, and I could see peering through the window several Laskar deckhands. On the faces of all was an expression of surprise and delight. Rose, in her role of entertainer, is a giver of innocent pleasure. She enhances the small pleasures of daily life, makes them shine with a special magic polish she rubs on them.

I was pushed close to Mrs Vexham in the crush in the exit afterwards.

'She brightens up the dull old world a bit, doesn't she?' I said.

But Mrs V. was not amused.

'It's dangerous to flout all the conventions at once as she does,' she remarked dourly. 'That sort of dancing – Why! It's like an African orgy!'

You are a nasty, dirty old woman, I wanted to say, swilling your disapproval where secretly you'd like to guzzle; but my indignation was tempered by your training in good manners. 'I can't see any harm in it,' I protested mildly.

'We shall see . . .' she muttered ominously.

What shall we see? I wondered. What prophecies of doom as yet unformulated were floating about in the imagination of this ship's Cassandra? I didn't have time to find out, because I had to put Lucy to bed; nor did I see more of Rose that night, so it wasn't till the morning that I was able to congratulate her on her performance.

'And Lucy's just mad about your tap dancing. She's been trying to do it up on deck.'

'OK' said Rose, 'I'll show her how. She's cute, and a real good dancer you know, Mrs Brunoye. Maybe we'll see her name in lights on Broadway one of these days.'

I glanced at Lucy dubiously. I didn't think Herbert would

take kindly to this suggestion; but the Major, who stood between them and was still wearing his baited-bull expression, stroked Lucy's hair. I noticed how his eyes suddenly melted with that tumultuous warmth which he had once turned on me.

After dinner I found him sitting alone, a brandy as usual in one hand, a cigar in the other. He looked sullen and unhappy as I sat down beside him.

'Where's Rose?' I asked.

He didn't reply, but picking up my remark of the previous evening as if it had been on his mind ever since he burst out angrily: '*Élan! Élan!* Why must you be so damned Frenchified? Though I've nothing against the Frogs. Fought magnificently at Verdun – poor devils!'

He paused and I waited.

'What she's got isn't *élan*. It's female animal attraction. Sexual attraction, don't you know?'

I said nothing.

'But that's not what she cares about at all. The pleasures of sex, I mean. What she's wild about is rhythm. She makes a fetish of it. It's a sort of religious exercise to her, like some damned Tibetan prayer-wheel or something. She says I haven't got it.' He emptied his glass quickly. 'Rhythm, she says, is a God-given grace. Seems I wasn't granted this, nor any other graces, come to think of it,' he finished gloomily.

I hastened to contradict him.

'To me dancing's just a way of getting to know girls; but to her it's a living! And because I haven't got this – no sense of this ragtime timing or something – I am a sort of *harayan*. An outcast.'

'Perhaps it's more than a difference in your timing,' I suggested. 'Perhaps it's a difference in your age.'

'What do you mean? A man is never too old!'

'Oh, Greg! What a Victorian you are! Rose is nearer to Lucy in the way she looks at things than to you. That's what I mean by the age difference.'

He was silent for some moments before he spoke again. 'You're a hard woman, Louise. You don't beat about the bush – but I daresay you're right.'

'And as to your being an outcast, that's rubbish! You were born with many advantages and many graces. Why! When you were a subaltern I thought you were the handsomest young man in London! I had quite a crush on you then – '

He looked into my face and then quickly out to sea through the porthole opposite. It was the first time either of us had admitted directly to a previous affection.

'That was a long time ago, Louise. A long time and a different life ago.'

The memory of it didn't seem to interest him greatly, because he came back quickly to the present.

'This rhythm thing seems to be what she lives for. She gets some kick out of it, almost like – like an addiction.'

'She's a very good dancer,' I said.

'What does it all amount to anyway?' he growled. 'Savages have rhythm, don't they? Beating the tom-toms and all that. She's nothing but a damned Yankee drummer. Drums with her feet!'

'Is she a professional dancer? On the stage, I mean?'

'Wanted to be; but her old man wouldn't hear of it. Said it was a low life, that she'd meet men who were bad guys and fall into all sorts of immorality and degradation. Wanted her to be a lady. Then she met this chap in the Indian Police.'

'How did she meet him?'

'Seems he stayed in her father's hotel in New York last summer. He was on leave and cricking his neck looking up at skyscrapers. Must have been a relief to look down again and see Rose.'

He sighed deeply.

'I suppose you're right. I'm getting old.'

'You're not old,' I remonstrated. But I reflected that he was twice Rose's age, and to her he might indeed seem old.

He was suffering, I could see. His great mass of curls, which when younger he had cropped close to his scalp, now fell over his forehead when he bowed his head. He looked rather like a lion, I thought, as he darted bloodshot eyes first at me and then at his empty glass, an enraged lion bathing his wounds in liquor.

'She's very young,' I said. 'Almost a child still. Probably this is the first time she's been let loose on her own, and she's enjoying it. Flirting, I mean.'

As I had done, I remembered; but neither of us mentioned that.

He shot me rather a venomous look, then rose and lurched off towards the bar for a refill. He never asked me if I wanted a drink too.

I left the room soon after him and went up on deck. It was a quiet, balmy night, the stars so bright they seemed to be exploding in the tropical darkness. I stood by the boatrail and listened to the black waters moving beneath the ship, slap-slapping our steel hull which was forever pushed forward by the pumping engines. It was like a great human heart pulsating while the days, like all our days, slipped past and slid away, merging one into the other in the ocean of the past. I let my thoughts drift with them.

It was easy to remember and to be amused by the memory of my schoolgirl crush on Greg twenty years ago, but much more difficult to believe that I had spent four weeks almost continuously in his company only seven years ago on a previous voyage in another ship. That was before the war, which has made such surprising changes in our attitudes. I was twenty-eight, engaged to be married, going out to dear Herbert to be his bride. But was that young woman, whom I now look back on after a mere seven years as at a stranger, really me? It was, as Greg put it, a long time ago and a different life then.

I suppose I was intoxicated by my sudden release from all those restraints of having to conform to accepted, but often absurd, social values. I was drunk with the delight of being young, of feeling the salt spray on my cheeks when I stood on deck in the wind, of standing close to Greg to watch the wake of water streaming endlessly away from us like time passing, passing: ecstatic days streaming away and each one bringing us closer to Calcutta and inevitable parting because, of course, Greg would never have married me. I knew that; but I didn't care. Greg . . . I had only to touch his sleeve and a sort of madness rushed through my body. When he kissed me I trembled as I clung to him. When with him I didn't see other people. I was dimly aware of them but I didn't in the least care what they said or thought about me. I can only recall those other passengers as blurred figures, dark against the brilliance of the sky up on deck when I stumbled down into the shade of a gangway on the way to my cabin, to fetch a book, to dress for dinner, to do all the hundred and one things I continued to do automatically, the dull actions of ordinary day-to-day living which I had before performed with interest but which then became trivial and remote from the blazing immediacy of my feelings in that strange period. All my former contacts with reality were loosened, vague, turned upside down. My only certain point of reference was Greg.

Love is a sort of sickness, *l'amour fou* . . . It makes men mad. And women too, as I remember. And now that I'm sane once more it's difficult for me to believe that I'm that same crazy girl.

Just as I was about to stop thinking of her and return to the present, Greg joined me. It was too dark to see his face but I knew by his slightly unsteady grabbing of the boatrail, and by a new muddled but more urgent speech and coarser growl in his voice that he was not only more than a little drunk but angry too.

'Women!' was what he was saying. 'Never really liked

'em, you know. Love 'em, want 'em – need 'em! Of course. That's natural. But not for long – ' He burst into derisive laughter.

'What don't you like about women?' I asked.

'Women?' he demanded, as if he'd forgotten he'd been talking about them. 'It's the way they cling,' he replied after a pause. 'Don't like the way they cling. Always wanting love for ever. As if anyone can love till death do us part!'

Knowing from my own experience how I have shed my past self as a snake sheds its skin and emerged a changed woman I could see the absurdity of the marriage promise, for the person who swears now to love another may not be the same person in seven years' time. Nor indeed may the recipient of love be the same recipient. So how can we swear for a future we don't know? In sickness or in health, or in riches or in rags maybe, but how when we change in character and philosophy? But Greg was following his own train of thought, not mine.

'Can't stand on their own feet. Not like you, Louise. You're different. Independent and outspoken. Don't make demands.'

Was Rose making demands, I wondered? But I didn't ask him. I didn't pursue the subject further because he suddenly seized my elbow.

'Something I've got to say, Louise,' he blurted out.

'Something about Rose?'

'No, no!' He gestured angrily as if trying to push a heap of papers into the sea. 'About you, Louise. About us.'

I felt my colour rising and was glad it was dark. 'Oh, Greg! That was years ago!' I protested.

'I know, I know. But there's something I want you to understand.'

'What? I was madly in love with you, that's all.' I spoke of love, but my voice was harsh.

He withdrew his hand from my arm. There was a long

silence. When next he spoke his voice was subdued, almost sad.

'It was what I'd always wanted. Love. I didn't get much as a child.'

I gave him time.

'When you gave it to me I wasn't allowed to take it.'

'Not *allowed*?'

'The Law – Society – all those things you respect so much. They can be cruel, Louise.'

'Yes?'

'Marriage impossible,' he struggled on. 'And all that. Prohibited. Indecent really.'

'Indecent?' I echoed. 'What do you mean?' And then the explanation flooded over me that he was trying to tell me he had been your lover in the past, that he couldn't marry a girl whose mother had been his mistress.

'You mean you loved my mother?'

There was a long silence. Then he burst out laughing.

'Oh no! Not like that at all!' He put his arm round my shoulders. 'You see she was my mother too. Bastard baby I was. Fostered out and not admitted to the family name. Never a real toff, you see.'

I was dumbfounded. Angry. Horrified. I shook myself free from his arm. I clutched the boatrail with both hands to steady myself.

'I don't believe it,' I said.

'No, I suppose you don't.'

And so we stood side by side in silence till a small feeling of pity for him began to melt my hostility.

'Was she kind?' I asked. 'Your foster-mother?'

'Lived on the other side of the river,' he replied shortly. Confession seemed to have sobered him because he began to speak more clearly and quickly then.

'Very clean she was, but not well-off. Too religious. Fair . . . but kind? Well, kind enough. My foster-father was more affectionate. He was a builder in a small way. Mother

– my real mother – visited me sometimes when she was home on leave. Paid for me to go to a good school. When she came she brought presents, chocolates and pocket money. Once or twice she took me out for a treat. We rode on the top of a bus, I remember. In those days it was a horse-drawn omnibus. And once we trotted through Hyde Park in a hansom-cab to tea with muffins in a teashop. My mother – your mother – always kissed me when she said goodbye.'

It was a long speech for Greg to make. It created in my mind a chilling picture of his childhood: of infrequent meetings with his mother, of pleasures sparsely scattered through the years, and kisses received only at partings with sad goodbyes.

'I was happy in the army,' he then said, as if trying to pull the picture straight. 'Mother helped me to get in – indirectly – pulling strings, don't you know?'

I did know. The *eminence grise* on the sidelines . . . .

'Yes, I did love her. She was so beautiful. But always from a distance.'

'So we're related?' I was still incredulous.

'You're my only living relative, Louise. But I suppose from your point of view I've never been anything but a bounder.'

His old-fashioned slang irritated me. Victoria was his sister too, but he had forgotten her. I felt as if a trap was closing over me. All sorts of new loyalties, duties and decencies were beginning to cling to me and tie me down.

'You're my half-brother then?' I asked. I thought: Seven years ago he knew, but I didn't. 'It was incest, wasn't it?'

To my surprise he laughed unconcernedly.

'Always straight to the point weren't you, Louise? Must be a bit of a shock to you, I know. But I had to tell you.'

And without another word, but still laughing, he turned and left me.

I realised he must have wanted to hurt me. If not, why

had he told me this awful secret? He was trying to punish me for being born in wedlock and for living on the right side of the river. Well, he had succeeded. I knew as I stood there staring at the moving sea that this burden thrown on me so unexpectedly would have to be carried alone, without help, in silence to the grave. Gradually there rose inside me anger and, hatred too, of you, my dearest mother. I saw you then, with the clear eyes of Alice Pillinger, and condemned you. She would have called you hypocrite, blamed you for allowing strangers to bring up your boy. She would of course have blamed you less for the indiscretion of your hot blood in allowing that unknown lover of long ago to come to your bed. (Or was it some dark and fragrant corner of an Indian garden on a stifling night awaiting the breaking of the monsoon?)

You should have rebelled, carrying your head high. You should have found a way of supporting your child by honest work, even by manual labour in poverty. Part of me accuses you thus, of preferring social position and ease to caring for your first child. But then I remember Grandmama Dambresac (whom Alice never knew), with her high authoritative nose, and Grandpapa Dambresac, whose translations of the Urdu poets made such a stir in the English newspapers of the day. Alice Pillinger never saw the old family photographs. She never understood the meaning of all those serried ranks of bearded cricketing and rowing uncles, left hands on left hips, as steely in their unarmed allegiance to the family as a corps of armoured knights, nor did she ever meet the aunts, pencil in hand, as ready to delineate a new botanical specimen as to strike off a lady's name from their social register.

I who have been so much influenced by Herbert's moderating intelligence, his ability to see all sides of any question, can't be so severe; but I wonder how you faced yourself during all those years after you had fallen from conventional grace and produced – how and where? – that beauti-

154

ful but shameful evidence of your fall. Did you regard yourself as wicked and deserving of punishment? Or did you rage against society and beat your fists on its barricaded doors? I believe you somehow contrived to balance the two opposed views. You were never a rebel abusing Establishment attitudes, nor were you a woman full of feelings of guilt. On the contrary you were confident, kind, honest and helpful to others around you whenever possible – and all this with a gaiety and a zest for living.

Herbert's presence has helped take the sting out of my anger, but can't make me feel any less unclean. I know I shall never again be able to have the same confidence in myself among others. I can't in reason blame you for my own affair with Greg; but I do. I am angry and hating you. It makes me feel sick when I think you might have prevented it. I can see that if I'd known who Greg was I would never have fallen in love with him. It was incest, you know. It's a nasty word. Because of it Lord Byron was outcast from all the drawing rooms of London and country houses of England and had to run away to exile in Italy. It is, after all, the ultimate taboo which, unwittingly, I admit, you have allowed me to break.

I walked slowly down to my cabin. Without turning on the light I washed my face and hands in the tepid water in my jug. Then I lay down fully dressed on my bunk.

Who was Greg's father? You must have known him before your marriage since Greg is some years older than me, and older too than Tom would have been. Perhaps you met Greg's father in India when you went out from school for your first season with the fishing fleet? Perhaps he was the great romantic lover of your life, and that's the reason you want your hair returned to India to be cremated with your youth. Why then didn't you marry him?

Did Father know you had a son by another man? If so, it must have been very bitter knowledge after Tom's death. Or did you keep your secret from him all through your life together? Was that why we never saw Greg at home till after you were widowed? I am sorry for Father. But no. I remember how happy and intimate you were. You were both in love. So perhaps he knew and understood and forgave your youthful mistake.

I shall never get answers to all my questions. No matter how long I live and how often I think about it I can never know the whole truth.

I felt dreadfully tired, but I knew that with this angry revulsion for your memory weighing on me I couldn't sleep. *Comprendre tout c'est pardonner tout*, you used to say; and so I tried to imagine in order to understand your feelings about the beautiful fire-headed boy, that first child of yours whom you had to abandon to the care of others. I tried to relive your earlier life. When you were away in India and I at boarding school in England you must have written letters to him as well as to me; and when you came home on leave you visited him before I came for the holidays. All the time I was growing up you hid this other child in your thoughts. Or did you manage to forget about him for months, and then sometimes, guiltily remembering, you sat down and wrote to him? Father, I think, encouraged you to be kind, but from a distance. You both agreed to banish him from your family life and social sphere. *Never a real toff, you see*. I thought how little I knew you. How little any of us know the secret lives of our nearest and dearest!

Rose isn't in love with Greg, nor with anyone else on board; and I'm glad for her sake she isn't. I wonder if Greg could possibly be in love with her, or whether his misery is not simply due to wounded pride? He certainly never was in love with me. He always took the view that my proper destination was in Herbert's arms. I am glad to say they never came face to face.

Although as Mrs Vexham says, Rose is not one of *us*, she

156

has by her success in our improvised theatre established herself as a special being in her own right. She carries with her an aura of magic. This is obvious in the way a great many eyes follow her entrance to a room, the way men move to find her a chair, to get her a drink, and the way the stewards give her a special, happy deference. Some of this attention is, I fear, sliding off on to Lucy's head; and I am beginning to worry that she is being spoiled.

'It's all due to sex,' she announced at the table. Rose has sex. That's what Groggy-legs says.'

I caught the captain's eye, and this time it was I who blushed.

Later that day, the Major, being at a loose end without Rose (who was walking her mile up on deck with her new friend the pianist), took Lucy down into the bowels of the ship to see the engines. Owing to the possible danger of her falling into the machinery she was never allowed to go there alone.

Lucy was visibly shaken when she emerged on deck.

'It won't stop!' she cried, running to me. 'it goes on munching and grinding!'

The engine was to her some sort of ogre, powerful and uncontrollable; and I know what she must have felt. When one sees the great wheels turning, pistons moving up and down, brass shining, black oil gliding, and feels all that jerking and shuddering, the perpetual vibration of the floor beneath one's feet, the fearful noise and above all the stunning, stifling heat one wonders how the engineers down below survive, let alone work at all.

Lucy soon forgot her fright and ran off to play with Sophie; but it must have made a sinister impression on her because she woke that night screaming. I jumped out of my bunk and caught her just as she tried to scramble out of hers.

'It's that albatross – that bad luck bird!' she sobbed. 'The Major held me tight and made me watch it!'

157

Something of her terror communicated itself to me. I realised that Greg with his shock of hair, his angry face and eyes full of unfocused hatred must have mingled in her memory with the sight and sound of the engine's inexorable energy. Perhaps she had been afraid he might push her into the machinery to be mangled. It had been to her some picture of hell so powerful that as she trembled and wept in my arms I too felt her fear. When we wake in the middle of the night reason is loosened and imagination leaps, sometimes to the truth. I too had a sudden glimpse of Greg peering down, not into the engine but into the turmoil of his own soul. Some of his agitation and distress, some of his rage against the world must have passed to Lucy through his hand as it held her.

'It's only an engine,' I said. 'A very big one of course, because it has to push a very big ship through the sea. The steam in the boilers and all those pistons going up and down push the wheels that push the paddles through the water.' She was snivelling less by now. 'Like when you swim,' I added. 'You push the water away with your arms like paddles, and so you shoot forwar .'

'Only I don't steam,' said Lucy, perfectly calm and rational once more.

'Let's read about naughty Peter Rabbit,' I suggested, 'and how Flopsy, Mopsy and Cottontail all went blackberrying together.'

So Beatrix Potter soothed our fears with pictures from her orderly world of little animals until Lucy, chewing the ear of her own battered Peter Pushkin fell asleep in my arms.

I laid her gently in her bunk and left her asleep. I didn't bother since it is now so hot, to cover her with a blanket. I took out my writing paper to continue this letter to you. In spite of what has happened to me, and although I feel in a sense unclean, even criminal when my imagination runs riot, I will try to get back to the ordinary routine I have set myself. It is habit, the pursuit of the humdrum, which keeps us going through an ordeal. So I will behave as I behaved yesterday and the day before; and Greg will not have the satisfaction of seeing me distracted and confused, nor the ship's gossips the pleasure of speculating on what has gone amiss.

December 30th

We docked in Colombo today. Quite hot and steamy. A large number of our passengers disembarked, some of them rather sadly and unwillingly, I thought, especially the younger women who realise that the peak in entertainment will be reached around the New Year. They are particularly sorry to miss the traditional New Year's Eve Fancy Dress Ball. The fact is that after the excitement of the Ship's Concert life at sea has been a bit dull. The only new sights worthy of note are the flying fish, flashing across the surface of the Indian Ocean in silver sprays.

Lucy's reading has improved enormously during our weeks on board. She is now able to read aloud not only the *Tale of Peter Rabbit* but quite a lot of *Jemima Puddleduck* as well. Her sums, too, are not bad. She is beginning to master addition and subtraction. I don't keep her at it too long, however, in case she gets angry or bored and like an obstinate pony at a new jump refuses to face the problem.

Christmas has passed quietly and happily. I made chintz cushions and covers for a tiny suite of wicker sofa and chairs, and dressed two little Japanese dolls to sit on them. These were all duly wrapped in red crêpe paper and dropped into Father Christmas' sack, which he solemnly dragged across the deck after our open air carol service on Christmas morning. When he gave Lucy her parcel she whispered to me:

'Who is it?'

She soon guessed it must be Dr Morton. Even the red

hood and white cotton-wool beard couldn't completely camouflage those steely blue eyes.

A Christmas teaparty was held for all the children on board in the First Class dining room. There are a good many more children travelling Second Class, which is what one would expect. As a matter of fact I have noticed that on this voyage there is considerable mixing of the classes. Everybody seems to mix for the dancing on deck after dinner as well as for the deck games. The only real separation seems to be for meals. At the children's party Lucy particularly enjoyed the ice-creams and iced lemonade. I am glad to say that plenty of ice has been available at table since we entered the Indian Ocean. The children had each a paper cracker at the party. Lucy turned round and pulled hers with the Major, who was standing behind her. He pretended he'd found a riddle inside it and read aloud:

'Why is a camel such a temperate animal when he works in a hot climate? Answer: because he can go for several days without a drink!'

All the grown-ups laughed, a few of us with embarrassment as we had heard the joke before, and others wishing that Greg could behave more like the camel.

Everybody is now beginning to look forward to the New Year. We all seem to be cherishing a belief that 1920 will somehow usher in a new era in history, a better feeling in politics, even a fairer, kinder society. Whether our hopes for the new decade will be fulfilled remains to be seen.

Our journey is coming to an end and I am trying to think less of the past and more of Herbert waiting for us on the quayside at Calcutta. I have kept safely hidden inside my trunk, and coiled like a white snake in its carved sandalwood box, the plait I made of your beautiful hair after you died. I have shown it to nobody. It is a secret between us. Your hair will be cremated according to your wishes on the banks of the Ganges, and its ashes returned to the India you felt a part of and loved so much.

Rose was as excited as Lucy about what she called the 'fancy ball' for New Year's Eve. She helped me rig up Lucy as Little Miss Muffet complete with a large grisly spider made out of eight pipe cleaners dyed in ink which it pleased Lucy to dangle over other people's hands and faces to tease them. Rose herself wore the white dress that caused such a furore at the concert, but added a broad sash round her hips bearing the message 'Miss 1920'.

I allowed Lucy to stay up till 10 p.m. so that she could watch some of the dancing. Rose was obviously exhilarated by the number of partners vying with each other for the privilege of dancing with her, but she very sweetly took Lucy by the hand and led her round the floor for several minutes before kissing her goodnight.

After putting Lucy to bed I caught sight through the doorway of Greg's back as he propped up the bar. He wore a pair of loud check trousers and a bowler hat. With his nose abloom after weeks of heavy drinking he could pass for a clown without dressing up, but Lucy said he was meant to be a bookie. At one end of the ballroom I spied Rose in the centre of a crowd of men keeping them at bay with a glass in each hand. She raised them both towards me as I approached and cried:

'This is one thing Miss 1920 won't enjoy back home, once they've made sure of Prohibition!' and promptly drained them one after another.

I felt momentarily worried by this exhibition of reckless-ness. I thought her English aunt might have allowed one but certainly not two glasses of champagne so early in the evening; but I am not her aunt.

I suddenly began to feel much too hot. I was aware of a slight headache, so I decided not to wait up to christen the newborn year in champagne. That was why I retired to bed before midnight and did not see Rose again.

The Twenties have not dawned auspiciously. On the contrary, new Year's Day has been full of anxiety and menace. The dining room was almost empty at breakfast. Most of the passengers were, I suppose, sleeping off the effects of the night's revelry. Lucy and I were alone at our table, and even she looked pale and down-in-the-mouth. Behind me the doctor's table was empty. The fact is something terrible has happened. I hardly know how to tell you, because I'm not quite sure what it is.

Lucy got up early this morning and dressed herself before racing off to visit Rose, who had promised to give her a New Year present. Only a few minutes later she ran back to me as I was sitting in front of the mirror brushing my hair. She was very distressed, sobbing and telling a garbled tale.

'She's not there!' she cried, holding my arm.

'Perhaps she's having a bath,' I suggested. 'We'll go and see her later. Don't worry, Lucy darling, you'll get your little present after breakfast.'

'The gramophone's broken. On its side – on the ground. And the record's smashed!'

'Oh dear! That *is* a pity!'

'It's not only that. It's her dress on the floor – all torn.'

'Her dress on the floor? Well, she was too sleepy to put it away.'

'Not her dress!' cried Lucy impatiently. 'Just the white fringe – torn off and lying in all the blood – '

'Blood?' This time I didn't make reassuring comments. 'Where?'

'Everywhere!' she blubbed. 'Broken glass and blood – in the basin – all over the floor!'

For a moment, neither of us said anything. Then Lucy released my arm as if remembering something important.

'You know her green necklace?' I nodded. 'Well, it was hanging on the handle of the porthole. It was going click,

click, click, click, with the boat.' She drew out of her pocket three green glass beads to show me.

'Then the necklace was broken too,' I said.

'Yes. Lots of beads on the floor. And her mirror was cracked. That's seven years' bad luck, isn't it?'

We went hand in hand to Rose's cabin and knocked on the door. When we got no reply I tried the handle. It was locked.

'I expect she wants to sleep late,' I said. 'Perhaps she cut her hand. That can cause a lot of bleeding. She'll be all right.'

I was appalled by the inadequacy of my explanation, but it seemed to satisfy Lucy, who stopped crying.

'Now I think we should make a solemn pact of secrecy, Lucy,' I said, drying her eyes with my handkerchief, 'and promise not to tell anyone about this till we've seen Rose. Promise?' She nodded. We stood in the corridor between the rows of closed cabin doors and crossed hands.

'Cross my heart,' she said.

'Now let's go up to breakfast.'

'Can we see her afterwards?'

I made no reply. I was having great difficulty controlling the shaking of my hands. All sorts of thoughts were tumbling around about my imagination. Had Rose perhaps disturbed a burglar in her cabin? Had some sailors' brawl exploded there in the early hours of this morning after all the other passengers had gone to sleep? If so, someone must have heard the noise. Had she herself taken part in drunken fighting, and above all was she injured? Perhaps she was already lying in the sick bay. Then certainly Dr Morton would know the facts.

But what if Lucy was the first witness of the signs of battle? I wondered if I should tell someone in authority what she'd seen, but decided as I sipped my black coffee that Rose's steward must surely have taken in her early morning tea and must then have noticed and doubtless reported the state of things.

'Let's take our constitutional first today, and do our reading later,' I suggested; and Lucy readily agreed.

The captain passed us on his way to the bridge as we went up on deck. I wished him a happy New Year. He returned my greetings; but I thought he seemed preoccupied.

On our second round of the deck I noticed that the engines had stopped. We began to lose speed. Other passengers noticed it too, and there was a rush to the boatrail to see what was happening. Somebody shouted 'Man Overboard!' – as a joke I believe. My heart began to beat uncomfortably fast as I told myself: Not man but woman overboard!

Then slowly the ship began to turn around on itself, and soon we were steaming back, retracing our course, which we continued to do for all the remaining hours of daylight. Meanwhile the Purser pinned up on the noticeboard a News Bulletin which, after the first crowd of passengers hungry for news had dispersed, I was able to read.

'It is with great regret that we have to announce the disappearance of a passenger who charmed us all so much when she entertained us at the Ship's Concert: Miss Rose Kelly. It is feared that she has fallen overboard. We will continue the search as long as necessary. Our wireless operator has alerted all ships in the area to be on the lookout. We are sorry that this accident will inevitably delay our arrival in Calcutta.

Poor Rose! She was a shooting star that after its brief transit fell into the sea.

January 2nd

A second bulletin has appeared on the noticeboard. 'It is with great regret that we have to report failure to find any signs of our missing passenger. We have therefore abandoned the search and resumed our course. We still hope that some other ship in the area may have picked her up. There is no further news at present.'

There is no sign of the Major either, who I fear must be ill. Lucy and I enquired at the sick bay only to be told he was too ill to have visitors. Someone else was told he wasn't there. So where is he? His table is empty. Rose is no longer there, and the doctor, it seems, doesn't care to sit alone. Rumours and speculation are flying about. Mrs Vexham told us she'd heard on reliable authority that Rose was seen astride the boatrail in the early hours of New Year's Day shrieking with laughter and declaring that she was riding a winner in the Derby. It is an electrifying thought.

Lucy very nearly broke her promise over our secrecy pact at lunch today. She didn't speak, but she pulled out of her pocket her three green glass beads and showed them to the captain. When she caught my eye she hurriedly hid them again. He said nothing but looked across the table at me. His face was grim, his eyes questioning. I immediately dropped mine to my plate. He knows now that Lucy entered Rose's cabin before it was locked; but so far he has said nothing about it. He is talking very little, and his expression repels conversation.

Mrs Vexham too, after her report on the Derby winner, seems to have become rather reticent. Whereas before Rose's disappearance Lucy was often the spark which fired a conversation, now she is the cold water that puts it out. Nobody wants to discuss the sad and perhaps shocking possibilities of the affair in front of a little girl, especially one who was made such a fuss of by the principle character in the drama. So now when Lucy and I enter the drawing room, or pass by a group leaning together in animated talk they are suddenly silent. They straighten up and move their heads apart, and some inanity drops loudly in the conversation's lull.

But Mrs Chinkwell, I notice, is talking still, especially to Lucy. I suspect that under her cloud of neurasthenia Mrs Chinkwell hides a sensitive heart. She wants to protect Lucy from the pain of hearing the worst. The worst, of course, is what I fear.

January 4th

Three days have passed and there is still no sign of the Major. This morning I was approached by Dr Morton. He spoke briefly and abruptly.

'The Major has been very ill. He's in the sick bay. He's asking to see you. Will you come now?'

Startled, I agreed at once. I left Lucy in the care of Sophie's mother for half an hour and followed the doctor, not immediately to Greg, but to the captain's cabin.

'I understand the Major was a family friend when you were children?' He offered me a seat and a drink, which I refused as I thought it too early in the day. Both men helped themselves to whisky as if they had all the time in the world to talk to me. There followed a long uncomfortable silence broken at last by the captain.

'I very much appreciate your discretion during these last few days,' he began. 'We would all be most grateful if you would continue to keep these matters to yourself, Mrs Brunoye. I realise of course that you entered Miss Kelly's cabin on New Year's Day.'

'As a matter of fact I didn't,' I said. 'It was only Lucy who went into the cabin. By the time I got there the door had been locked.'

'Only little Lucy?' He seemed surprised. 'Well Miss Kelly has disappeared, you know. Gone. Nowhere to be found. We can only assume she has fallen overboard.'

'Or been pushed,' said the doctor.

'That remains to be proven,' said the captain.

They looked at me expecting a gasp of horror, some comment, a murmur of concern at least. I gave them none. I had already accustomed myself in imagination to hearing all this. Moreover an instinct for self-preservation made me silent. I felt I myself was under scrutiny, almost as if I were in the dock being interrogated.

'The Major, who was of course her – her friend, has naturally been very upset,' continued the captain.

'You'll find him very subdued now,' interrupted Dr Morton. 'He is under sedation. It was necessary to control his agitation. He was very excitable, even wild, at first.'

The captain raised his eyes from his glass and gazed gloomily out to sea through the porthole above my head.

'He has asked to see you, Mrs Brunoye,' he said. 'We think it would be a kindness to let him talk to somebody. We can't deny him that.'

'Is he under restraint?' I asked sharply.

There was another long silence.

'You understand that while at sea I represent the law on my ship,' the captain said at last. 'But Doc here has been looking after him.'

'He has been threatening to do away with himself,' explained the doctor. 'He was very violent at first. It took a lot of paraldehyde to get him under control; but he's calmer now. You'll be quite safe. I shall remain in my surgery throughout your visit. If you need help you only have to raise your voice.'

I nodded. I began to understand why they thought I might need a drink before seeing poor Greg.

'Has he succumbed to grief or to delirium tremens?' I asked.

'His emotions, of whatever sort, are inextricably confused with his DTs,' the Doc pronounced somewhat pompously. 'But he is being dried out now. He is under the influence

167

of chloral today, and is as meek as a lamb. You'll notice a change in him.'

Greg was indeed much changed. He was sitting up in bed. He looked so thin, as if he had somehow shrunk in the wash; but the obvious change in his appearance was due to the bizzare way his beard had been shaved away from the left side of his face revealing a jagged laceration that had been stitched up. It extended from his left cheek and lips into the cleft of his chin and down into his neck. There were purplish bruises on his face too, and his right hand and wrist were bandaged.

'Good to see you, Louise,' he said. 'Sorry about this.' He pointed to the wound with his left hand, which shook. The stitches in his lips contorted his speech a bit. 'I can explain.' His eyes closed wearily.

He had no need to explain. I guessed immediately I saw him how it happened. Rose had done it. She had snatched her water jug and smashed it against the edge of her wash-basin. She had used the jagged edge of glass as a weapon to defend herself. It was Greg's blood, not hers, which had splashed across her cabin.

I sat down beside the bed and took his hand. An unpleasant sweetish, slightly fruity smell hung on his breath. I supposed it was the chloral.

'What happened?' I asked.

'She did it!' he exclaimed, as indignant as a child who believes himself unjustly treated. 'Piece of broken glass. Like a wild cat. Jumped at me.' He paused and withdrew his hand from mine. 'She would have – would have cut my throat, if I hadn't – if I hadn't – '

'Caught her waist?' I suggested.

'Killed her.'

I sat still, clasping my hands together, repeating to myself what I had just heard. Could it be true?

I heard myself speak, marvelling as I did so at the steady progression of my thoughts and the evenness of my voice.

168

My surprising calmness at this moment of crisis was certainly the result of all your training to achieve the necessary degree of self control. It is what Herbert calls the Dambresac armour-plating. 'How did you do it?' I asked.

'Thuggee,' he said calmly. 'The old Indian way.'

I waited. I must have been sweating because I felt cold.

'I found this sash in my hand. Part of her fancy-dress. Just the thing.'

It was only then that I felt a desperate desire to run away. I was beginning to tremble. I feared I might be sick all over the bed; but I forced myself to speak.

'What made you do it, Greg? I mean – did a quarrel start?'

'Mistake really – ' he murmured.

I looked sideways at him and saw his eyelids closing. His desire to speak was losing the battle with the chloral for his attention. I decided to go and tried to rise; but he caught my sleeve.

'Don't go. Need you, Louise – '

'I'll come back tomorrow, Greg,' I said; but it wasn't until I added 'I promise' that he released me.

I must have looked pale as I emerged from the sick bay because Dr Morton, who was waiting outside, took my arm firmly and led me into the captain's cabin where he pushed me into a chair.

'Put your head down on your lap,' he ordered.

I obeyed meekly. This time I accepted the whisky proferred.

They said nothing. They waited for me to recover, and as I did so I became cautious and more hostile towards them. It was obvious they wanted me to talk. Perhaps they needed my evidence to charge Greg. I was horrified by the idea that I might have to appear as a witness in a public trial during which events in my own past and even in yours might come to light. And Herbert would be sitting listening at the back of the Court.

'My interview with the major was absolutely confidential,' I declared.

'Have no fear, Mrs Brunoye,' said the captain. 'No one will ask you to give evidence.' He had read my thoughts. He hesitated and then added: 'Since you yourself did not enter Miss Kelly's cabin on New Year's Day you could only tell the Court what Lucy told you.'

'And that of course would be merely circumstantial evidence,' broke in the doctor. He sounded disappointed.

'Naturally we wouldn't dream of putting little Lucy in the witness box.'

So they had been hoping to use my evidence. I had been correct in my apprehension. Only the fact that Lucy had run to Rose's cabin alone that morning while I was still brushing my hair had saved me from a court appearance. The palms of my hands began to feel clammy. I took my handkerchief from my pocket and rolled it into a ball between my fingers.

The captain then told me that two passengers whose cabin was opposite Rose's had heard a lot of noise in the early hours of New Year's Day, shouting, singing and laughing in the corridor, and the slamming of a door. A couple of junior ship's officers, too, had owned up to being among the group of men who had escorted her to bed. That was 2 a.m. Her Steward found her cabin empty and in disorder at 7 a.m. So they knew of her disappearance at most six or seven hours (allowing a little time for how long it took to search the rest of the ship) after it happened.

'We have all the evidence we need,' explained the doctor. 'First of all the major claims he killed Miss Kelly, although his lawyers may plead that when he confessed he was suffering from delirium tremens with all the distortion of fact and the hallucinations which it can cause. We believe she smashed her glass jug and attacked him, but he didn't report his injuries. He was found lying on the floor of his own cabin at about 7 a.m. on January first, exsanguinated and semi-conscious. We had to carry him on a stretcher to the sick bay; but we had to tie him down as soon as he came to. He was confused and noisy, and very frightened.'

'What we don't know,' said the captain, 'is what he did to Miss Kelly before – before – '

'Before she disappeared?'

'Exactly.'

Thuggee, I thought, while a cold trickle of horror ran down my back, the ancient rite of strangulation with a silken cord for the sake of the goddess Kali whose gaping mouth dripped blood. But I had no intention of telling them.

'No,' I agreed. 'She has simply disappeared.' I sipped my whisky. I too wanted to know more. 'I promised I'd visit him again tomorrow,' I said after a moment's hesitation.

'Ah!' they both sighed.

'He seems to feel the need to talk about the past. I can understand it. But if he wants me to spend time with him I'll have to make some arrangements about Lucy.'

'I'll teach her to play chess,' offered Dr Morton. 'That will use up her energies as much as dancing.'

'That would be a help.' I threw him a grateful glance; but I was longing to get away, to be alone, to think over and, yes, subdue with honest reasoning all the terrible images that were thronging my mind.

Of course I couldn't sleep that night. I lay on my bunk staring up at the darkened ceiling. I felt the throb of the engines under me and the gentle sway of water under the ship. Thugs strangled their victims with a cord. It was a tribal rite, but it was also in pursuit of robbery. Had Greg robbed Rose? Not, I thought, before death, because she had obviously struggled violently to defend herself. That he had tried was suggested by that fringe torn from her dress and his own admission of the sash in his hand. But could he – was it possible that he had done it after death? Rape

171

is the word, I told myself, and I must face it. Rape of a corpse. It was a horrible thought.

He had not raped me. I did not resist. Perhaps that's why I'm alive today. It was Rose, so criticised and frowned on by the Mrs Vexhams of this world, who had fought like a tiger, had indeed given her life in defence of her virtue like any Christian martyr. But no – ! I hastened to tell myself, he wouldn't have done such a thing to me. For one thing he wasn't drinking so much seven years ago. I began to think he must have been pushed into crime by the sickness produced in him by alcohol poisoning as much as by his passions.

What surprised me more than anything was the lack of compunction he showed. He obviously wanted to talk, to confess, but he didn't seem to feel much guilt about it all. He spoke in such a matter-of-fact way. *I found this sash in my hand. Part of her fancy dress. Just the thing.*

This curious lack of emotion was even more noticeable when I visited him next day. He looked much better. The ship's barber had shaved him properly and washed his hair, which shone with some of its old glory. If he didn't quite look like the Greek warrior of old at least he wore his copper-tinted helmet.

He was also less drowsy. He seemed glad to see me and smiled when I sat down beside him. I was nervous, not because of the possibility of any assault such as Dr Morton thought I feared, but because I was afraid of what Greg would tell me; and yet I was eager to hear it.

'How is Lucy?' he asked.

'Playing chess with Dr Morton,' I replied. I didn't add that his place outside the door had been taken by a sick-berth attendant on guard duty.

He nodded almost happily.

'How do you feel today?' I took his hand.

'Better, better . . .' And then he sighed, although he didn't look sad.

'I'm in a mess, Louise.'

'How did it all start? I mean on New Year's Eve?'

'I was drunk.'

'More than usually drunk?'

'If you like,' he agreed, making a defensive grimace. 'I got mad with Rose. She's a tease you know. Calls a man on, and then slams the door in his face. Couldn't get near her because of the crowd. Other fellas.'

'Yes. She seemed very popular on the dance floor.'

'So I went down to her cabin. She never locked it you know. I sat there with a bottle of whisky and waited for her.' He released my hand. 'They all came down to the cabin with her,' he continued, and his voice took on that disturbing growl I'd heard before. 'Crowd of them. Laughing and singing. Said they wanted kisses. Wanted to undress her. Wanted to put her to bed. I could hear them. Outside the door.'

'Did they come into the cabin?'

'No. She managed to get rid of them. Banged the door. And then she saw me. Sitting on her bunk.'

He paused and shut his eyes wearily.

'She was probably very tired and wanted to get to bed,' I suggested.

'Far from it,' he said. 'She ran amok. Snatched the bottle out of my hand and threw it out of the porthole. Called me names. She can be devilish cruel sometimes.'

He stopped. He would say no more. He sighed deeply.

'I've made a mess of things, Louise,' he repeated after a while.

'What did you do with her body?' I asked coldly.

'Pushed her through the porthole,' he replied promptly. 'Easier than you'd think really. Of course Rose is a little thing – small boned.' He spoke of her in the present as if she were still alive. 'Head went first, and then the shoulders. Had to give her rump a bit of a push.' He might have been describing a game of football.

I suddenly though of Lucy's description of the green necklace broken and dangling on the handle of the porthole window. *Click, click, click, click.* I looked at him, examining his face closely. Perhaps the chloral was damping down his feelings. Or was it the whisky that had washed away his guilt?

Demonic energy he certainly had, but no compassion.

I glanced at him quickly, at his head resting against the high pillows, the large, flabby, plethoric face with its angry, disappointed expression, and thought, Was it possible that I had once loved this man? Certainly he is sick, probably he is my half-brother, but I am not his keeper. I imagined that perhaps in his desperation he might want to catch hold of me and through me of Herbert and his position in India, begging for help. But Greg wasn't begging. He was not desperate at all. He seemed to have no feelings.

'Goodbye, Greg,' I said. I held out my hand. Courtesy is a humdrum habit, and sometimes a reassurance ritual.

'Must you go, Louise?'

I went.

January 5th

I was unable to eat any lunch today, nor could I pay much attention to the conversation at table; but the captain did his best to keep the ball rolling by joking with Lucy, who was bursting with information about chess.

'The horse can jump sideways as well as forwards.'

'The knight,' Mr Vexham corrected her.

'The knight on his charger,' Lucy conceded. 'And the bishop can slide across the board.'

'Do bishops slide?' asked Mr Vexham, producing a few smiles between us at his suggestion. 'And what about the queen?'

'I don't understand kings and queens yet,' she admitted.

Although tired and lethargic I dragged myself away from

the dark thoughts pressing on my imagination and forced myself, with Lucy's help, to begin sorting and packing our trunks. As we knelt on the cabin floor Lucy handed me a pair of socks.

'Rose can swim, you know,' she said.

I was startled.

'People say she fell overboard. Perhaps,' she considered the possibility thoughtfully, 'perhaps when she cut her hand she couldn't hold onto the rail so tight.'

I nodded.

'Mrs Chinkwell thinks they threw her a lifebelt to keep her up in the water.'

'That's more than likely – '

'And the water's warm, she says. So if she can keep afloat until a rescue boat sees her she'll be all right.'

I blessed Mrs Chinkwell's kindness.

'Mrs Chinkwell says there are lots of ships in the Bay of Bengal. So someone's sure to see her.' Lucy was smoothing and folding a vest. 'And then she'll be picked up out of the water.'

'So we must just hope,' I said.

When at last Lucy was asleep in her bunk I lay awake in mine. I didn't go up to dinner that night but lay in the darkened cabin letting the images come, images of puppets with inanimate limbs folding and falling, being pulled and pushed, then slipping and sliding. I must have fallen asleep because I woke suddenly, feeling myself dropping helplessly into a vortex of inexorably whirling machinery. I shook myself awake and sat up. But no! Of course it was not Louise; it was Rose who fell.

January 7th

I think I must have looked wretched at breakfast next morning because I noticed several people glancing at me with some concern. No doubt they are all gossiping with

175

relish. Lucy has already informed everybody that I am visiting Groggy-Legs who is very ill in the ship's hospital; but I am too tired to wonder what is the general conjecture, too tired even to smile. I suspect Lucy must have dropped a few hints by now (perhaps to Mrs Chinkwell?) about the cabin. And the blood.

I drank black coffee at breakfast and revived a little. Dr Morton came across to our table and challenged Lucy to a game of chess at 10 a.m. I looked up at him beseechingly, and thought his cold eyes seemed kinder; but he said quietly: 'The Major has asked if you'll visit him this morning.'

The nasty thought struck me that perhaps in his ravings before he was dried out he had blurted out all sorts of things about our affair, perhaps about our family ties, to Dr Morton. If so this would explain his willingness, eagerness even, for my visits to his patient.

'Of course,' I said, though I greatly dreaded another meeting with him.

The sick-berth attendant showed me in before stationing himself outside the door. Greg was sitting up fully dressed in a chair. His hands still shook, but the smell of chloral had gone from his breath.

'What day is it?' he asked.

'Wednesday,' I said, sitting down opposite him. 'We're due to dock tomorrow.'

'How's Lucy?'

'Playing chess with Dr Morton.'

He nodded approvingly, smiling happily. It was almost as if having told me about the past – got it off his chest – he no longer cared about it. In some extraordinary way he seemed to be accepting all the outrageous events of last week as inevitable, and even (as if that were possible!) as natural.

Then he pulled out of his pocket Rose's little silver ash tray with the blue butterfly enamelled on its lid.

'It's Lucy's butterfly-box,' he said. 'Rose meant to give it to her on New Year's Day. Will you keep it for her? Give it to her one day?'

He was handing me this burden, charging me to explain things to Lucy, begging to be remembered by her. I was indignant. I had no intention of allowing Lucy to be dragged through this mess.

'It was sweet of Rose,' I said.

He sighed and relapsed into silence.

The sick-berth attendant knocked and brought in two cups of tea.

'No whisky?' laughed Greg.

'Not allowed, sir!'

'Not allowed? Shame! Shame!' Greg made a face.

'It is a shame, sir,' agreed the sailor. 'But we've got to get you well again. See?'

If he was a prisoner he was being treated kindly by his gaolers. I couldn't help foreseeing rather grimly how his situation would change as soon as we landed. He would no longer be a patient then. He would be a prisoner charged with murder, handed over to a posse from the Indian Police.

We sipped our tea.

'I'll give it to Lucy,' I promised him. 'She always wanted it. And it's very pretty too.' I turned it over, pressed the clasp and let the lid fly open to reveal a small heap of ash inside.

'Tell Lucy old Groggy-legs is better,' he suggested. 'No need to say any more.'

'Of course.' I stood up. 'Goodbye, Greg. And good luck!'

'I'll need that,' he grinned. 'You're a good sort, Louise. A real brick!'

It was an object I did not wish to resemble. It was a word which immediately emphasised the incongruity of our minds and the difference in our upbringing. But I accepted his compliment. I held out my hand, which he clasped; and then suddenly he raised and kissed it clumsily.

I fled as quickly as I could and ran straight to my cabin. I decided I would tell the captain and Dr Morton nothing whatever of what Greg has told me. As to the method of Rose's killing and the disposal of her body – they can go on guessing till the cows come home. What I know I will keep to myself.

I couldn't sit for ever in my cabin. I still had to do my final packing. Lucy had to have her reading lesson, had to have her sums checked, had to be washed and brushed before meals and put to bed at last, excited at the prospect of seeing her daddy again tomorrow, but tired enough at the end of her day, I'm glad to say, to fall asleep quickly.

I decided not to change for dinner. I couldn't face the dining room – all those eyes probing. I turned out the light in the cabin and sat there allowing all the events of the last few days to stalk through my mind dragging their accompanying violent feelings with them. After a while I became calmer. Herbert was waiting for us in Calcutta, only twelve hours away, and I would meet him with my mind and heart in disorder and my face distorted by worry and lack of sleep. Sleep I longed for but could not achieve. It was the third night I'd been deprived of it.

How long I sat thus I don't know; but it was very dark when I looked across at Lucy and heard her regular breathing. A little light from the sky beyond the porthole fell on her clothes folded neatly at the foot of her bunk, ready to wear tomorrow; her new white drill sailor suit with its wide navy collar and her white straw hat. I suddenly knew what I must do.

I began to take off my clothes, these mourning weeds as they are called. I folded them up one by one. I put on my dressing gown and slippers and carrying the black garments under my arm I made my way up on deck. As far as I could see it was deserted. I knew there were officers and men on watch who perhaps could see me as a shadow moving, but I couldn't see them. I hurried to the ship's stern and stood for a moment gazing down at the moonlit wake of water streaming away. Time passing, passing . . . How many millions of tiny sea creatures churned up by the ship's turbines were tumbling in that phosphorescent plume? Somewhere out there in the great expanse of the Bay of Bengal, among the other bodies, victims of cholera or simply starvation, poor wretched victims washed out along the Hooghli River, Rose was floating. Buried at sea. Six days away.

I took my mourning clothes and rolled them up, and one by one I flung them into the water. As I watched them turning and sinking I felt my spirits begin to rise. Then I left the rail and walked back along the deck. I felt calm, even happy after my action. Burial at sea. Now I knew I could sleep.

I have officiated at a ritual burial: death of my former self. I am no longer your obedient, subservient daughter, but I think I understand you better. Nor am I that palpitating girl with a crush on a handsome face behind whose mask lurked God knows what childhood hatreds and humiliations waiting for revenge. Nor am I that young woman who was briefly caught up in a web of emotions, personal and ancestral, which I couldn't possibly understand. I am not even the hesitant young wife eager to please. I am myself at last.

All that miserable past is behind me, washed clean in the wake of water and time passing. Tomorrow I shall begin afresh. Tomorrow I shall wear a new dress, a pretty cream-coloured cotton dress with a frilled neckline. It is the latest fashion, short, the hem just below the knee, loose at the waist and fitting snugly over the hips. I shall take out of my hatbox my new cream-coloured straw with a large, silk-petalled red rose under its brim. I shall go down the gangway to Herbert feeling like a bride. I am going to be Herbert's wife, the wife of that young DC with ideas and integrity, the one people say will have a part to play in history. I too will have a part to play for Herbert, but also for myself in the scheme of things to come.

January 15th

On crawling into my bunk I must have fallen asleep immediately. I slept so long and so soundly that I didn't hear Lucy get up and run out to the bathroom. When I did wake I realised that it was already late for breakfast.

By the time we arrived in the dining room most of the passengers had left to fasten their trunks and supervise their collection for disembarkation.

I thought we should never get everything inside the great zinc-lined wooden box, nor ever get it closed, but at last with Lucy sitting on its lid and bouncing up and down I managed to snap the fastenings to and turn the key in the lock. We were then left with a small suitcase for our last minute needs as well as my hatbox containing several fragile creations with which I was hoping to dazzle not only Herbert but the whole of Bankipore.

Although we were already late I took my time dressing. I wanted to look my best for Herbert. After all I had gone through, all the skins I felt I had shed, I was putting on a new self. Perhaps for the first time I could really be his wife.

It was while I was fixing my lovely wide-brimmed straw with a long hatpin that Lucy emitted a wail. Her beloved Peter Pushkin was nowhere to be found, not in any corner, nor under either bunk. I could see Lucy's distress mounting. I didn't want a tearful scene to spoil our joyful arrival, and I knew she needed Peter Pushkin, who had to be carried not only to bed but also during any new and challenging venture, for it supplied reassurance with its familiar, worn surface, soothed her nerves and gave her courage. Just as the tears were beginning to rise the Bath

180

Steward knocked on our door and held out the missing rabbit by its flaccid ears. Lucy seized it with cries of joy.

A deckhand then appeared to pick up our luggage. We should have been ready, but Lucy suddenly demanded to go to the lavatory, and since she was squirming and complaining of collywobbles I knew I should have to take her there at once. The result of all these delays was that we were amongst the very last passengers to leave the boat.

'Ah! Mrs Brunoye!' The captain greeted me rather apprehensively, I thought, as I approached the group around the head of the gangway. I followed his glance down towards the quayside where I had already spotted Herbert's dapper white figure topped by his pith topee coming towards us from the left. I knew he would be looking out for a woman in mourning. I was just about to wave to attract his attention when the captain, standing a little in front of the purser, took Lucy's hand.

'Goodbye, Lucy,' he said. 'It's been an experience having you on my ship.' Did I detect a little huskiness in his voice?

The purser laughed. 'We've all enjoyed your company, Lucy,' he said.

The captain bent lower, perhaps to hide his face, and raising Lucy's hand to his lips he kissed it.

'Ooh! That tickles!' she giggled as his eyebrows brushed her arm.

'Goodbye, Mrs Brunoye,' he said gravely, turning to me.

'Goodbye, and thank you, Captain.' I would have said more, but Lucy, in her new white sailor suit and white straw boater, was already tripping down the gangway, so I hastily tried to follow her sure-footed, rapid, fairy-queen flight.

Had we left earlier we wouldn't have seen Greg. The captain must have telegraphed the police ashore before our arrival, because there were several of them waiting, one tall police officer in conversation with our ship surgeon, and a pair of policemen, one on each side of Greg at the bottom of the gangway. Lucy recognised him at once in spite of all the work the ship's barber had done on him and the scar still livid on his cheek. She ran towards him waving her hand and calling out in her grandmother's best memsahib manner:

'Why, Major! What a lovely surprise! I'm so glad to see you!'

He stood stiffly to attention, but as she reached him he seemed to melt suddenly and stooped to greet her. A glint of reflected sunshine shone from his wrist and I realised he was handcuffed. His sudden movement had pulled one of the policemen down with him. Lucy threw her arms round Greg's neck and kissed him, and in doing so her hat was pushed off her head revealing her hair. I could see the three faces close together as they all looked up at me: the momentary surprise on the face of the darker police-man above, with Greg and Lucy parallel, laughing, their bright china-blue eyes beckoning me, their red-gold curls close enough to be intertwined. It was suddenly and hor-rifyingly obvious: the same hair (God in heaven, dearest Mother!) as red-gold as your own used to be, the same hereditary liquid fire erupting from some distant ancestral source and running down the generations, through Grand-mama, so much admired for it by that coterie of pre-Raphaelite hangers-on, through you and me down to Lucy. That Greg was her uncle I now knew; that he was her father I could not be absolutely certain. But the likeness between them was unmistakable.

Feelings of panic began to fly about inside me like terri-fied caged birds. I determined that Herbert, who was by now quite close, should not, must not see them together. I tried to hurry down the gangway, but I stumbled and nearly fell. The captain's voice, tinged with concern, floated down to me.

'Are we all right, Mrs Brunoye?'

This time I didn't reply. I didn't even glance back over

my shoulder. I was trying to run and my curved heels were catching in the anti-slip crossbars. It was like one of those nightmares in which you are desperately trying to get away and something grasps your ankles to hold you down. My fashionable hat with its red rose blooming under the brim began to slip backwards on my neck and I had to clutch the crown to keep it on.

Greg stood up as I reached them. I was at once immensely relieved by the separation of their faces. I glanced at the somewhat embarrassed police officer, and wondered if Rose's fiancé was on the quay.

'Goodbye, Louise,' said Greg.

I didn't look at him. I didn't dare. I snatched Lucy with one hand and with the other scooped up her straw boater which had fallen in the dust.

'You suddenly look so young, Louise,' Greg was saying to my back. 'Be happy, won't you?'

It was what I hoped and planned to be; but it was not what I was feeling at that moment. All I could feel then was terror at Herbert's approach. I wish now that I had looked back, said a few words, smiled perhaps. Greg was in need of kindness; but my own feelings were so overwhelming that pity was pushed aside. I heard him say: 'God bless you both!' Was he stating some claim on us? As I dragged Lucy away he called after us: 'It's young Lucy who's going to be Miss Twenties: it's Lucy who's going to shake the bad old world to bits!'

But Lucy didn't hear him. She had spied Herbert with Bearer Abdul carrying garlands of marigolds to place round our necks, and ran towards them calling 'Daddy!' Then she saw Agatha, so patient and humble in the background, her hands pressed together in the *namaskar* gesture of respectful greeting, waiting to fold the Babamemsahib in her loving arms, into which, waving the battered Pushkin in front of her, Lucy ran.

I fell into Herbert's embrace. Dear, safe, reliable Herbert!

I began to weep uncontrollably, all the fears and tensions of the past week suddenly released on to the spotless expanse of Herbert's white jacket.

'Steady on, old girl!' he remonstrated, alarmed at my uncharacteristic outburst but pleased, too, at my emotion, which he took to be on account of our long-delayed reunion. 'Take it easy, Louise! You must have been through a very trying time, I know. So long-drawn-out. Your poor mother!' He put his arm around my waist and led me away.

'Welcome Memsahib!' Bearer greeted me, placing the garland round my neck.

I began to smile. I blew my nose, adjusted my hat which in spite of its holding hatpin had been knocked sideways to a very unfashionable tilt by the violence with which I'd thrown myself on Herbert, smoothed down my dress which was already looking crumpled, and apologised.

'I hope I haven't ruined your jacket, Herbert.'

'A little salt water soon dries out,' he assured me as he shepherded us all towards a taxicab. While Bearer was overseeing porters and luggage he remarked: 'I'm glad you've discarded your mourning, Louise. So sensible of you. You look beautiful too – better even than the first time you arrived out here. The sea voyage has done you good.'

'I'm glad,' I said.

All would be well. All would be as I hoped.

'Who was that fellow making a fuss of Lucy?' he asked when we were settled in the private compartment he had booked on the overnight train to Patna. It was going to be a long journey, warm and sticky though mercifully, since it was still only January, not unbearably so. I began to realise how unsuitably I was dressed for travelling. I really must have been a bit mad during the last few days to decide on this semi-bridal outfit which, unless we kept our carriage windows permanently closed, would soon be begrimed with specks of soot flying back from the engine.

184

I wondered if I looked a complete clown. I had not received any strange glances from other British travellers at the station, so perhaps they presumed we had been to a wedding or had been attending some garden party. You, I know, would have frowned. With your sense of occasion you would have criticised me for appearing too flamboyant, *outrée*, and therefore in bad taste; but Herbert didn't notice anything unusual. He was just pleased to see me and pleased that I looked well.

'Which fellow?' I asked, taking the cold lemonade Bearer brought out of the tiffin basket.

'The fellow standing between the policemen,' Herbert replied.

'Oh him! Well,' I said, glancing at Lucy to see that her attention was fully occupied by the game she was playing with her ayah, 'it's a very long story which may take me days to tell you. Darling Herbert we have had a very eventful voyage, and – yes – rather alarming.' I leaned across and whispered to him: 'He has been arrested on a murder charge.'

'Good God!' he exclaimed, and would have turned pale if his suntan had permitted it. 'Did you know this man? I mean to say, Lucy seemed quite familiar with him on the quay just now.'

'Lucy has no idea what has happened,' I assured him. But yes, I did know him. Quite well in fact.' And I told him about our childhood friendship and my girlish crush on him in the old days.

'I say! How awful!' Herbert was sympathetic. 'Dear girl, what an ordeal this must have been for you! No wonder you seemed a bit put off your stroke when you arrived!'

By the time we reached Patna I had told him my story, or at least those parts of it which I considered he must know. It was already losing some of its immediacy in my mind as we travelled north, away from the wide brown

185

water of the Ganges delta. Mother Ganga, I thought, sacred river of healing and forgetfulness.

Within a week of our arrival in Bankipore Herbert began to hear rumours from informants in the bazaar and the riverside quays, bits of gossip brought up river on commercial steamboats and by travellers on the railway. Within a fortnight the scandal broke with a wealth of detail which I had not guessed before. It seems there had been a previous occasion when a lady friend of Greg's had died suddenly. She fell downstairs and broke her neck in a Calcutta hotel – Greg's hotel in fact, for that was what it was, a rather sleazy one with restaurant and nightclub which had been running for some years. A verdict of death by misadventure had been brought in at the inquest, but there had been gossip at the time based on suspicion that her fall had not been altogether accidental. A chambermaid had given evidence that she'd heard angry voices shouting in the lady's room and had seen Greg coming out of it, his face red and distorted with rage. The lady with the broken neck was his wife, a beautiful Eurasian girl, people said. It was after this that Greg, who had always been a heavy drinker, began to drink too heavily.

We also learned he'd been dismissed from the army, cashiered for some undisclosed misdemeanour. He was no longer a serving officer, not a major at all. That was a rank he had bestowed upon himself.

Now I am resuming my normal life once more with its familiar routine of supervising the servants, the table, the garden, and that daredevil gardener's boy who swings so recklessly on the pulley above the well, making Lucy squeal with fear that he'll fall in, I shall find time and opportunity to fulfil the promise I gave you. Herbert will help me. He does not consider it macabre. He understands.

Herbert was much too delicate to ask about your will, although of course he expected me to tell him in my own good time, which I did.

'The capital is to remain yours, Louise, entirely yours to do exactly what you like with.'

'Well, you must advise me,' I said, which he did with pleasure and I think a certain relief, because my inheritance has removed from him some of the burden of providing for our uncertain future in an India which is one day going to become independent. And it seems to be the case, doesn't it, that the white man in India doesn't last as long as his mate?

We have decided to use some of the money to endow a fund for the education of two Eurasian sisters orphaned in early childhood, a project close to our hearts since he believes passionately in education, and I in education for women.

The sandalwood box will be burnt with this letter. I will tie it up with pink tapes filched from Herbert's office, and seal it so that it will look like a pile of official documents. We intend doing it tomorrow evening when Herbert and I go for our daily stroll across the compound. I have arranged with the gardener and his boy to have a bonfire ready. I have told Herbert the pink tape enclosed your old love-letters. The mystery and romance hidden in this white lie makes his eyes sparkle. He is happy to join in our ceremony of your last rites. It is a game he will enjoy playing. Lucy will enjoy it too. She will say: 'Is it really Granny's hair?' and her eyes will grow big and solemn as she is held spellbound, watching the flames curl and crimp those long white tresses to our common ash. And I shall think of your portrait (still hanging in the drawing room of the Kensington house, and respected, I hope, by the new tenants) in which your red-gold hair is piled up on top of your head in the Edwardian fashion, unadorned but more beautiful in its natural shining than bound by any jewellers diadem. We have decided to scatter the ashes not over the banks of the Ganges, where we would be altogether too conspicuous, but under the peach trees. I think you'd like that. Perhaps then your spirit will return to India, to the Hindu Whole of things.

All will be well. All will be as I hoped. And never, I vow solemnly to myself and to you, never will I tell him after a quarrel that Lucy is probably not his daughter, that I may not have conceived this child by him, that perhaps I won't, perhaps can't have a son by him. Nor will I ever, even in old age made bitter by widowhood in that cold, grey Kensington house, and lonely by Lucy (ardently pursuing the affairs and activities natural to an exuberant young woman in which an ageing mother can't take part), never will I vindictively repay this hurt by revealing to her the truth. Some truths should not be disinterred. They are best left buried, especially when they are dead.

Louise stared at her daughter anxiously when Lucy brought her breakfast tray to her bedroom next morning. She hugged her, clinging desperately for a moment before freeing herself.

'Yes,' said Lucy, 'I've read the whole thing. And do you know? I believe you've missed your vocation. You should have been a writer. I couldn't put it down!'

Her frail body relaxed, and she smiled. 'Ah well! You're not exactly an impartial critic, are you?'

Lucy picked up the pretty, pale blue bed-jacket Louise wore in bed, and gave it to her.

'I'm surprised you take it so calmly,' Louise said.

'That's something you taught me – to remain calm in the face of powerful emotions. Power comes from self-control is what you said. Remember?'

'I was afraid to tell you before. I thought you'd never forgive me.'

'I'm glad you didn't tell me when I was a girl. It would have worried me then, but I think I can take it now. Greg may be my genetic father (though you can't be absolutely sure, can you?) but it was Herbert who brought me up. And it was Herbert I knew and loved.'

'He was such a good man!' she sighed; and smoothing the coverlet over her knees, and bowing her head over her hands she added: 'But I've always carried this load of guilt for wronging him.'

'All this has left a dreadful mark on your conscience. But, Mummy darling, it was all so long ago! What does it really matter now? what matters is Herbert loved you and you always loved him.'

Louise leaned back against her pillows, and the tears flowed unchecked.

'You must remember the good things you've done,' Lucy urged her. 'You were an awfully good mum to me. And nobody could have looked after Daddy as you did – all those years of nursing him, when he must have been at times trying beyond endurance.' She gave her a tissue.

'I do believe,' Louise said sniffing, 'that by dedicating myself entirely to him during that awful illness, and until death, I did expiate my guilt. That's what I hope anyway. It was God's punishment, of course.'

Lucy was indignant. 'If so it was very unfair of God to punish Herbert even more severely than you when he was entirely innocent of your crime!'

Louise laughed then, her unique laugh full of energy, fresh, derisive, healing.

'That's better,' said Lucy. 'That's more like the old Louise!' She bent over her, shaking out and readjusting her pillows. 'And what about the garden you created? You made that as a memorial to him,' she reminded her. ' "A thing of beauty and a joy forever" for all who walk in it. An oasis of serenity. You've planted a place of healing you know, for all people who are falling apart from disillusionment or insecurity.' She tried to say all the right things, all the things Louise wanted to hear.

189

'You're a good nurse, Lucy,' her mother said. 'Even if you are only a doctor!'

'Was he hanged, by the way?' Lucy asked.

'Greg? Well no, as a matter of fact. He died of a heart attack while awaiting trial.'

When Lucy left her room and walked through into their den she glanced at the portrait and saw with a shock how prophetic it was. How could he have known, that Viennese painter of the turn-of-the-century Secessionist school, trying to express in images the new surge of feeling and ideas tearing apart the conventional bandages in which eroticism was swaddled, how could he have foreseen this clinging together of the women of their family? Was he painting something which all women hold and pass on to one another from generation to generation? Lucy refused to see the menace in the painting, she looked only at the great gold cloak of love, telling herself she would outwit that painter, she would shake her fist even at death itself. Louise had loved and given much. *Datta, dayadhvam, damyatta:* Give, sympathise, control. She had followed the precepts of the Upanishad, and would, with Dr Gillow's help and Lucy's, be granted *Shantih:* the Great Peace. Lucy would make sure she didn't go out with a whimper but in a blaze of glory, serene, fulfilled, forgiven, her body piled high and smothered by all the flowers she grew and loved.

Later Lucy thought about the papers a lot: murder. Her father was a murderer. She was born of an incestuous relationship. Every time she remembered it she felt a shock of horror. But it wasn't the end of the world. She tried to distance the emotional impact of these revelations by thinking of them biologically. She couldn't be absolutely sure that Greg, a rather ridiculous figure, was her father. Both he and Herbert had offered spermatozoa to her mother's egg within fifteen or sixteen days of each other; but which of them had won the race for the waiting ovum nobody after this long lapse of time could possibly know.

190

Louise and Herbert were married in January 1913 and Lucy was born in October, so Herbert had a pretty good chance of being her father too. She wondered if murderers were different from the rest of us, whether they carried some special inheritable trait, or whether any one of us in special circumstances, cornered and seeing no other way out, would kill. Of course the weapon had to be handy. Perhaps that was, after all the real reason why men were more often killers than women; perhaps it was just that extra strength and speed that made them hunters half a million years ago, soldiers in past centuries, trigger-happy cowboys in more recent times, and if a weapon was near enough at the moment of rage, occasionally murderers in our own. Perhaps the killing instinct is embedded deep down in all of us. She remembered her own darling Nicky shooting down all those Messerschmidts, each one containing a live German. It was a form of chess played amongst the clouds; the prize for winning was survival. Killing was a necessity then, an obligation in defence of cherished beliefs, glorious even. No guilt – though had Nicky lived he might have suffered nightmares later in life. During her psychiatric work Lucy had seen one or two cases of middle-aged men with depressive breakdowns who were feeling obsessive guilt and remorse for what they'd done during the war.

She thought about Herbert – a great and good man if ever there was one. He too had killed, not with his own hands, but indirectly. Once when he was up-country in Chota Nagpur two British soldiers murdered an Indian who had cheated them. Between them they kicked him to death. Herbert as acting magistrate found them guilty and sentenced them to be hanged. The colonel of their regiment visited him to ask if the sentence might not in some way be commuted, since hanging would disgrace, not only the regiment, but also the fair name of Britain in the eyes of her subject peoples. But Herbert was adamant: murder, not the sentence, was disgraceful. 'We can't bend the Law to

191

suit the colour of a skin,' he said. 'Nor to save the face of the regiment.' Justice must be done, and must be seen to be done. 'It's something we're going to leave behind us in India when we go,' he said. 'It's more important than the regiment – more important even than the Empire.' So in a way he was guilty too: judicial killing, a sort of permissible revenge. And were not the juries of twelve good men and true, who sat on English murder trials before capital punishment was suspended, responsible for the hangings? They took upon themselves for all of us the collective decision to kill. But there is a difference, of course, between the willingness to kill in self-defence, defence of country or of ideology, which most of us share, and the determination to commit murder in rage or for greed. Is this instinct, or ability, or some absence of fellow-feeling, or possibly some gene, inherent in the few? If so, Lucy and her descendants were among that number.

All this chewing over of her mother's confession did not alter the image she now carried with her forever of a squalid struggle in a hot, stuffy cabin, attempted rape by a drunken male animal of a young woman who desperately broke some glass and used its sharp edge to defend herself. She was killed, and her body was pushed through a port-hole into the Bay of Bengal.

It was something she would never be able to tell Beena.

'You will make sure that diary of mine is destroyed, won't you?' Louise had asked her.

'It will go with you,' Lucy had promised her. But she did hesitate when it came to the point. Such a pity, she thought, to lose forever this piece of family history – social history too! She couldn't help thinking of all those burning women who tried to keep secret the sins of their loved, or once-loved ones: Florence helping Hardy to pile letters, note-books and diaries on bonfires in the garden of his home at Max Gate in order to twist the record straight into an authorised version of his life for posterity; Lady Burton lighting bonfires which burned for days after her husband's death to obliterate much, but not all, of his traveller's tales and erotica; and Lady Millbanke, Byron's wife, who was the instigator, if not the arsonist, at the burning of Byron's memoirs by Murray, his publisher, and Moore his friend (poor fellow!) always so short of cash. Lucy regarded them all as traitors to their friends and the truth. But Louise (thank heaven!) was no literary giant; she owed no testament of truth to literature; she was just her mother, a very private person. So Lucy placed the papers under her feet in the coffin.

Lucy was glad she died in June because that was when her peonies were at their best. They are named after Paeon, that Greek physician who healed the wounds of Trojan warriors. Lucy cut them all, great armfuls of her favourites: the full, blowsy, double pink Sarah Bernhardt, the delicate single White Wings, and the open carmine Bowl of Beauty with its startling crown of stamens. She arranged them herself all over and around her coffin before the cremation service. *Man that is born of woman hath but a short time to live. He cometh up and is cut down like a flower.* Like a flower . . . How glad she was that they had the sonorous language of the King James Bible to console them on that day, instead of the homespun, not to say bedraggled prose of the New to reduce even the great drama of death to the level of the everyday! She gave orders that the peonies were not to be sent to some old people's home to wilt in vases unobserved but were to be burned with her.

Beena was upset by this.

'Great-grandmother Dambresac sent her hair back to India to be burned there when she died,' Lucy told her. 'It was a tribute to the country where she lived and loved when she was young. And her peonies with her own body are Louise's gift to the earth here.' She scattered the ashes around the statue at the bottom of the garden, where

Louise used to stand and stare out over the vale of Frenester.

'I think it's horrible! Horrible!' Beena declared.

Lucy suspected her daughter was afraid Louise's ghost would rise with the mist from the valley below on still autumn evenings. Perhaps she was really afraid of death itself . . . though why she should be, when she believed so firmly in the resurrection of the body and a glorious after-life in heaven, Lucy couldn't imagine. Bailey wasn't afraid of Louise's ghost; Lucy believed he hoped to see her. He was certainly haunted by her memory. It was Bailey who wept at her funeral. When everybody else stood up to sing: 'The Lord is my shepherd. I shall not want. He maketh me to lie down in green pastures' Bailey suddenly sat down and buried his face in his hands. Lucy could see him from where she stood on the other side of the aisle. It was he who helped her spread the ashes, so he knew where they lay. He used to spend quite a lot of time sitting there and staring into the distance where earth and sky meet; and once when Lucy found him there he said; 'The earth is our mother as well as our mourner.' So she sat down beside him at the foot of the statue, and they cried a little together.

Sadly, Bailey no longer worked for them. Beena employed a couple of odd-job gardeners of a different, less imaginative mettle.

Lucy dragged herself back to the present as Beena hustled into the den to pick up the breakfast tray.

'Back already?' said Lucy dreamily.

'It's after ten, and you're not even dressed yet!' Beena accused her.

'Only my dress to put on, and then do something for the poor old face. What time are they all expected?'

'Twelve noon,' said Beena. 'And let's hope the drinks lot won't stay too long, or the rest of us will be kept waiting all afternoon for lunch.' She moved towards the door, which she held back with one foot. Lucy suddenly jumped to catch it before it slammed.

All this fuss about her eightieth birthday was rather absurd really. It might of course be her last; that was what they were all thinking, and probably celebrating; her death day was only round the corner. She considered the probability (since she suffered no disease other than some stiffness of her joints and a little shortness of breath when she walked the mile uphill from Frenester, which she was still able to do if she took the last two hundred yards slowly) that she might survive till eighty-five; but not – please God – to the brainless creeping-about-of-the-snail stage of ageing. Sweet death, be sudden when you come! she prayed silently. A philosopher had once said that death was not an event in life because it was not lived through. She thought it rather a silly thing for a philosopher to say. Of course you didn't come through death, which was the end, the ultimate cul-de-sac; but you certainly lived through dying. She was not afraid of death as Beena was, only of the process of dying in all its possible forms. That was something she thought about daily nowadays; but it was not something she could discuss with anybody else. Death is the twentieth-century taboo, she thought, just as sex was for the Victorians. We cover it up with just as many layers of self deception.

FOUR

The Birthday Party

The three hikers returned later than planned, and had to rush upstairs to wash and change in time for the guests expected at noon. As Joanna stepped on to the landing and was about to descend into the hall she caught sight of Joss and Danielle standing by the last curve of the bannisters. Danielle was pulling away a tendril of hair from the back of her neck, and as she did so Joss stooped and kissed her fingers. The shock of surprise Joanna felt made her stop. She turned away pretending to examine an etching on the wall. She couldn't read the title because hot tears spurted unexpectedly across her eyes. I don't really know much about him, she thought, although we've made joyful love quite often for at least six months. He seldom spoke about himself. She knew about his childhood home above the railway embankment, and the fact that he used to borrow illustrated books about artists from his local library. His teacher, catching him poring over a life of Van Gogh, was bewildered and a bit suspicious. She could understand the attachment of boys to science fiction, that they like imagining themselves inside plastic shells in space shooting laser beams at other plastic shells containing other-planet aliens, but that one of her pupils seemed more interested in the brush strokes of Van Gogh worried her. So Joanna stood,

197

staring unseeing at the framed etching, and felt like that school mistress, worried and suspicious. Of course he must have had many love affairs before he met her. He must have acquired a lot of sexual experience to become such a good and understanding lover; but he never talked about other women, and Joanna in her innocence imagined that he had left all women now except herself. He'd told her: 'You're the nicest girl I know. The most beautiful and the best.' And that had always satisfied her; but now she was suddenly assailed by all sorts of questions about him she'd never bothered to ask herself before. Perhaps he didn't love her much after all? Perhaps he didn't think of her as his best friend and companion, but just as a convenient comfort. Was this love which she had been treasuring nothing more than a passing affair to him? Perhaps it was already over. She stood still for a moment longer to brush away her tears, knowing she must not allow herself to be overcome by them. This was Lucy's day. It must be a success, a day of joy unclouded by any shadow. So she put aside her own apprehensions of personal disaster. She was a girl who could do so. She lifted her chin, shook back her hair, smoothed down the front of her dress and walked calmly downstairs. Joss and Danielle had disappeared into the drawing room. When Joanna entered she was immediately surrounded by the clamour of friendly greetings.

She walked towards her grandmother, who stood near the fire, a glass of champagne held in the sparkling semicircle of her right hand. Joanna thought she looked magnificent in her loose flowing dress of sea-greens and nightblues, which seemed to mingle and merge as she moved, while on her breast shone the big diamond star.

'A happy birthday, Lucy darling!'

Lucy smiled and made kissing gestures with her lips; but her attention was immediately occupied by the necessity of having to greet new arrivals, neighbours, a couple from a cottage bought as a retreat from the too-fast lane of city living, then a farmer and his wife from the other side of Frenester, and two surviving medical colleagues who, tall, thin and angular like a pair of grizzled herons, formed a gothic arch as they leaned over her.

'Well, Lucy my dear, it must be some satisfaction for you to reach this day and still look younger than superannuable age, what?'

'I daresay you've cured the odd patient or two in your time, Lucy – even in psychiatry, eh?'

'I was never much more than a listening ear,' said Lucy, 'or a basin of warm water, if you like, in which my patients washed their hands.'

'Oh come! That's far too modest!'

Lucy smiled up at them, professional optimists that they were, and patronising too; but she was thinking: You can't alter the human condition. We are what we are. Sometimes you can ease the pain till it becomes bearable.

'At any rate you've survived them and their miseries, Lucy. That's the great thing,' one said.

'Though it does make one feel a bit guilty to be old and healthy nowadays on our overcrowded planet,' said the other.

'There's one good thing about us though – we're not so wasteful as the young. My grandchildren are downright profligate with energy resources, judging by my fuel bills after they've been to visit me!'

'Conservation and population control must be the gospel of the future.'

'Of the present,' said Lucy. 'If it isn't already too late.'

'It does look rather as if we'll have to minister to a sick planet rather than to sick people.'

'The community physician as an environmentologist?'

They all three agreed that perhaps this would be the new order of things in medicine; and each was secretly rather glad to be too old to bother with it all any more.

Although Beena was kept busy feeding people with

delicious morsels of smoked salmon rolled up in thin bread and butter, with olives and salted peanuts and other mouth-watering tit-bits, she was not forgetting to keep her eye on Danielle. She was pleased to note that Danielle was not with Joss. She had cornered Duncan, the middle-aged Canadian, with tinkling laughter and a chiming of all her bracelets and was focusing her laser beam of sexuality on him. He was obviously not used to being singled out by sirens at parties, and stood dumbly pink with pleasure and embarrassment, but sipping his champagne with the determination of one clinging to a lifeline.

Joanna saw them as she threaded her way through the crowd and thought: Perhaps flirting is a sort of addiction she has; perhaps it's just a game she plays, and Joss is of no more permanent interest to her than Duncan; and immediately Joanna's hopes began to rise that Danielle would forget Joss after the weekend and leave him alone.

Beena glanced across the crowded room at Joanna and at once felt happy and proud, although she couldn't help wondering if Joanna had any suspicions about Joss and Danielle. Joanna looked so serene and confident; but Beena knew about her daughter's force of will, which would override any emotional misgivings she might have, and if she chose to do so her face would show little of her inner torments. Beena recognised in Joanna something she herself had never had, and wondered if this faculty was something that belonged to the younger generation.

Joss found himself pushed very close to a man of about fifty who had wisely grown a beard to hide his lack of chin, and who was shouting in order to be heard above the alcohol-amplification of the party sound: 'Havelock! Will unlock!' he uttered a braying laugh, but seeing Joss' blank expression he laboriously explained: 'Name is Havelock. Timothy Havelock.'

'He's our local historian.' shouted Beena at his elbow

with a plate of appetizing savouries, from which both grabbed pieces as she passed.

'House was built by a rich wool merchant,' confided Havelock in loud, rapid, urgent tones. 'Originally sixteenth century. You can still see some of the old beams at the back of the house. But it was partly burned down during the Civil War when a couple of Royalists were found hiding in the cellar.'

'Oh?' Joss swallowed half his champagne in one gulp.

'And then in the eighteenth century it was updated into a Georgian residence to match the rising status of its new owner. Cloth weaver, he was. Owned the mill on the Frene in the valley below. All very well documented. Am I boring you?' But without waiting for a reply he raced on: 'A lot of wealth round here for a long time, you know. All grown on the backs of our fat sheep. Our small Cotswold towns have been occupied for centuries by a fairly well-to-do middle class – as well, of course, as the inevitable poor who are always with us.' He brayed again.

'I daresay they carried the wool sacks and got bitten by fleas,' suggested Joss. 'And were paid as little as was necessary to keep them alive.'

'Sure – sure,' agreed Havelock irritably, peering at Joss over the tops of his semi-lunar specs. He didn't like being checked in mid-flow. He popped one of Beena's tit-bits in his mouth. 'Do you know' he asked rhetorically, 'the other day my son called me *bourgeois*! It was intended as an insult. Though I ask you, what's wrong with being middle-class?' He spread his hands, waving his glass carelessly as he slightly shifted the meaning of the word in translation. 'When you consider that it's really the middle-classes who have made us wealthy, discovered and invented things, and – yes! – instigated all the reforms. Most of them anyway. Wilberforce was one of us. I grant you Aneurin Bevan was a miner before he gave us the NHS; but Lord Beveridge was a middle-class administrator; he wasn't born into the purple; he achieved lordliness by thinking so long about our welfare.'

Joss was no longer listening. He was watching Joanna over the man's shoulder as she moved about with that wonderful serenity she possessed, smiling and looking stunning in her close-fitting black dress whose collar was embroidered with glittering green and silver threads. She knew everybody, and they all seemed pleased to see her.

Lucy was sitting in her big armchair when Ellen and Dewey presented their parcel.

'It's for your birthday, Granma,' said Dewey. 'From Ellen and me.'

'Oh how lovely! You open it for me. Otherwise I might spill my drink.' He did so to reveal a small black box and tiny ear-pieces with wires attached.

'What is it?' she asked.

Dewey was dumbfounded. Was it possible she didn't know what a Walkman was? 'You slip your favourite cassette in here,' he explained, 'and put it in your pocket, and the ear-pieces in your ears. And then you an walk about and listen to music without interrupting anybody else.'

Lucy considered the contraption might be attractive to the young who had so little in their heads to think about; but to her, who had so many sequences to run through in memory before it was too late, the thing was not going to be much use.

'How very sweet and thoughtful of you both,' she said gravely.

'Of course you're not really my granma, are you?' asked Dewey. 'You're a sort of great-aunt.'

'Not that either,' Lucy explained. 'Your grandfather Robbie was my first cousin. I grew up with Robbie and Charlotte and Patsy in the same house in Wimbledon. At any rate I spent most of my school holidays with them. My father was an invalid you see; and my mother thought I'd have more fun with them. So they were like brothers and sisters to me. Robbie was a lovely man. But I don't mind being your granma. Not at all. In fact I rather like it.'

'I'm Joanna's Auntie Patsy,' said the elderly woman who touched Joss's glass with her own. He knew she was Lucy's younger sister, so she must be a great-aunt to Joanna, hiding her age, though she certainly didn't look anything like as old as Lucy. She was slim and elegantly dressed in a *café-au-lait* outfit with perfectly colour-matched shoes; there was not a hair out of place in her coiffure, the colour of gilded dust. Beside her was her husband, a good deal younger, but a good deal less healthy-looking. Porcine, thought Joss. That was the contemporary Brit. No longer John Bulldog challenging the world, but Pig with his trotters in the trough, swilling his way to an untimely death. He eyed the man's belly as it bulged out of the top of his trousers.

'Bully darling,' said Patsy, 'get me a fill-up won't you?' Taking her glass, Bully, who was quite nimble in spite of his rolls of fat, lurched off to do her bidding.

In the kitchen sat Mrs Colbert on a chair in the corner away from the mainstream of fast-moving feet. She, who used to think High House would fall down if she wasn't there, found herself no longer indispensable. She had insisted on arriving early to help, although it was a Sunday. She didn't trust these new-fangled caterers to do anything right; and of course she didn't want to miss the party and all the family gossip that went with it. She managed to spread the largest white damask tablecloth on the dining room table before the caterers arrived; but after that she was pushed out of the way. She was happy though, when the enormous joint of beef was put in the oven. She approved of roast beef. That was what Sunday was for, wasn't it? The Sunday roast of lamb for the usual, but beef for the special. All this talk of bovine-what's-its-brain disease wasn't going to put her off beef. 'Tis my belief the poor beasts picked it up from the farmers,' was what she said. 'And nobody's going to eat *them*!' This line of logic seemed to her irrefutable. Roast beef and Yorkshire pudding with roast potatoes was the proper dish for a festive day, except Christmas, of course, because that was turkey. Unfortunately Brussels sprouts were not yet in season, but this new-fangled calabrese was a good substitute. The meat was to be followed by a large array of tempting desserts including raspberry flan, the defrosted raspberries set in redcurrant jelly, and lots of chocolate mousse heavily laced with brandy and served in all the small glass dishes the house could muster. She was looking forward to a mouthful of that leftover at least.

'There's only eleven for lunch!' she shouted stridently from her corner, trying to keep her end up. 'All the rest'll have to go!' She jerked her head towards the source of the noise.

'Trouble is they're taking so bloody long about it!' grumbled the chef, who was ready to serve and didn't want his meat overdone.

The crowd was thinning gradually. The two old doctors placed dessicated kisses on Lucy's cheeks, collected their wives and departed for their own Sunday lunches. Havelock the historian presented Lucy with a copy of his latest book, *Woolpack Inns of the Cotswolds*, and said goodbye, and the rest went home, some more reluctantly than others, leaving the houseparty consisting of relatives and Joss to sit down and eat at last.

At one end of the big table sat Beena, with Patsy and Bully on either side of her; and at the other end sat Lucy, with Charlotte on one side and Dewey on the other. She explained to him that it was proper for the youngest to sit by the oldest, and had filled up his glass with very good Châteauneuf-du-Pape. Lucy could hear, although not every word was clear, what Beena was saying.

'It's the story of my life. It's how I get into these fixes I can't get out of!' There was a ripple of laughter.

Lucy was glad Beena had an audience; and Joanna, in the middle of the table opposite Joss was glad too, since as she'd heard the story before she had no need to listen and could concentrate on Joss. The red wine was making his fine profile flush. She wondered uncomfortably if he was playing footsie with Danielle, who sat beside him. All the many little charms and chains and bangles on her wrists tinkled whenever she moved. Joanna wondered, too, how long it would be before their incessant chiming drove him mad.

Beena's story was all about the time a fat man sat on her hand as it rested on the seat beside her in a train on the district line. She'd been too shy to remove it from under him. Nor had he complained, but went on sitting on it. 'Wimbledon Park went by, Putney passed, and Fulham Broadway, and still he sat on it, staring straight ahead. I was getting pins and needles and was afraid the circulation was being cut off, and that I'd be left with gangrene of the fingers, unable to type . . . But at last at Earl's Court he rose without a word, without a backward look, and left the carriage. Earl's Court has always seemed like a place of deliverance since.'

Dewey uttered a loud slightly tipsy laugh and shouted: 'He was a dirty old man!' His father laughed, and said: 'Let him have his day!' In fact Dewey wasn't drinking the red wine, which he found too strong and strange, but he'd already swallowed quite a lot of champagne, which excited him, chiefly because it was the stuff sports champions on telly squirted all over the place.

Patsy was examining Lucy through the bifocals she was forced to put on her nose at meals. She thought Lucy looked really half-dead. What a pity she didn't use more make-up! After all it was the duty of all women of sense to make an effort to grow old gracefully. If Lucy had taken

205

more trouble with her face she might have married again after that Steve disaster. It was only years after it was all over that Charlotte let this particular skeleton out of the family cupboard. Patsy glanced across the table at Bully, who was having second helpings of everything. He wasn't the perfect answer to a maiden's prayer. He was eating too much as he always did; but at least he wasn't eating carrots and fussing about fibre. And he did fuss a bit over her. It was pleasant showing off in company how willingly he ran errands for her. But undoubtedly he was overweight. She compared his plate with that of Ellen, who sat next to him. She wondered about Ellen, so reserved and quiet you couldn't tell what she was thinking. She rather wished she had a daughter like that: well behaved and no trouble, and not good-looking enough to put her mother in the shade. Patsy had no children by her first marriage, and by the time Bully came along she was too old.

Ellen laughed at Beena's story: a sudden, unexpectedly vigorous laugh from such a quiet girl, and Lucy at the other end of the table felt a shock because she'd heard that laugh before. It was Louise's special characteristic laugh, incisive, joyful and a bit aggressive, putting pomposity and pretence to flight. How could it be that Ellen who had never known, never even met the dead woman, had learned her laugh? And the possibility passed through Lucy's mind that a laugh might be an inheritable family trait, linked in some way to a group of genes among our million of them, just as much as facial features or the colour and texture of hair. It was a mystery that the next decade might unravel, after she was dead.

The desserts were so good they produced a short silence while they were savoured. Lucy had ordered a sweet wine to be served with this course, not Muscat de Beaumes de Venise, which was trendy now, but really too expensive and a bit over the top even for today, but a really nice Sauternes recommended by the Wine Society's List.

'Coffee will be served in the drawing room,' Beena announced.

One by one they left the table. Joanna took the opportunity to slip into the kitchen carrying two puddings to Mrs Colbert, whose sweet tooth she'd known since the days when they shared such things as Mars Bars and even sucked an iced-lolly together, when out for walks or shopping in Frenester.

'How's things going on in there?' asked Mrs Colbert, adding without a pause: 'You do look tip-top in that dress, my love. Ravishing. I only hope that young man of yours appreciates what he's getting.'

'Oh yes, I think he does.'

'And I 'opes you're not such an unmerciful little tyrant to him as you was to me when you were in your pram!'

'Oh, he gets lots of mercy,' said Joanna.

In the drawing room a neat, white-pinafored maid was pouring out coffee into small cups. There were only ten of them left, with nine saucers, but Lucy wanted them used because they were so pretty, their fine translucent bodies decorated with trailing Edwardian violets. She thought Ellen and Dewey could be given the coarser cups, since they were the youngest and least sophisticated guests.

Duncan took his coffee to the piano and, opening the lid, tried a few runs along the keyboard. He looked across at Lucy guessing that she must still play sometimes, and met her smiling approval. So he sat down and immediately raced into an old jazz classic he knew she'd like: 'Singin' in the rain! I'm singin' in the rain!' A murmur of pleasure mixed with the clinking of cups greeted him. He sang loudly and happily. 'What a glorious feeling! I'm happy again!' This was the life, this was what he should be doing, not slaving away at airline business. Playing the piano always filled him with such expanding happiness; and jazz rhythms made him love his neighbour better than any number of preachers could.

'Ellen!' he called out. 'What about giving them a song from Montreal?'

Lucy was delighted that he played so well, seemingly without effort, all from memory and sometimes improvising. He changed key and began to play an old, and to Lucy a familiar melody. Without any shyness Ellen began to sing in French, with an accent which Lucy guessed must be Quebecquois:

> *'Plaisir d'amour ne dure qu'un moment.*
> *Chagrin d'amour dure toute la vie.'*

The girl's unaffected singing of that sweet sad song silenced the room; the maid stood still in the half-open door, and Mrs Colbert and the others came into the hallway to listen. Lucy's eyes filled with tears. The song was carrying her back to a forgotten evening so long ago she'd been a school-girl then. In this very room Louise sang that same song. The french windows were open because it was summer, and you could see over the edge of the terrace scarlet oriental poppies hanging their heavy heads. Her father, sitting in his wheelchair, wept. Lucy didn't know why. Louise, seeing his tears, stopped abruptly. 'Cruel Louise – that's what you are!' he cried out. Lucy could still hear the pain in his voice, but had no idea what cruelty her mother could have committed. 'Oh my dear, my dear!' Louise was bending over him, caressing the back of his neck. 'I didn't mean – I didn't think – ' And in that moment it was revealed to Lucy what his long illness was doing to them both. Its demands and its duration were slowly destroying their love rendering him impotent perhaps, reducing her to exhaustion, probably both.

When Ellen finished singing her audience applauded enthusiastically. She could see tears in Lucy's eyes, and artlessly believing her talent had produced this wonderful effect on her grandmother, she hurried over to Lucy's winged chair.

'Was I OK then, Granma?'

'You sang it beautifully,' Lucy said.

Duncan was already moving into another rhythm and another country with Albeniz in 'Granada Serenata' when Charlotte put down her coffee and rose, clicking her fingers like castanets. She stamped her heels, made a few half-turns and tossed her head in a sham Flamenco, and then suddenly shouted out: 'Give us some syncopated rhythm, Duncan – some real hot stuff!' Without pausing for a single bar he plunged straight into "I can't give you anything but love, Baby!" He sang it too, in a charming diffident way: 'That's the only thing I've plenty of, Baby!'

Lucy couldn't help thinking how times had changed. What hopes of love requited were there at this money-worshipping end of the century without a bank balance (even one in the red), or at least an expectation of affluence? She supposed that in the Thirties, when that song was popular, most people were poor.

'Let's show them how to do the Charleston, shall we, Lucy? Show them what dancing really is?' cried Charlotte, pulling Lucy to her feet, and as she hesitated: 'Show a leg, Lucy! You've still got good legs, so don't be afraid of showing them off!' And before she quite knew what she was doing Lucy was 'shakin' out yo' feet', and her arms as well, literally throwing herself with joyous abandon into the dance.

Everybody else was in fits of laughter, so she knew their movements must be inappropriate to their age and appearance; they must look like puppets violently jerked about by strings attached to their wooden joints; but at the same time she felt she was twelve years old, doing the Charleston with Charlotte on the landing at the Chestnuts while Robbie beat time like a metronome with a ruler on the bannisters.

Lucy stopped dancing when she suddenly felt giddy. She must have swayed because the laughter died away. Joanna stood up; but it was Dewey who took her arm and led her to a chair exclaiming: 'Gee! You were great, Granma! Just great!' while Duncan rose from the piano and demanded a round of applause for the old Wizz Kids.

Conversation was muted after the clapping and there was a general feeling that the party was over. Duncan tried to revive it by bravely strumming 'Putting on the Ritz' at sizzling speed; but Patsy decided it was time to go.

'I wonder, Bully darling,' she said, 'could you fetch Lucy's birthday present from the car?' And while her obedient husband was out of the room she sat down between Lucy and Charlotte, who lit a cigarette.

'Do you remember that time in Wimbledon – during the Charleston craze at school?' asked Patsy. 'We were practising the Charleston on the landing.'

'And Mummy stood at the bottom of the stairs wringing her hands and wailing: "The girls are going wild Toby! Going wild!" ' Charlotte mimed her mother.

'And Uncle Toby came out of his study on a whiff of Balkan Sobranie and asked "What's this? A Jungle Jamboree?" ' said Lucy.

'He was always so out of touch and old-fashioned!' snorted Charlotte. 'I shouted down the stairs: "It's the Charleston!" But of course he'd never heard of it.'

'I remember his comment,' added Lucy. ' "Ah! Confederacy Capers!" was what he said.'

Charlotte stubbed out her cigarette on the saucer of her coffee-cup, as Bully returned to the room with a big pot of Nerines in his arms.

'How lovely!' cried Lucy. 'How really lovely of you, Patsy – of you both! Nerines . . . romantic flowers . . .'They were indelibly associated in her mind with Lillie Langtry, the Jersey Lily, and that song 'Lily of Laguna' which Louise had loved. Tears made Lucy's voice unsteady. She was filled with happiness, but also with grief. It was the kind of emotion she felt on listening to a Puccini aria: a sudden lifting of the heart with joy, and then the stab of recognition that joy is transitory, that flowers wither and even love dies. Events and people, she thought, do possess a certain life even after they have passed, as long as they are remembered; but who will remember Louise and all her vanished Edwardian age when I am gone?

Joanna, feeling Lucy's pain but not understanding its cause hesitated beside her chair. 'Let me take the flowers,' she said gently. 'Let me take them to your den.'

Lucy nodded. 'Yes,' she said and repeated: 'Yes.' Then turning to Joss: 'I'd like to show you the painting now.'

He was a bit sleepy after all that food and wine; but he woke up. He was glad there were to be no more displays of family talent. No more geriatric music-hall, thank heaven!

'Come and talk to me, *Ćhérie*,' Charlotte said to Danielle who was sulking because she had been excluded from Lucy's den. 'What's the matter then?'

'I wanted to see the picture too,' pouted Danielle.

'You haven't missed much. It's rather nasty. If you looked at it late at night you'd have bad dreams. Lucy loves it of course; but she's so used to it I don't think she really sees it any more.'

Joss looked around the den with interest. It was a narrow room whose window looked out over the garden at the back of the house. A fire was smouldering in the small grate. On one side of the fireplace stood a Davenport writing desk, obviously in constant use to judge by the papers scattered on its slope and the full wastepaper basket below. On the other side of the fire was Lucy's chair, and an Indian curio in the shape of a disdainful camel whose back supported Lucy's tea-making things on a brass tray. Opposite the window a *chaise-longue*, or day bed, stood against the wall, and immediately above it hung the paint-

211

ing. He stared at it in silence. It certainly was a great painting. What struck him first was the extraordinary likeness of the main figure to Joanna. If Joanna wore her hair long and piled up on her head like that it could have been a photocopy of her.

'That's my grandmother Dambresac,' Lucy explained.

'She's awfully like Joanna.'

'I'm not so sure I like her likeness to me,' objected Joanna. 'I hope I don't look quite so formidable.'

'My grandparents spent most of their year's leave from India in Vienna,' said Lucy. 'It was 1900 – or was it 1901? Louise – that's my mother – was only fifteen then. She's the dark-haired girl in the picture.'

He listened, his eyes moving systematically over the canvas. He walked towards it to examine it more closely, murmuring: 'It's marvellous! Marvellous! Klimt was so innovative – before his time really . . . but is it by Klimt?' There in the right corner, where his name in detached capitals like an Egyptian hieroglyph should have been, was a blank space. It was probably not genuine. But he particularly liked the numerous decorative designs scattered in the folds of the gold cloak among the babies' heads: the eye that can be seen on the prows of Greek fishing boats, and geometric patterns such as are found on old Japanese Satsuma ware. Then he stood back to study the whole. In the background was a sombre shadowy wood. Half-hidden behind the main figures was a strange ghost-woman, entirely colourless, naked, grey and shrivelled. The condition of her senility – or might it be death? – was made more starkly horrible by contrast to the bold vibrant colours in which the young living women were depicted. But what was the meaning of the very lively green serpent coiled about her neck? He thought the painting was an allegory, an allegory of the life of women, of the great mysteries of sex, childbirth and death, the continuity of human

212

existence and culture over which women preside and hold power.

'Have you got it insured?' he asked suddenly. 'It might be priceless.'

'I have no idea what it's worth today,' said Lucy. 'I hoped you'd be able to tell me.'

'It must have been a very exciting time in Vienna,' Joss said. 'All the old conventions and attitudes bursting out at the seams . . . the feeling that a new century was being born . . . Did your grandmother ever talk about it?'

'Not to me; but my mother sometimes did. I was very small when Grandmama Dambresac died. I can't remember much about her except the burning of her hair.'

'Good heavens!' exclaimed Joss. Joanna laughed at his surprise.

'My mother cut off Grandmama's white plait of hair when she died and put it in a sandalwood box which she took to India with her. I remember seeing it burning – the box with the hair inside it. She wanted it to rejoin the soil beside the great river Mother Ganges.'

Joss felt his own hair rise on the back of his neck at the conjuring up of this macabre image. Burning was that woman's way of killing the snake. Even in death she was a destroyer. Her own hair, coiled like a white cobra in its sandalwood box, was cremated in a distant foreign land, where she probably had experienced sexual joy. That was certainly an ambiguous act showing as much anger as tenderness.

'I think they went to Vienna in the first place for the music. Mahler was conducting the Vienna State Orchestra at the time. Louise was musical, you see, and I believe they were seriously considering the possibility of her taking up music as a profession. She was only fifteen. But it never came to anything. She told me she wasn't good enough. But she did hear Mahler conduct. And once they met Alma

Mahler – the future Alma Mahler. She was Alma Schindler then.'

'What was she like?' asked Joss.

'Proud and beautiful was how my mother described her. Lots of distinguished admirers – Klimt among them. There's an amusing story told about her later life. Three times married and still in middle age a *femme fatale* she met a Viennese couple on the Riviera and the husband, overcome by Alma Mahler's celebrity and sex appeal, kissed her hand declaring he would marry her in heaven. His wife standing just behind, said tartly: "And even there you'll have to wait your turn!" '

Joss and Joanna were sitting side by side on the day bed and Lucy in her armchair when Mrs Colbert came in with a tray of tea.

'Thank you, Mrs Colbert,' said Lucy, 'And thank you for all your help today.'

'And a very happy birthday to you – what's left of it,' said Mrs Colbert, who had brought the tray in order to get a closer look at Joss. 'I hopes as 'ow you're not too fagged out by it all.'

'Not too tired yet, my dear,' Lucy assured her. 'But I shall go to bed early.'

'You do that,' agreed Mrs Colbert. As she put down the tray and then straightened up her eye met the imperial stare of Grandmama Dambresac, who over the years she had come to detest, and then shifted uneasily to the naked figure behind her. She grimaced with distaste. 'Indecent, that's what she is!' she had once complained to Joanna. 'Showing her nakedness when she's as old as that! She should have a pair of knickers on at least!'

Joanna caught her glance and smiled; and Mrs Colbert gave her an almost imperceptible wink as she left the room.

'The Dambresac ancestor was rather a *femme fatale* too, wasn't she?' prompted Joanna.

'She had lots of admirers, but also great sadness in her

214

life.' Lucy stood up and went over to the Davenport, whose top drawer she pulled open. Out of it she took a small, enamelled silver box. 'This is for you Joanna. I want you to keep it. But let Joss tell us what he thinks of it first.'

He took a jeweller's eyeglass out of his pocket to examine it more closely. 'It's a lady's cigarette case,' he said. 'Art Nouveau . . . very much of the period.' It was beautiful in design, made by a gifted craftsman, with a blue butterfly on its lid. He opened it to reveal another smaller lid which covered a tiny well. 'That must be to collect the ash. It was still rather daring for a lady to smoke then, wasn't it? I suppose that's why she had to hide the ash?' He squinted at it inside and outside. 'I thought it might be Lalique; but I can't see a signature anywhere.'

'It was probably made in America,' Lucy explained. 'It was not my grandmother's. It belonged to an American girl on the boat which took Mummy and me out to India in 1919. Rose was her name; and it was Rose who taught me how to do the Charleston. She was murdered before we reached Calcutta.'

Joss closed the lid softly. Joanna had seen the box before, but never heard the story.

'She was murdered by another passenger on the boat, who had once been Louise's lover. It was he who gave my mother this cigarette case. How it came into his hands we don't know. He probably stole it. It seems he wanted me to have it.'

'Why you, Lucy? You must have been a small child then.'

'It seems he may have been my natural father. It's a strange legacy to inherit.'

There was a long silence. Joss put the pretty *objet d'art* down on the tray, and wiped his hands on his handkerchief.

'So it's likely that my real father was a murderer.' Lucy took up her story. 'It's ironic, isn't it? When you think my other father – Herbert – was such an upholder of the Law, and brought me up to believe that the essence of a civilised society was to be judged by it's justice . . .'

'What was the man's name?' asked Joanna.

'Greg was what Louise called him.'

'So this Greg was my great-grandfather?'

'So I believe. And what makes it worse is that he was Louise's half-brother. For many years she didn't know that. Grandmama Dambresac had an illegitimate son before marriage. He was cared for by foster parents. They were paid for by the family to keep him out of the way. That must have been a great sadness in her life. Louise didn't know anything about all this until it was too late.'

Joss was very uncomfortable. His collar felt sticky, and the palms of his hands were damp. He felt like an eavesdropper on the Confessional. Why on earth had the old woman wanted to spoil her birthday by telling them all these unpleasant things?

'Was he hanged?' asked Joanna.

'No. He was considerate enough to die of a heart attack while in custody awaiting trial.'

'Why did you tell me all this, Lucy? V "1y now?'

'I believe the truth should be known. Louise didn't tell me till she was dying, and I've never told Beena; but I think it's something you should both know.'

'I don't see much sign of *your* dying,' said Joanna cheerfully. 'And anyway, what the hell? It was all such a long time ago it's rather like reading about the Tudors in a history book.'

'There's a rogue in most families,' said Joss stiffly; but silently he decided that most families don't parade their skeletons. He stood up and began to examine the painting again. 'It does make you see Klimt in another light though. Prophetic . . . uncanny really . . . the secret poison that was passed through the women . . . and that green serpent round the ghost's neck – do you think it was that which prompted Grandmama to burn her hair? It would be destroying the snake in a way, wouldn't it?' He turned to smile at Lucy. 'The old woman shadowing the beautiful Dambresac lady is certainly a very strange figure.'

'I've always thought of her as Eve, the ancestress of us all,' said Joanna. 'Poor Eve was cast out of Eden, cursed, wasn't she, and had to wear round her neck, as a punishment forever, the snake which tempted her.'

'That's an ingenious idea, Joanna,' said Joss. 'The serpent which was coiled round the tree of knowledge in the garden now coiled round the first female in this matrilinear tree of life?'

'And all women being liable to evil forever too?' laughed Joanna.

'The serpent wasn't always a symbol of sin, you know,' was Lucy's comment. 'The Greeks considered the serpent endowed with wisdom and subtlety, and therefore a guardian spirit. Aesculapius, god of healing, held a staff entwined with a snake; and temples and shrines were often homes to pet snakes. If Klimt was thinking along those lines he might have intended to represent the old woman in her frailty and fading as being garlanded with wisdom.'

He made wisdom very unpalatable then, thought Joss, as he sat down to finish his tea. It was cold, and tasted nasty.

'Mrs Colbert was right,' said Lucy. 'I do feel rather tired now. I think I'll just sit here and doze for a while.' That was what eighty-year-olds were supposed to do. It was really a bit over the top to dance the Charleston with Charlotte! It had tired her out. It was time now to sit and doze. She remembered the reply of an old Gloucestershire woman when asked what she did all day: 'Sometimes I sits and thinks; and sometimes I just sits.' That was what Lucy intended doing: just sitting and letting her brain slip into free-wheel.

Beena and Mrs Colbert were at the front door to oversee

the departure of the caterers, who had cleared up, washed up, packed up, and were about to leave. Joanna poked her head around the drawing-room door to make sure the rest of the party was happily occupied before she went out. Charlotte sat by the french windows staring at the garden while she smoked; the others were playing Trivial Pursuits, at which Danielle squealed a lot, shaking her bangles, and Dewey seemed to be winning on the Sports section. There was always the telly to amuse them when they finished the game; and the oldies would certainly want to hear the news later.

Joanna wandered into the garden with Joss. They didn't talk, but using what remained of the daylight he took a snapshot of her standing in her black dress among the fiery maples before they strolled down past the statue to the gate, where they stared in silence at the view.

'It's a strange painting,' said Joss at last. 'Wonderful but strange. And menacing too. Worth a lot of money. Difficult to know how much, because I don't think a Klimt has come on the market for some time. If it were to prove to be a genuine Klimt you'd have here a very important painting – important historically, because Klimt was a key figure in the Vienna Secessionist Movement, and probably the most influential Art Nouveau painter of all. It would make a great stir in the art world. I'd be surprised if it fetched much less than a million, even perhaps two million.'

'Really, Joss? I had no idea it was so valuable.'

'Well, I said if, if, if . . . My own view is that it's not authentic. But then that period is not my thing. As you know Italian Renaissance is my line. I think you should get an opinion from someone whose speciality is that Viennese school – even two or more opinions might be needed.'

'So you think it's a fake?'

'Not exactly fake, Joanna; but I don't think Klimt painted it. He certainly didn't sign it. Perhaps – who knows – he drew the outline of the head and neck, and then a student

218

or a friend did the rest in a pastiche of his style. I think the gold cloak with all its intricate patterns was painted by another hand – wonderful work, whoever did it . . . And if it went up for sale there would be a lot of interest, perhaps from Japanese buyers because Japanese design and its influence are so obvious in the decoration.'

'But as it isn't signed, and probably not authentic, it won't fetch two million.'

'Oh no! Nothing like! All the same I do hope your grandmother hasn't left it to Beena in her will.'

'I don't think she'd do that, because of course Beena would sell it and use the money to set up a dogs' home, with all mod cons and hospital attached – a sort of Bupacum-Hilton for dogs.' Joanna laughed.

'Would she leave it to you?'

'I don't think so. I wouldn't be able to afford the insurance, would I?'

'I daresay a major gallery would insure it for you if you loaned the painting to them.'

'Well, I hope she leaves it to the Nation when the time comes,' said Joanna. 'Although I've always loved it. It's always been mysterious to me. Every time I look at it it means something different. Mostly I think it represents the ages of woman; but today it spoke of death and dying.' She began stripping a maple leaf down to its veins. 'I daresay that's because that's the way my mind is running just now – I mean, being thrown headlong into clinical work in the Wards and seeing the sick and dying all around you – it's bound to affect you, isn't it?'

He drew closer to her and put his arm round her shoulders. 'Poor Joanna! I thought you'd been rather quiet all weekend.'

'Of course I knew what to expect. People warned me; but you don't really know until you're there beside it. That's what the painter is saying too: *In the midst of life we are in death*.'

219

'It must be beastly for you. How can you take it all so calmly? But you'll pull through, I know.'

'Oh yes. I'll pull through. Have to. Must.' They fell silent again till she asked: 'Do you find Danielle very attractive?'

'Danielle? Well you can't help liking her, can you? She's so pretty. She has a sort of delicate beauty like a Watteau drawing.' He wondered if Joanna could have noticed anything during lunch. When he rubbed his shoe against Danielle's sandal he felt to his surprise her hand on his thigh, caressing him. He was grateful for the overlap of the damask tablecloth which was ample enough to conceal his erection. 'But I daresay she's rather silly too.' He changed the subject. 'Your grandmother surprised me.'

'Me too.'

'What a horrendous tale! Why did she want to spoil her birthday with nasty revelations? And those Pandora's boxes! The little cigarette case – wonderful decorative workmanship of course; but it really was a poisoned gift, wasn't it?'

'Was it?'

'And the other one: the one that carried her hair out to India to be burned – Ugh!' He shuddered. 'A white snake coiled up in a wooden box . . . That was dramatic sexual symbolism! Frightening too . . .'

'Yes. But old history now, Joss. Finished. Done with.'

'The past has a way of clinging to us, Joanna.'

'Yes. I know; but we can learn from it – change things – see they don't happen again.'

Joanna is a born optimist, thought Joss. She always looks on the bright side. All the same those two Pandora's boxes did throw a shadow between them. They stood silently looking down into the great green bowl of the vale of Frenester. Long shadows thrown by the sinking sun crept upwards from west-facing hedges and a broad band of shade advanced from the screen of trees below them. Joanna touched the little cigarette case in her pocket and thought: Joss is right. The past does have a way of clinging to you. She felt a tingle of excitement in her fingers. She took it out and lifted the lid. There was nothing in it, not even a speck of ash left by the pretty dancer on that steamer chugging its slow way to Calcutta through gradually warming seas. It was empty, but to Joanna it was packed with electrifying drama. It was, she knew, an heirloom of a very special kind Lucy had given her, because it contained with its memories the history of her forerunners: the passions, joys and miseries, triumphs and mistakes of all those women's lives in which the poor little butterfly, poor pretty dancer, had become entangled. This little butterfly box, she told herself, is something I must never lose.

'I think it's awfully exciting, Joss . . . so full of happenings!' But he was irritated that she was unable to share his disgust. 'I think what Lucy was trying to say,' she struggled to express it, 'was that we are what we have done. And what has happened to us becomes ourselves. I know she believes that in order to be fully grown, sane and whole, we must know and accept it – see what we are, however painful that may be. In a way it's like the food we eat: it has to be digested and transformed into energy and growth.'

He stared at her coldly. He saw her transfigured in that evening's light, as if a layer had been stripped off an old master to reveal a different painting underneath, and was surprised at his own feelings of distaste. This was not how he'd seen her, felt about her, twenty-four hours ago. But he knew now how she would be in middle age, the soft outlines of her serene and beautiful face, and no doubt of her character, hardened by time, because she would inevitably become folded in, enclosed inside that painted golden cloak. She would grow to be like the other formidable matriarchs, absorbed in her ancestry and in her own young; and he would be made marginal. He would be made to feel even more excluded than he felt now. He was irritated, too, by Joanna's romantic fancies about that silver cigarette case. No souls of fragile butterflies slept in it. The one and only, the pretty dancer – was she called Rose? – was killed and trapped forever in the blue enamel on the lid.

'That's all my eye, Joanna! Just look at your family! Are they sane and whole and fully grown? Just take a look at all that bunch sitting round the lunch table!' He chose the easiest target first. 'That silly Auntie Patsy with her flawless profile and her disgusting fat Bully darling—!'

Joanna was suddenly shaken out of her musings by his contempt.

'Patsy?' she repeated foolishly. 'And Bully darling?' She laughed. 'I've always thought of them as rather comic. I suppose I've never really thought about them much at all. I've just taken them for granted as part of my environment – same as the old house, and the animals when I was growing up.'

'Well, you're grown up now, Joanna. You should be more critical.'

She felt stung. Science demanded a sharpened critical faculty, she knew; but should this be turned on your relatives too? She said: 'They're distant relatives you know. Not very important.'

'And your mother,' he continued accusingly, 'she's not exactly mature, is she? Living in a child's paradise!'

'Just leave my mother out of this, will you? You don't know a thing about her! She has her own way of going about things which suits her – so just leave her alone.'

'The whole lot,' he added savagely, 'except perhaps your grandmother – they're all absolute Philistines!'

'And Danielle, is she a Philistine too?'

'Probably,' he admitted, turning away his face. 'She's not important.' He thought he was telling the truth, half-hoping it was, half-hoping it wasn't.

'Do you think kissing a woman's neck so unimportant?'

Joanna demanded. 'I saw you as I was coming down the stairs.'

That made him blush suddenly and unexpectedly, and his voice became quietly sarcastic. 'Were you spying on us then? And are you suggesting I've made any vows of faithfulness to you alone? You're trying to limit my freedom, Joanna – just like other women! You're all the same in the end.' He turned away from her abruptly, and staring out towards the horizon asked: 'Are you trying to trap me into marriage? I suppose that's why you brought me to this birthday party.'

'You know that isn't true!' Joanna threw away the maple leaf with a gesture of impatience. 'I wanted you to enjoy a weekend with my family. And you wanted to see the family portrait.'

'Yes, I did. And in a curious way it's been a revelation – about your family, about all women. They're a threat, women, a threat to a man's freedom.'

'You don't really like women, Joss, do you? What you really want is power over them, not love. What you want is to keep a stable of fine women in the same way as some rich men keep horses to show off their charisma and success.' She didn't know she thought these things till she found herself saying them. 'And you're vain, Joss. Did you know that? You want women to admire, to worship you even, while you reserve the right to withdraw love from them.'

He felt furious, but bewildered too. He had never seen Joanna in such a rage. What was happening to her? She was changing before his eyes. It was all due to that beastly little box! Butterflies indeed! The ghosts haunting it were arachnids, big female cannibal spiders which ate their males after mating, black widows with eight legs and several pairs of eyes, spinning yards of silk to trap the naive and unwary. Well, he had no intention of being caught and eaten alive. The very thought made him burst out: 'All this talk of power and vanity! It's sheer hypocrisy! Why, your family is riddled with them both! Where do you think they got their wealth and importance then? From exploiting the poor under the British Raj, that's where! It's nothing but ex-colonialist power, Joanna. I'm not deceived.' He pursed his lips in a peculiar way which made Joanna see him suddenly as a pinched puritanical preacher.

'Nor am I,' she said. 'I'm not deceived any longer either.' She gripped the top of the gate sharply; and then she shivered. The last of the daylight was fading, and the air felt cold. 'Let's go in,' she said quietly. 'It's too cold in the garden now.'

They were silent as they climbed the slope up to the house.

'We might join in Trivial Pursuits with the others,' she suggested. 'Or would that be beneath you?'

Outside her attic door Joanna said to Joss: 'I'm sorry, darling. I didn't mean half I said, you know. It was just jealous temper.' But Joss was not in a forgiving mood. He pursed his lips in an expression of disapproval.

'You've hurt me, Joanna. Hurt me more than I thought possible.' He turned away and shut the door firmly between them.

He will not forgive me, she thought, not because I have withdrawn my love, but because I spoke a few home truths. She lay awake for a long time on the narrow iron bed. She lay fully dressed with her hands clasped behind her neck on the pillow. She wriggled herself down and pushing her feet between the bars at the end she dropped her shoes on the floor. She wriggled up again and tried to read a book, but couldn't concentrate; she picked up a glossy magazine and flipped through the fashion adverts, but they didn't hold her attention. So she decided to stare at her own thoughts flickering across the ceiling where they were projected by the movie camera of her mind.

She felt uncertain about many things. Dismay and elation were chasing through her alternately. She picked up the silver cigarette case, which she'd placed on the bedside table. Its delicate beauty gave her a thrill, but the most thrilling thing about it was that it contained the past. She thought: Lucy has made me the recipient of ancestral memories. I am myself a box into which all those who have gone before me have packed their substances — their stories, their characteristics and their looks, their hair and temperaments, their very genes . . . And if she had children she would pass on to them their family history together with these little twists of DNA, indelibly marked, but also capable of infinite variety owing to the mingling of so many millions of them in any human coupling.

She made a face remembering the quarrel. Joss had called her uncritical; and perhaps he was right. Perhaps she was too easy-going or lazy, taking people as they seemed. Perhaps she should have turned her critical faculty on Joss when she first met him. The trouble was that sexual attraction blinded your critical faculty. Sex so filled all your senses it made you unaware of faults or incompatibilities till passion died. In sex Nature, whose purposes are in diversity not harmony, stopped you thinking too much. And so did jealous rage when it suddenly shot through you.

Joanna was thinking quietly now; but though she was no longer in a rage she was still jealous. She still disliked Danielle in spite of all her prettiness and charm. She believed Danielle was a girl who was quite willing to poach on other women's love territories. Was Joanna then claiming territorial rights? There was, she had to admit, some truth in Joss's accusations about her trying to tie him up. But Danielle was a bandit in matters of love. No doubt about that. Joanna wondered if Danielle would give her heart in exchange for those stolen goods, because if she did, Joanna thought grimly, she'd suffer for it when Joss left her. Yes! Joanna hoped she would one day feel the pain she herself was feeling now – the humiliation of being jilted, but also the pain of missing him, which she knew would go on and on until enough events and days passing had healed the wound.

She had certainly loved Joss, or thought so when she first met him in the spring and they walked in the park in the cool blue sunlight and admired the daffodils – or *she* had admired them. He didn't seem to notice them; he was too busy telling her which paintings she ought to like and what she should despise. They had just visited a gallery near Bond Street; and his speciality, she was discovering, was Renaissance Art.

'I don't know much about Art,' she said.

'You don't need to – a girl like you, so much more beautiful than any painting!'

Of course she was pleased to find she could be lazy and still be loved; but as time went on she found he did expect her to know. He used to be irritated by her lack of taste, or understanding, or failure to observe some detail he'd pointed out before. (Although he often failed to notice other things – daffodils – himself.) He made it all a lovely time for her though: pleasant, relaxing, never disturbing or harrowing like her hospital life. She enjoyed her love affair with Joss. He rescued her from time to time from the blood and stress of the operating theatre, and took her out to some little restaurant in the West End where they ate scrumptious food undreamed of in her Students' Hostel. Once or twice he took her to see a play, and afterwards they strolled along the Embankment in silence, savouring the night and the black river reflecting a thousand lamps, in the quiet time when traffic has left the city. They made love in the bedroom of his orderly flat, which was white and uncluttered as a monk's cell. There were no bean-bags in his sitting room, but proper high-backed chairs of Rennie Mackintosh design, very elegant, very expensive, and not at all comfortable. It was a measured sort of love. There were no agonies, but no ecstasies either, nothing even unexpected; and by September she was beginning to ask herself, wasn't she just a tiny bit bored by it all?

She stirred uneasily on the bed. She got up and unzipped her dress. Perhaps it wasn't after all what Lucy had sometimes talked about on those long walks they used to take along the Edges: the real thing, the once in a lifetime sort of love. And was Joss, she wondered, lying awake next door and thinking the same thing? Was this why he compared Danielle with a Watteau drawing?

And why was he so upset by Lucy's story? What did it matter if her great-grandfather murdered a pretty girl on a ship long ago and her great-grandmother had unwittingly committed incest? Louise had outlived all that horror, had planted an avenue of beeches and a copse of maples; she had created a place of peace and order and a safe, welcoming home. In Joanna's eyes she was a sort of heroine. Joss was pusillanimous, she thought. That was the word. Pusillanimous: he lacked courage, he was afraid of scandal; underneath all that love of Art, all his avowed admiration of the innovative and adventurous, he was basically conventional; he wanted desperately to conform. He would never, after all, be like Fra Lippi who braved the might of the church, the anger of the Pope, the possibility of excommunication, of hellfire itself for the love of his little nun. Joss was afraid of the demons locked up inside her butterfly box; and these had made an unholy alliance with the fluffy prettiness of Danielle strong enough to drive him away.

On one of their long walks Lucy had once said: 'Love winds in and out of a woman's life like a piece of scarlet silk threaded through a garment; but family life is the garment she wears.' It was true. Love comes and goes, Joanna thought, but your family persists. Even the most single woman has a family of some kind. She has no being without parents. They are more than a garment; they are your skin. Inside it all are your ancestors, and they are you.

When Lucy woke up it was dark. She felt cold and her joints ached. For a few moments she didn't know where she was. She must have been dreaming because she thought she was seven years old and had just rushed out of the Rice Collector's bungalow in Bankipore to stand under the overflowing gutters and let heavenly cool rain pour down on her hot naked skin. The monsoon had broken at last, and the bad, sultry summer's heat would soon be washed away. Ayah was calling from the verandah: 'Keep your drawers on!' Even at seven you had to observe the proprieties.

Lucy noticed the curtains in her den were wide apart, and she was still in her party dress. Beena had not looked in to say good night. Perhaps when she peeped in and saw her mother asleep she had not wanted to disturb her. It was just as well she hadn't. Lucy knew her way with doors. She would rush out again, leaving the door open to let all the heat from the room evaporate upstairs, or else slam it shut with such force the whole house trembled, and anyone lucky enough to be asleep woke up with a start.

She struggled out of her chair, holding one of the arms to steady herself for a second before going into her bedroom to fetch the duvet. She threw another log on the sinking fire, and wrapping the duvet round herself she sat down again, trying to remember her dream. It was a pleasant dream, and wisps of it still stuck to her. She could see the bungalow standing on a small hill overlooking but not too near the river. It was a large one-storeyed building with spacious collonaded verandahs on all four sides. The north being the coolest was reserved for her parents, the east for the entrance, arrived at by a flight of steps, and for the administrative offices. From here an avenue of very old banyan trees led to the ironwork gates, beyond which there was a dirt road to the Ganges, that great expanse of brown water which flowed glistening in the sun half a mile away. On the south and west and hottest sides the servants worked, cooking, washing and scrubbing, and heating water slowly on charcoal embers for the evening tubs. The house-servants lived round the edge of the compound, but clerks and secretaries came into work from Patna, several miles away, on bicycles or walked.

By the time she was seven years old Lucy already understood some of the social divisions and the pecking order in that complex, multi-racial, multi-religious, hierarchical world. At the top her father, a big man with a high forehead and well-shaped nose above a stiff, short moustache sat at an enormous desk of Burmese teak, beside him Krishna, his Babu, a Bengali secretary, who was small, thin and diffident with delicate apologetic hands. He was often joked about on account of the peculiar English in some of his letters ('I thank you from the bottom of my heart, and from my wife's bottom also'), but possessed a sense of humour and an astringent snigger which when adroitly used could most effectively dissolve pomposity.

Behind her father sat the *punkah-wallah*. He came low in the order of things, crouched as he was cross-legged on the floor, sometimes asleep because of the heat and perhaps through sheer boredom, and sometimes, especially when he'd been shouted at, frantically pulling the ropes which flapped the fringed folds of cloth suspended from the ceiling to create a small stir of air in the torpor at noon. Her father never slept during the siesta hour. He was too busy toiling at Administration and Land Reforms, and at Rice Collection, which Lucy understood better, and something called the Franchise which he was introducing into the province, and which she didn't understand at all.

'One day Indians will be doing all this for themselves. And pretty soon too, if this Gandhi fellow gets his way.' He sighed. 'I feel like Sisyphus!'

229

'What's Sisyphus?'

'He was a man condemned to roll a heavy stone up a steep hill, and every time he got there it rolled down and he had to start again.'

'What a silly man!'

Daddy laughed then. He was a serious man and seldom laughed. Lucy never saw him during the day; but sometimes in the cool of the evening when he sat on the verandah sipping chota-peg and smoking a cigarette to keep away mosquitos she was allowed to climb on his knee and talk to him, or read to him from one of her Beatrix Potter books.

Bearer came to refill his glass. He was a tall Moslem from the North. He wore a brown coat over white cotton trousers, and a wide red cummerbund round his ample middle. His brown feet were bare and made no sound as he moved gravely about the house. He was the head servant, second in authority only to Mummy and sometimes, when she couldn't hear what he was saying, above even her. Moslems, Lucy knew, didn't think too highly of women.

After the monsoon there was a plague of frogs. They were everywhere, in corners, hiding under sofas, behind curtains, and one morning when Lucy put on her shoe and felt something slithering in the toe she screeched aloud and kicked out a fat wet creature with pop eyes.

'Herbert,' said Mummy, 'you'll have to do something about the frogs.' He sighed. It was another of those Sisyphus things: easier said than done. It was impossible to kill them outright without inciting a Hindu riot, because as Mummy explained to Lucy, Hindus believed that frogs like all animal creatures had souls inside, living out a phase of existence as they climbed slowly towards higher and at last human forms. Luckily Bearer was not averse to frog-catching; and Lucy ran around after him picking up one or two with tongs and dropping them into empty oil cans which were too tall for them to leap out of. The drums were then taken to the furthest limit of the compound and abandoned.

'It's not nice for the frogs,' said Lucy.

'No,' agreed Mummy.

Lucy learned early the difference between killing and allowing unofficiously to die.

When later she asked Ayah: 'Who is this Gandhi fellow?' Agatha replied: 'He is the Mahatma. He is a Holy Man.' Ayah was a Christian; but she bowed her head when she spoke of this Hindu leader. So Lucy knew at once that Gandhi must be Someone.

'Will you rule India one day?' Lucy asked Bearer.

'The Sahib says so,' he said. 'But not I — ' and he sighed.

'Why do people sigh when they talk about ruling India?'

'Perhaps it is too difficult. Perhaps it will never be.'

The Hindu who was polishing her mother's silver rose bowl looked up quickly.

'If the Sahib says so,' he said, and suddenly he laughed, at which Bearer made a small, deprecating clicking movement with his fingers and a tutting sound with his tongue, and the Hindu polisher bent his head, breathed on the silver, rubbing it vigorously, and said no more.

Mummy was second in importance on the compound because although only a woman she was the Memsahib. She had lots of dark hair piled up on top of her head. She moved quickly and her voice was clear and forthright. She laughed often. There was nothing devious about her, no feminine wiles, no frills and flounces about her clothes, no perfume more subtle than eau de Colgone. Although she was nervous about driving in the new car, Daddy said she was brave.

'She was brave enough to marry me!' They exchanged glances over Lucy's head and smiled happily.

Mummy was devoted to Daddy and to music in about equal measures. She gave musical parties in the big drawing room whose bamboo armchairs and sofas held chintz-covered cushions decorated with large pink roses. Two carved wooden camels raised disdainful nostrils on either side of the fireplace — for there was a fireplace, and sometimes a fire burned in it in winter when Lucy wore her brown serge skirt. The camels carried, instead of the usual humps, brass tables on which Bearer placed sweetmeats and cigarettes for the tea parties. People who could sing or play a musical instrument converged on the bungalow in cars and pony-traps. Mummy, who could play both violin and piano, used to accompany Mrs Ezekiel, the soprano, a robust lady with a great expanse of cream throat which wobbled when she sang.

'She does swoop and tremulo a bit,' Mummy admitted, 'but she can hit top C at times.'

Hitting top C was something Lucy tried to emulate sitting at the keyboard but could never achieve. She was considered too young and too distracting for the artists, so she was not allowed to attend these parties, but was sent out with Betty Ezekiel, who was the same age, or to Charlie's house — wet Charlie they called him because he drank so much water he wet his pants. It was annoying to be excluded, but Bearer comforted Lucy when it was all over by beckoning her into the dining room.

'Babamemsahib's favourite,' he would say softly and conspiratorially as he removed a net and bead anti-fly cover to reveal two small pink-iced sponge cakes which he had saved for her. Their sweetness was of a heavenly intensity which transcended even the taste of baked custard served in individual moulds.

On one occasion when they returned too early from Charlie's house the music was still in full swing and Lucy caught a glimpse of a stout baritone with a red face and a bow tie bellowing:

Du meine Seele
Du mein Herz!

She gazed at him in alarm over her shoulder as Bearer whisked her away into the dining room; but afterwards Mummy reassured her.

'No. He wasn't in a rage. It was a love song.' She laughed. 'He's not really out of the top drawer; but he can sing in tune.' Lucy was puzzled by the idea of such a fat man being able to get into a large bottom drawer let alone out of a small top one; but she did understand that singing in tune was a much more important feat.

Lucy dragged herself back to the present by opening her eyes and wondering what time it was; but she was too tired to bother to undress now and go to bed. Home . . . she remembered. They were going Home . . . They were going home in a big ship, and the journey would take a whole month on the ocean. Bearer and Ayah came to the foot of the gangway to see them off, Bearer all smiles because Daddy had given him a large sum of money as a parting gift, but Agatha in tears with her sari pulled down over her face to hide her grief. Mummy bent and embraced her before mounting the gangway.

'We shall see you in one year from now,' she said.

Agatha pressed into Lucy's arms a bunch of green bananas, which would ripen on the journey one by one. Lucy kissed her and clung to her for a moment, but oncoming passengers jostled her forwards. At the top of the gangway she turned before stepping on deck and looked down, shouting with the unconscious cruelty of children:

'It's lovely to be going home!'

She had only a vague memory of what home was or England meant. She had heard those words repeated in tones of awe and longing. To Ayah they must have meant the loss of her job and happiness in working for a family she loved. She looked up, waving her thin hands. She was smiling but tears ran down her cheeks.

'Ayah is crying,' Lucy remarked, butting Mummy in the

back with her head. She couldn't pull her sleeves because her arms were full of bananas.

'Yes, I know, dear. It's sad for her.' Mummy said. 'But we have given her quite a lot of money. She'll be able to travel to Madras to see her son.'

So Lucy dismissed Agatha from her thoughts, and as it turned out from her life, because they never returned to India. During the journey home her father contracted an obscure disease which the French doctor on board called *fièvre cerebrale*. Daddy couldn't control the jerking of his limbs, and lay in his bunk twitching and unable to sleep. Into his cabin the doctor brought a glass jar full of black slugs which he stuck on the back of Daddy's neck.

'Leeches,' explained Mummy. 'They suck blood.' They did indeed, and bulged with it when the doctor pulled them off. Lucy saw the little wounds their fangs made in the skin. Daddy fell asleep afterwards. He slept then for a week, and could only be roused with difficulty to eat, drink and be washed. The ship's nurse helped Mummy to look after him; and as Lucy's bananas slowly ripened he seemed to get better, so that by the end of the voyage he could dress and come to the dining room for meals. Mummy was overjoyed by his recovery.

But during the year of leave it became gradually apparent that he was no longer quite the same man. In London a Harley Street neurologist was consulted and pronounced the diagnosis: *Encephalitis Lethargica*. He explained to Louise, and she in later years to Lucy, that his mind and body would undergo a stiffening process, a slowing down due to muscle rigidity, a blocking of his ability to express himself, and finally a destruction, very gradual, of his personality.

That was all finished now, over and done with, all so far away and long ago; but when Lucy shut her eyes she could see Ayah's face tilted towards her as she turned at the top of the ship's gangway and called down: 'Goodbye! Good-

234

bye! We'll see you in a year from now!' And Ayah's expression was saying silently: 'Perhaps. Perhaps not', accepting the impermanence of human relationships, accepting the uncertainty of the future, which is the common lot of the poor, feeling the resignation of all those accustomed to the snatching away of hopes. She was waving her thin hands. How Lucy used to love those fingers, fluttering like moths, when they tickled her to make her laugh! And how she hated them when they pulled her hair during the morning brushings! She belonged to the humble unsuccessful majority into whose hands Lucy would have to entrust so much. Gandhi described women as the better half of mankind, better fitted by nature for *satyagraha*, the great non-violent struggle for freedom and fulfilment which continues after him, and is now world-embracing. It was not going to be a sudden, spectacular revolution, but a slow change towards relief from oppressive and destructive customs, from the burden of excessive and unwanted childbearing, and an enlightenment leading to a better way of doing things, including perhaps even the outlawing of war. Gandhi was right. Lucy nodded sleepily. We are going to have to depend on women everywhere on the planet for its safe keeping.

FIVE

Monday morning

Joss woke up suddenly, jolted by a tremor which he guessed would be fairly low on the Richter scale. He remembered the sound of a door loudly banging. A dog was barking outside, and he could hear rapid footsteps in the house underneath. The first thing he thought of was a possible break-in. With a groan he got out of bed and glanced at his watch: 4.30 a.m. Still dark, but Monday. He could see, since his curtains had not been drawn, light shining out from the room below, which must be Lucy's bedroom or her den. The guest rooms were, he knew, on the other side of the stairwell. There were no sounds from the other attic where Joanna was sleeping; but as soon as he opened his door, wrapping a towelling bathrobe round himself as he did so, Joanna's sleepy voice called: 'What's up? I heard noises.'

Joss opened her door and was about to speak when a series of moans rose up the attic stairs. Joanna leaped out of bed, snatched her dressing gown and ran past him muttering: 'That's Beena. It's not like her to wail.'

The doors to Beena's room and Lucy's room were open and light flooded out over the landing.

'What is it, Beena?' Joanna called out.

Beena ran to meet her. She clutched a folded paper in her

237

hand, which was crossed over her chest, and she moaned as if in pain. Joanna put her arms round her repeating: 'What's the matter?' But Beena was unable to speak.

Joss pushed past them into Lucy's den where Lucy lay curled up in a heap, face downwards on the carpet. Oh God! he thought. She's had a stroke! And what on earth do I do now? Her left arm was stretched out, and he noticed that although she was still fully dressed in her party clothes no rings sparkled on her fingers. He stared at the dead body, for that's what he thought she must be: dead. He'd never seen a corpse before. His heart beat very fast, and his hands felt clammy. He rubbed them on the belt of his dressing-gown and saw that they were shaking. His whole body began to tremble uncontrollably; he was ashamed of it, but couldn't stop it. Was she dead or was she still alive? He tried to listen, but couldn't hear her breathing, distracted as he was by the noise of Beena's sobbing. He didn't want to touch Lucy. He glanced round the room and saw her rings glistening in a Chinese porcelain bowl on the table by her chair. She must have taken them off before she fell. The bottom drawer of the Davenport was open, and papers had been pulled out roughly and dropped in disarray. As he hesitated Joanna pushed her mother into the room, and Joss saw to his amazement that Lucy's diamond star pendant blazed on Beena's chest as she stood there, a ridiculous figure in a flimsy nightgown, with bare feet, blubbing. It hadn't taken her long to snatch that symbol of authority from Lucy's neck and hang it round her own!

Joanna ran immediately to Lucy, rolled her over on to her back, listened and felt with her fingers for breathing, put a hand on her chest to feel for heartbeat, and tried to find a pulse. Joss thought: If I keep out of it and stay in the background no one will notice I'm shaking. At the same time he was annoyed with himself for being so useless. He watched Beena as she sat down in Lucy's chair, and wished her nightie didn't reveal quite so much to his embarrassed vision. His innate fastidiousnes was offended by the sight of her squat shape and her hardly hidden large, floppy breasts.

'I think she's dead,' said Joanna.

At that moment Dewey walked in, barefooted and in a long T-shirt emblazoned with the Flintstones cartoon.

'Rufus was barking. He woke me up,' he explained. 'Is it burglars?' He sounded hopeful. Beena sniffed her crying to a stop.

Joanna knew without thinking about it that Lucy's role had fallen on her. It was she who would have to take control at High House now. She glanced at Joss and realised that he was not going to lift a finger to help her. He was going to punish her for what she'd said to him yesterday. Well, she could do without him. She touched Dewey's arm. 'It's Lucy,' she said. 'I think we'd better lay her on the day bed Dewey. Give me a hand, will you?'

Without a word he helped her to lift the body. One arm dangled loosely, the fingers brushing the carpet, and her mouth fell open. The cousins looked across her at each other.

'Poor Granma!' he said. 'She won't use the Walkman now, will she? She was so nice!' He began to cry. Joanna took him in her arms, and for a few moments they stood hugging each other for comfort.

By this time Charlotte, woken by voices, joined them. She looked very old, frail and shrunken in her dressing gown without her make-up and the aggressive armoury of her vivid clothes and ethnic jewellery. She was wearing bifocals, but had to grope her way across the landing. It was a miracle, Joss thought, that she was still alive when her younger cousin lay dead. She crept in; she didn't ask any questions, but bent over Lucy murmuring: 'Poor Lucy! Poor Lucy!' She lifted the dangling hand, which she kissed before tucking it in under Lucy's hip, and pulling the hem of Lucy's sea-green dress over her knees she exclaimed: 'Still in her glad-rags to!' She picked up the duvet, which was on the floor beside Lucy's chair and spread it out over the corpse. She touched Lucy's forehead. 'Cold!' she murmured. 'Cold already!'

Then Charlotte went over to Beena and, kneeling beside her, asked: 'When did it happen?'

'About an hour – no, half an hour ago. I heard the bump when she fell. She was still breathing when I got here – a sort of snoring breathing.' Beena seemed matter-of-fact; but suddenly she burst into loud lamentations: 'It's unjust – terribly unjust! Wicked really to do this to me!'

'Dear Beena,' Charlotte's voice was soothing with sweet reason. 'I know it's hard for you; but Lucy was eighty after all. She had a good long life with plenty of fun. You couldn't expect her to live forever.'

'No! No!' cried Beena. 'Nobody wants that. It's just that – and I'm glad she died suddenly because that's what she always wanted. It's just that – this awful will!'

'Don't, Mother! Don't' begged Joanna. She knelt down on the other side of the chair and held the hand that clutched the folded paper; but Beena freed herself and thrust the document in their faces.

'Read it! Read it!' she shouted. 'Better still – burn it!' And jumping up she threw it on the still smouldering fire; but the embers were not hot enough to make it catch alight. While Joss watched in dismay Charlotte snatched the paper from the grate.

'Naughty Beena,' she chided. 'That's naughty. And anyway it won't do you any good, because Lucy's solicitor is bound to have the original locked up in his safe.' She unfolded the paper and fixing her specs glanced at it rapidly. 'As I thought, it's only a copy.'

'It's so unfair,' lamented Beena. 'I gave my youth to her, to looking after High House – to looking after her. I gave my whole life to her really – and now she does this to me! It's so ungrateful.'

A silence followed her outburst. Joanna could see Dewey was shocked. Joss stood with his head bowed so she couldn't read his face; but she guessed he must be horrified. He was calculating that Beena must have found her mother dead some time ago, that she had immediately taken from her body the diamond pendant and the rings, and that she had then searched for the will. It was the contents of this will and not her mother's death that made her scream in the first place, and that were so distressing to her now. Charlotte spoke sharply.

'If I remember rightly, Beena, it was Lucy who looked after you when you were young, and for many years after that. So let's hear what wrong she's done you. And where did you find her will so quickly anyway?'

Beena intimated the Davenport with a jerk of her head. She was still angry but the force of her feelings was reduced to grumbling: 'She should have left everything to me to look after. I'm her nearest relative – her only daughter. Why didn't she leave High House to me? It's my home. It's always been my home.'

'Beena dear, be sensible.' Charlotte spoke for them all. 'This house is much too big for one middle-aged lady to live in by herself. You'd rattle in it all alone. And anyway, how could you afford to keep it up? It would be far too expensive for you to run. I'm sure Lucy thought of all these things.' She looked again at the will. 'I see the solicitor is executor as well.'

Joss felt rather sick. He longed to get out of the room which was oppressing him with its smallness, its highly charged atmosphere, and with all these people who seemed complete strangers to him. Even Joanna, so cool and businesslike over the body, and now so occupied with trying to calm her mother, seemed to have cut him adrift. He was an outsider; he didn't belong. Worse than that he'd been witness to a disgusting scene which he wanted to wipe entirely from his mind; but he also wanted to hear what fate Lucy had ordained for the painting, so he waited. Charlotte was reading rapidly, translating legal-speak into plainer English. He had to admit that in spite of her frail appearance and the likelihood of her following her cousin into the abyss any day now she had certainly not lost her marbles.

'First there's all that stuff about debts and taxes being duly paid; but here now is the nitty-gritty.' She paused. Even at such a moment she was playing to the gallery. 'The house is to be sold and the proceeds divided into three: two thirds of the sum for my daughter Sabrina Marshall, and one third for my granddaughter Joanna Marshall.' Charlotte peered over the tops of her lenses. 'Well, that's fair, Beena. Joanna's portion will cover the costs of her medical training, and your portion will buy you a small house — a nice one, more manageable and warmer than this one — as well as leaving you something over to invest for income. There's no need for you to move away from your roots. You can still live near Frenester and your friends. And you can always find work looking after people, which is something you do so well.' She read another paragraph. 'I see she's left you all her jewellery and any of the house contents you want to keep.'

Joss could restrain himself no longer.

'Has she left the family portrait to the Nation?' he asked.

'No,' replied Charlotte. 'No. She hasn't. This is what she says: "the painting of my grandmother Amelia Dambresac, painted in Vienna in 1900, is to be sold, and the capital so obtained to be donated to – this ah – um – Indian medical college. The medical school of Chota Burrapur to be endowed with the capital sum released by the sale of the painting will use the income generated by investing this capital sum for the training of Indian women students as doctors, who could not otherwise afford to pay the cost of medical education for themselves." ' She took off her specs. 'A bit rum, all that, Beena, I agree. But that's her wish. She always had rather a thing about India, didn't she? Like her mother and grandmother too. They all felt they owed India something.'

There was a short silence.

'I ought to ring her doctor,' said Joanna. But Beena, suddenly remembering she was a Brown Owl and ought to pull herself together, and thinking it was time to assert her new authority as well as to resume her older role as servant-of-all, intervened: 'Let the poor man have another hour or two's sleep. He can't raise the dead. He can't do anything now except certify the cause of death.'

'You're quite right, Beena,' Charlotte agreed. 'So what we all need now is a cup of tea.'

Joss slipped out of the room followed by Dewey who ran to wake his parents with the news. Joss held on to the bannisters as he descended the stairs. He made his way to the cloakroom at the back of the hall. He knew there was a basin there where he could wash his hands. He felt an urgent desire to wash them. He hadn't touched the body, but his hands felt unclean. As he dried them he caught sight of his own white face in the mirror above the taps and thought: I am afraid of death; and Joanna isn't. It made him angry to have to admit it. He blamed what had happened in that den for making death seem so dirty, undignified and horrible. I hate this house he thought. How on earth have I got tangled up with all these women? It was not a home but a tomb, haunted by all those ancestors with the evil they did living after them. Panic was rising inside him like a gale, shaking him and thrusting him where he didn't want to go, making him think things he didn't want to think. He felt trapped, ensnared by the events of the last forty-eight hours. At all costs he wanted to escape.

He ran into the drawing room, towards the french windows, and with clumsy fingers undid at last the locks. He stepped out on to the terrace and felt with relief the cold air on his face and neck. It was still dark, but he could see at the far end of the shadowy beech avenue a splash of lighter sky gleaming – no warmth from the sun as yet, simply a promise of another day. Thank heaven it was Monday! His work in London now could decently extricate him from High House, and he could return to sanity, to the humdrum workaday world. People died, many were dying every day, everywhere at this moment; but life had to go on. There was no need for him to stay here, he told himself, and felt calmer at once. Beena and Joanna would manage all the business of the disposing of the dead between them. It was not his affair. He wondered if Joanna would expect him to attend the funeral; he hoped not. He would send flowers, of course. And later he would send Joanna copies of the photos he'd taken in the garden. He walked about on the terrace till the cold air drove him inside to sit by the Aga in the kitchen. Then he filled the kettle with water, and put it on the hot plate. Nothing would persuade him to take tea up to that den; but he would make it and get someone else to go up with a tray – Dewey perhaps.

He was immensely relieved when Danielle sidled sleepily into the kitchen and sat down at the table without a word. There was no need for speech. Even in her crumpled early morning state she emitted powerful sexual vibes. He didn't greet her. He wondered if she knew about Lucy's death yet; but decided not to speak of it until she did. All the silver charms on her bracelets sang siren songs to captivate him'; not one of them clinked out a single warning tocsin. He made the tea and sat down opposite; and when he handed her a mug she smiled at him. It was then he suddenly saw her grey and shrivelled and naked except for a green serpent-like scarf round her neck. He put down his mug noisily on the table and thought: My God! I'm sick! The night's events and lack of sleep must have deranged my imagination, making my mind play games of hide and seek with common sense. It was that horrible painting. He wondered would he ever again be able to look at pretty women and see them untainted?

Danielle sipped her tea and sighed with satisfaction: 'Ah! That is good!' Her lazy, contented voice banished his neurotic fantasies, and he began to relax. Her very ordinariness was a healing balm.

'Are you going back to London today?' he asked.

'I must catch a plane at Heathrow,' she said. 'But *Grand-mère* will stay in London now, of course. And I must travel alone.' So she did know . . .

'Let me give you a lift,' he suggested. 'Heathrow is on my way up the M4.'

She lifted her eyes to his and sighed: 'That would be marvellous!'

Gradually the house woke up. Guests stumbled downstairs to get breakfast, had showers, got dressed, moved about, following their routine habits, but Beena did not. She decided to go back to bed and let Charlotte bring her breakfast on a tray.

'You just let me look after *you* for once,' said Charlotte. 'And don't bother about goodbyes. Joanna will see them all off.'

'I never did discover why he's called Joss,' said Beena from her pillow. 'I wonder what his real name is.'

'I can tell you that, Mother,' offered Joanna from the doorway. 'It's Martin.'

'Martin?' echoed Charlotte. 'That's a long way from Joss!'

'It was all due to a stink-bomb,' explained Joanna. 'When he was a kid at school one of the dare-devils in his class let off a stink-bomb to annoy the Maths teacher. He sniffed, asking: "Do I smell incense?" and Joss shouted "Yes, sir! Joss-sticks, sir!" And ever afterwards the nickname stuck. The sticks fell off in time!' She laughed a trifle apologetically.

245

'Darling Joanna!' said Beena. 'Come here and let me hug you.'

'We three will have to stick together now,' said Charlotte.

'We'll have to pick up the pieces, tidy up, and just go on,' said Beena.

Joanna thought: That's where the courage of women lies – in picking up the pieces of broken lives, and mending them. Surviving . . . that's what we're good at. And in the end that's what counts.

The Canadians decided to continue their tour of the UK including Scotland, and return within the week in time to attend the funeral. Charlotte would remain at High House to support Beena and help Joanna on whom most of the practical work and decision-making would fall. Lucy lay covered with a white sheet. The doctor was on his way; and after he had certified the cause of death if he knew it, or informed the coroner if he thought a post-mortem to discover it was necessary, the undertakers would arrive and take away the body.

When Joanna stood in the porch saying goodbye and watching everybody leave, Duncan said: 'What about coming to Canada next winter?' and Dewey shouted excitedly: 'Oh gee! Yes! Do come, Joanna! There's super skiing! I'll show you!' Ellen echoed, 'Skiing's great! You'd love it!' Then suddenly remembering the dead body upstairs she felt ashamed of her own exuberance and added in a low voice: 'When you've got over the shock of course . . .'

'It sounds wonderful,' said Joanna. 'Well maybe . . . I'll think about it seriously.' They all kissed her cheeks in turn, and Dewey hugged her.

'Till next Monday then!'

With faces appropriately sobered by the mention of Monday and its attendant funeral solemnities they drove off, hands waving out of the car's windows as they disappeared down the drive.

Joss explained he was dropping Danielle off at Heathrow

to catch her plane. Danielle kissed Joanna, smiled, but wouldn't meet her eye. 'I am so sorry. It is sad for you,' she said, leaving Joanna to guess if she was referring to Lucy's death or to her own hi-jacking of Joss.

'I'm afraid I'm rather letting you down in this crisis, Joanna,' he said. 'But if there's anything I can do . . .' He took a card from a pocket. 'Perhaps Lucy's executor should have this. He'll need professional help over the portrait.'

'I'll see he gets it,' said Joanna. 'No doubt he'll contact you at Frithby's when he needs you.'

'We'll do our best for you, of course.'

'Of course.' Then suddenly deciding to sting she added: 'It was nice knowing you.' She was admitting that the Joss of yesterday already belonged to the past. So this was how it was. Lucy had always told her: 'Love is not all, love passes. Affection, loyalty, work remain.' And now she knew that it was true.

'Goodbye, Joanna.' Joss kissed her cheek. 'You know how bad I feel about all this. You're a great girl. You'll pull through, I know.'

She smiled wryly as she watched them go. There was something so quaintly like the hearty Boy Scout image in his turn of phrase. And yet he was neither a Boy Scout nor hearty. He simply presumed that whatever happened she would survive. Or did he just not care? Her whole world had turned upside down in one night, but because he thought of her as a survivor he expected her to be immune from suffering and offered her no help. Death, the great tester, had found him wanting. He had run away from her and her basket of troubles and gone off with Danielle instead. To be pushed aside by what Mrs Colbert had once described as 'that French piece with her head full of feathers' was humiliating to say the least but it did show her she couldn't rely on him in time of need. Lucy would have understood her pain; Lucy knew about private agonies as well as those more publicly displayed; but Lucy was no longer there in the old house. Never again would Joanna catch and hold that firm hand, nor feel the stones of its rings stroke her cheek when she sat on the floor beside Lucy's chair. Never again would she walk with Lucy along the Edges as far as Betty Bugler's Tump, pausing to lean on a gate and stare down at the immense green pasture stretching as far as the eye could see to a horizon of blue remembered hills, and talk, arguing about everything under the sun. What had Lucy thought of Joss, and what would she say now? Joanna knew what Beena would say: 'Plenty of fish in the sea, even in our polluted times, and plenty of time to catch them too!' Joanna guessed that her mother would be pleased Joss had gone off with Danielle and left her alone. Charlotte's reaction too, she could guess: 'He's handsome and has good manners, but not much sense of humour, has he, darling? A bit of a solemn pontiff, don't you think?'

And then she heard Lucy's voice speaking inside her head as clearly as if she stood beside her staring at the space where the Volvo had accelerated and where a single beech leaf, brittle and dry, spiralled slowly down into the settling dust. ' "Man's love is of man's life a thing apart. 'Tis woman's whole existence." That might have been true in Byron's day. But not any more! The twentieth century has been the century for women. It has changed us all.'

Joanna was not so sure. The Dambresac ancestor was so passionately in love she risked social ostracism, and even marriage because of it, Great-grandmother Louise fell so madly in love she conceived before she married another man, and Beena became pregnant outside marriage. The fact was that in their eagerness and disregard for the rules they all jumped the gun. Only Lucy didn't, and that was probably because she married in a hurry during the Battle of Britain. In all of them, at least for a brief period, love was their whole existence. No, she decided, women hadn't really changed much. What had changed was their existence. And Joanna replied to Lucy silently in her head: Yes. OK. There's work to be done, responsibilities to be accepted, decisions to be made, which was seldom the case for Byron's ladies. But it was all very well for Lucy to preach caution and common sense. She was old, her hormones dried up and her spirit resigned to the failure of desire. I'm young, Joanna argued. I shall certainly make a grab for love when it comes my way again. She stared sadly down the empty driveway wishing Joss had kissed her lovingly just once more before saying goodbye, there and then in front of that Watteau drawing of an air-head who had defeated her in sexual combat. She flushed with anger, and feelings of jealousy and self-pity mingling with her sense of Lucy's loss made sudden hot tears spurt from her eyes;' but as she turned to go into the house she spoke aloud: 'No. It's not my whole existence . . .'

Read on for the first chapter . . .

'Stand up please!' shouted the Clerk. As the Magistrates rose, picking up their scattered papers, everybody in the courtroom stood up too. The Clerk stood up himself. He cast a quick look over his shoulder at his newest Justice of the Peace as she pushed back a stray lock of blonde hair from her face and slipped behind the heavy curtain into the retiring room behind the bench. He was glad to see her disappear. Mary Chicon was the first lady magistrate he had ever dealt with, this was her very first court session, and her presence made him feel uneasy. Then, leaning his left elbow on the edge of his high desk, he scraped with his right forefinger a flake of breakfast eggyolk congealed on the pot-belly of his waistcoat.

Gregory Barton was a clever, uncultivated man. He had come to Frenester nearly fifty years ago, a skinny, thread-bare, bespectacled boy (so Higgs the local ironmonger told Mary) to work as a clerk in the offices of Preene, Parsons and Parsons, and through his native wit and persistence had qualified himself as a solicitor. The old-fashioned gentlemen of the law, not recognising their cuckoo in the nest, fostered his talent and encouraged him. In time he completely ousted Messrs Parsons and Parsons. Poor old Preene by then had faded away from senility and weari-ness. Gregory Barton took control not only of that rather bumbling firm but also indirectly of many lives. Higgs used to say there wasn't a pie in the district into which he hadn't poked a finger. Mary's father described him as Dickensian. As a matter of fact everything about that rural court was Dickensian.

'Even more archaic than Dickens,' Colonel Chicon said.

'The other magistrates are not like you, Colly,' said Mary.

'I don't believe they've altered much since Shakespeare's day. That Mr Justice Shallow of Gloucester in *The Merry Wives of Windsor* still sits on the Frenester Bench.'

'Perhaps it doesn't matter much,' said Mary thoughtfully. 'As magistrates we only take the place of the jury. The average judgement of society is what is needed. Twelve good men and true and all that . . .'

Mentally he clicked his heels and in soldierly fashion saluted her common sense. 'That's about the ticket. They're judge and jury rolled into one. No great intelligence is asked of magistrates, provided they be good men and true. But it is your job to try to make things a little better,' he exhorted her. 'I believe I improved things a bit, and you must carry on my work. I'm a great believer in the little leaven that leavens the whole.'

Mary had to admit that Gregory Barton was a hard worker. And many people felt affection for him. Some were grateful for his cranky benevolence; and it was even rumoured that he occasionally helped the guilty, *sub rosa* of course, and through their families, if they kow-towed to him enough. He died rich, 'the uncrowned king of Frenester' to quote old Higgs again; but he lived frugally and remained throughout life, as he liked to tell people, a humble man. At the time of Mary's first meeting with him he was very far from dead.

He had an immense respect for the Law; but he didn't like Mary, especially on what he called 'My Bench', as a member of 'My Magistrates'. When he first shook her hand he looked her over rudely and openly, sizing her up pretty shrewdly too. He knew her to be an inexperienced female who had led a more or less protected existence hitherto, running her own Girl Guide platoon to be sure, and dabbling a bit with calf-rearing on her father's farm, but a middle-class spinster who had never had to earn here own living. He cautioned himself that she was her father's daughter, and might not be easily cowed. Many were the times, in the days when old Francis Chicon was Chairman of the Bench, they had crossed swords, and usually Barton got the worst of those crossings. In his own opinion the proper place for a woman was in the kitchen or in bed, though he realised (and Mary could guess his thoughts as his sour glance slid over her) she would not be desirable in either place. She had an angular figure, she knew, and too big a nose; but by the time she reached her late forties she had grown to accept her own appearance, and was able to acknowledge her disadvantages without bitterness.

The Law demands that each Juvenile Court must be constituted of not more than three magistrates and shall include a man and a woman. So Gregory Barton had to put up with her, not only on the juvenile bench but in adult courts where she had to take her turn as well. He treated her with mildly sarcastic gallantry, egging on the other justices to feel amused contempt for her. She suspected that behind her back, at Bisons' Club dinners and the like, when they were all boys together, he was more ribald. She could hear him saying: 'I don't think she'd be profitable in bed.' And Turner would laugh, adding: 'No. She'd be a dead loss there.' Their imaginations, she felt sure, would be anchored to the concepts of profit and loss. Perhaps they said even worse things about her; but of course all this could not be tolerated in the courtroom, where Barton liked to cover the proceedings with a veil of pomp. This was often very rudely torn by his own bad manners, his bullying of witnesses when irritated, and by his undignified, sometimes ungrammatical speech. In Francis Chicon's day as Chairman he had managed to check the Clerk, cutting short some of his rhetoric, and forbidding absolutely his attempts to join the justices' deliberations in their retiring room, 'to prevent any mistakes', as Gregory Barton put it. But the Colonel had dismissed him promptly. 'It's your duty to keep us inside the Law,' he said. 'It's not for you to influence our verdict.' So Barton had been a bit afraid of Mary Chicon's father.

Mary once overheard old Higgs describe her father to a customer who wanted to buy some four-inch nails. She hid in the doorway, overcome with embarrassment at being an eavesdropper; but she couldn't help hearing what was said: 'Old Colonel Chicon was a Desert Rat, you know. Blown in up in a cloud of sand at Alamein. Riddled with shrapnel, and left for dead. Terrible thing – in that heat! But he survived, you see. A strong man, the Colonel. And good at laying down the Law. Best for folks to keep on the right side of him – and the Law!' Higgs laughed, and so did his customer.

Higgs was right about Chicon's being good at laying down the Law, which he had done for years in petty sessional driblets to the fear of some and the satisfaction of many, as is required in the magistrates' courts, but he was wrong, Mary knew, about his being a Desert Rat. Strictly speaking, that honour belonged only to the Seventh Armoured Division, which alone bore the insignia of the little rodent. He had fought at El Alamein. That battle finished his army career. He was hospitalised, invalided out and then discharged, limping badly, into civilian life when he visited her at school towards the end of the war. He was a brave man, a survivor, and very sure of himself.

Mary was much less confident. She did not take easily to her new office. Sometimes she felt totally bewildered. She slept badly after days in court. She was most anxious to do the right thing, but often feared she'd done the opposite. She had sudied all those dull little red handbooks for new justices, attended some lectures and visited a prison, a remand home and a detention centre in her conscientious efforts to learn how to cope with her new job; but she felt very keenly her inadequacies and the weight of her responsibilities.

On that first morning, which she always looked back on

with hot embarrassment, the defendant before them was a poor fellow who had pinched some frilly knickers off his neighbour's washing line. Mary wondered what on earth he could want them for. The Chairman, Mr Turner, explained shortly: 'He's a pervert. That's why.' They were sitting in a little room no bigger than an alcove behind the bench, hidden from view and out of earshot of the rest of the court.

'If that's the case,' she said, 'he should see a psychiatrist.'

The other magistrates looked at her pityingly. Mr Dunster, who was a farmer and a mild man, said: 'I don't suppose that would do much good, Miss Chicon, would it?'

'Well, if it hasn't been tried it should be,' she insisted.

Mr Turner laughed. 'OK', he said. This man has done this before, and fines haven't stopped him yet. So let's try it.' He was a very busy man, a builder, able and active in local affairs and a District Councillor as well, and was anxious to get through the list of cases as soon as possible.

When Barton heard their decision he was dumbfounded for a moment, but agreed to adjourn the case for reports from Probation Officer and Psychiatrist. He addressed the defendant in a loud, sarcastic voice. 'One of my magistrates thinks a psychiatrist would do you good. I don't think much of psychiatry myself; but in the circumstances we'll give it a go.'

Mary was furious. He had no right to express his opinion in defiance of theirs. Battle between them was thus declared after that very first case she heard. He won the first round. Six months later the same man was brought before them again on the same charge. When in the dock he spoke up for himself: 'I seen the psychiatry doctor, and he says as how I can't help myself.' This time he was fined amid laughter in court, and Mary was made to look a fool, which perhaps she was. The other magistrates enjoyed themselves laughing at her later over a pint with Barton in the pub. But later still (it must have been in the second year after her appointment) Turner and Dunster took a liking to her. It happened over a young man with very long hair. He was brought before the court by an irate matron who had heard him using obscene language at a bus stop. Barton explained to the justices that there was still in existence some quaint law or by-law forbidding the use of obscene language in a public place; and the lady thought she was doing a public service by bringing up the case. The young man in question had been standing in the street with a macho friend who accused him of being a sissy. The policewoman read aloud the indictment in a steady expressionless voice without dropping a single H: 'The defendant then said: "I've got more fucking hairs on my fucking balls than you've got on your fucking head!" '

It was Mary who burst out laughing first. Her laughter was checked only when across the courtroom she caught the steely blue gaze of the policewoman, who was understandably offended because she'd tried so hard to state her case in a professional manner. She didn't even smile; but the magistrates were finding it difficult to suppress their hilarity. They retired as quickly as possible to consider their verdict, and in the little room behind the bench they broke down into loud guffaws.

'Why! It's the kind of language farm workers use all the time!' said Mary. 'They don't mean any harm. They just haven't enough vocabulary to find the right adjectives.'

Mr Dunster wiped his eyes. 'It's all a bit silly, isn't it? But if it's the Law . . .'

'That young man has read nothing at school except comics, and only the tabloids since,' she declared, riding one of her hobby-horses, 'and probably has a reading age of nine. We should regard him as a juvenile.'

'We can't do that,' said Turner. 'He's obviously got too much hair.' And they both dissolved into laughter again.

'What a pity we can't make him sit in the police station

until he has copied out a page of the dictionary,' Mary said. 'That might teach him a few more words.'

'No, seriously, what can we do? It's obviously a trivial charge. The woman who brought it has been wasting the time of the court. It's she who should be fined.'

'Why not an Absolute Discharge?' suggested Dunster.

'OK,' agreed Turner. 'We'll find him guilty, but give him an Absolute Discharge.'

And that was what they did, to the relief of the defendant and the outrage of the irate woman. This incident for some reason softened her colleagues' attitude towards her, though it did not alter Barton's; and from then on, at least while she was in the magistrates' retiring room, she became almost one of the boys.

By the time Hannah Batherswick was brought before them as a juvenile in Moral Danger and in need of Care or Protection Mary's whole outlook was more relaxed. Nevertheless it gave her a shock, especially when she learned that the girl was Maeve Delaney's daughter, to see her standing there, and yes, it gave her heart a nasty wrench to note her astonishing beauty. Although she drooped her head Hannah carried an air of wounded, indignant innocence. Mary remembered her mother well. As children they often went riding together when Mary was home for the holidays. After all the evidence had been heard, and the magistrates had retired to consider the case, Mr Turner began to mutter: 'What a shocking business! At her age too!'

'What can we do with her, Miss Chicon?' Dunster turned his troubled eyes to her.

'She's fifteen next month,' Mary said hesitantly. 'Care or Protection must continue till the age of eighteen, I believe?'

'Hannah Batherswick is an old-fashioned sounding name,' mused Dunster, 'but she's not exactly an old-fashioned girl, is she?'

'She's a trollop!' said Turner. 'And a disgrace to our town!

Her own father has refused to have her back home. And I'm not surprised. She's quite out of control.'

'Her father is a ruffian,' Mary said.

Turner continued as if she hadn't spoken: 'Running away and living with all sorts of men! Going to pubs, and then trying to do away with herself by drinking a bottle of lysol ... She was picked up, I see, in a public lavatory, where she passed out.'

Mary was reading the Probation Officer's report, from which images of the child's first seduction, so baldly described, stuck in her mind like thorns: 'He pushed me down in the back of his lorry,' she said. 'It was a gravel lorry, but it wasn't· ordinary gravel. It was red earth and dust from the reddle mine down Madstock way; and the driver's clothes, and even his skin was stained red with that dye. He'd given me a lovely meal of egg, bacon, sausage and chips at a transport caff, so I was grateful. I was scared, too, because I didn't know what he'd do. You don't, do you? Till it happens to you. Gran never told me anything about sex. Whenever I asked her any questions about it she used to say: "I'll tell you when you're old enough"; but she never did, because she died too soon. Of course I knew lambs were pushed out between the ewe's hind legs, and I'd often seen young steers playing at mounting heifers in a field. Sometimes the girls in my class used to huddle into a heap in some corner to tell a sexy joke, and then burst apart laughing; but I never used to see the point of it. So when I came to lie down in that lorry I didn't know much; and I was scared.

'He undid my blouse and lifted my breasts as if he was weighing bags of sugar. "Like apple dumpling they are," he said. "Like my Mum used to make, with a little pastry knob on top. So nice I could eat them." For a moment I thought he might; but he didn't use his teeth. I cried out when he pushed his Thing inside me. He stopped then for a moment. He must have realised I was a virgin. "Take it easy kiddo," he said, and waited while he stroked my bum. He was quite nice really. Afterwards I was grateful for the quiet. I thought how strange it was. Not a bit nice, not for me anyway. I wondered what my Dad's blondes did it for.

'When morning came and I saw how covered in red sand I was I decided to move off. I bided my time till he parked the lorry near a pub and went inside for a pint. Then I jumped down and ran as fast as I could back along the road we'd travelled to a Service Station I'd spotted on the way. I reckoned there'd be a toilet there, and perhaps a wash-basin too. It was while I was standing naked over the basin to wash my pants and bra that a woman came in and began to eye me suspiciously. No wonder, since all the water in the basin was bright red. She must have thought I was bleeding and needed an ambulance. So I grabbed my clothes and rushed into the toilet to dress.' The Probation Officer added her own bleak comment to Hannah's story: 'She seemed more upset by the colour of her underclothes than by the loss of her virginity.'

Mary picked up the Psychiatrist's report next. It was not too puzzling because he'd taken the trouble to write it in plain English: 'She described her adventures as if talking about something which had happened to someone else. Apart from the shelter she found in vans and the cabs and backs of lorries she seems to have been homeless. She said all this was okay until it got really cold in December. She couldn't stand the cold, she said. When asked wasn't her father's house better than a lorry in winter she suddenly came to life. "Please don't send me back to him," she begged. "Please! Please! He killed my Mum driving drunk with her in his car. It's because of him I've got no Mum. He used to hit me too. Black and blue I was sometimes. That's why I ran away."

'Presumably her hatred of her father and her homelessness gave rise to an insoluble dilemma, which was what drove her to attempt suicide. She was picked up in a public lavatory after having swallowed some lysol she found on the window-sill. "A black woman came into the toilet as I was staggering about," was how she described the incident to me. "You having a haemorrhage or something?" Hannah remembered throwing the empty lysol bottle in a litter bin, but can't remember anything more until she found herself in hospital. I think if she were sent back to live with her father the whole history would repeat itself. What she needs is a calm, secure and affectionate family background for the remainder of her adolescence. She is a girl of above average intelligence; with care, and a bit of luck, her cognitive ability might yet steer her out of the emotional traumas of her childhood.'

Dunster sighed as he looked up from the papers. 'No relative has come forward,' he said gloomily. 'Her grandmother is dead, and the aunt can't look after her, since she herself is a chronic invalid in a nursing home.'

'We'll have to send her to an Approved School then?' said Turner briskly. He was used to making quick decisions in business, and that's how he wanted justice to be done.

'No! No!' Mary protested vehemently. 'She's not a criminal. In that Approved School she'd mix with all sorts of bad girls who'd teach her all sorts of bad habits. Even taking drugs, perhaps. And then perhaps finish up in a Borstal before she's eighteen.'

'She's a very bad girl herself,' said Turner indignantly. He had no children himself. 'If I had,' he once modestly explained to Mary, 'I wouldn't be able to give so much time to public life.' Her own opinion of his altruism was that the addition of JP to his name weighted the scales slightly to his advantage when he applied for planning permission to extend a Grade II Listed Building, or to spread new houses on a green site. So she argued with him.

'But the child's had no mother since she was four years old. It's obvious the father's no good.' She thought of him sitting there in the courtroom turning his big flabby face this way and that, fiddling with those enormous moustaches grown to emphasise his virility. 'You can see that. What she needs is Care or Protection, a mother in other words – not incarceration in an Approved School.'

The two men looked at her in silence. She could read their thoughts: That was the worst of women on the bench! Always letting their feeling run away with their judgment–!

'Well, what else can we do, Miss Chicon?' asked Dunster kindly, with a little helpless gesture of one hand.

'There's no alternative then?' said Turner.

So they filed back into Court.

'Stand up Hannah Batherswick!' shouted the Clerk.

When Hannah heard that she was going to be shut up in an institution where it was hoped she would be trained to lead a sober and industrious life she suddenly uttered a piercing scream, and leaning across the table where her father calmly sat, who had publicly disowned her by declaring he was unable to keep her under control, and was, it seemed to her, the cause of this terrible punishment, she bared her teeth like a carnivore, and cried out: 'You viper! You dirty snake!'

The Court was shocked into complete silence. The scorching venom in her strong, young voice rushed through Mary's soul, making her shudder. She supposed that after a lifetime of discipline in her father's house she was an exceptionally orderly person. Her days were certainly planned, quiet and composed, her hours pigeonholed. Hannah's rage swept through the tidy compartments of her mind like a hot wind, leaving them strewn with dust. Her mouth felt dry. She knew she was inexperienced, foolish even, but she felt in her bones the suffering and need of the girl standing, savage but quivering and wounded, only a few feet away from her. In spite of her history there was a sort of innocence in Hannah's face, and her big beautiful eyes blazed with a sense of outrage. She obviously felt an abominable injustice was being done to her. And so did Mary. She remembered the lessons learned from her handbook for new magistrates: 'In dealing with the adult criminal your first duty is to protect society; but in dealing with the juvenile delinquent your first duty is to consider the welfare of the child.'

She must have turned pale, because her cheeks felt suddenly cold; but she took a deep breath, and leaning forward she tapped Gregory Barton on the shoulder.

'I will offer myself as a foster mother,' she said. He turned crossly to stare at her. Everybody must have heard what she said. The silence was intense and seemed interminable. At last Barton rose and turned towards his magistrates.

'This is most unusual, if not irregular,' he whispered hoarsely. His eyes, behind his spectacles, bulged over purple cheeks at the enormity of what had been suggested. The other two magistrates stared at Mary in stunned disbelief. The Clerk's clerk, whose job it was to copy into a big book the whole proceedings laboriously in longhand, stopped writing and stared at his pen. The policewoman and Hannah's father eyed each other in consternation, and Hannah's sobbing died away to a whine.

'Are you sure you understand what you're suggesting, Miss – Madam?' asked Barton with a highly audible hiss.

'I think so,' she replied.

'I've never in all my experience known such a situation,' he grumbled – and then, turning to the Chairman: 'Do you agree to this?'

Mary felt the blood rushing to her cheeks, and spoke quickly. 'Is there any reason in Law why I may not foster this girl?'

'Well, no,' he admitted. 'But it's most unusual.'

The Chairman now intervened. He stood up and spoke firmly: 'We shall retire again to consider these further aspects of the case.' And again they filed into the alcove.

'Do you really have any idea what you're suggesting?' asked Turner irritably.

264

'She wouldn't be an easy girl to manage,' said Dunster.

This time Mary did let her emotions go in a torrent of words. 'We knew her grandmother quite well, you see. The Delaneys used to supply a lot of our winter cattle feed in the old days. And I knew Hannah's mother. Maeve was younger than me, but we did ride together a few times. I can remember the day my father sold her one of our ponies. The Delaneys were keen for her to learn to ride, and I taught her a few things about horses myself. And then she married this ruffian. God knows why! He was good looking, of course. Women are so foolish in love.'

She could see Turner gesturing in an attempt to stem the flow of her story, but she refused to be stemmed. 'Then she was killed in that terrible car crash. New Year's Eve it was. The man was probably drunk. Everybody knew about it. Everybody was shocked. And now here's this child. She hasn't had much luck really, has she? All the dice loaded against her . . . . Her life in tatters already. . . .' She choked and for a few appalled seconds the men must have thought she was going to weep. They didn't know her. It wasn't grief, it was rage that choked her. There was a short silence.

'Well, of course I can see that in the circumstances . . .' said Dunster. 'There are special circumstances in this case, are there not?'

'No relative has come forward,' said Turner slowly. 'And perhaps in a way you are as near as possible to a relative as we are likely to find.' He spoke grudgingly. 'How do you think your father will take it?'

She was beginning to wonder about that herself.

'The Colonel might supply the order and discipline the girl needs,' was Dunster's comment.

Gregory Barton, who had believed the other magistrates would persuade Mary to drop her silly idea, was very put out when he heard their decision. He shook his head and muttered loud enough for everybody in the court to hear, 'I'm sure this won't be the end of the matter!' Then sitting down again in his high desk he shouted: 'Hannah Batherswick stand up please!'

The Chairman then announced the Magistrates' decision that an Interim Care Order committing Hannah to the care of the local authority for twenty-eight days would be made to enable full reports to be put before the Court for proper assessment of the foster home offered.

As Hannah was led out Mary could hear her protesting, 'I don't want to be fostered by that mangy old cat!' Barton grinned openly, and the Clerk's clerk bent his head to hide his smile as he scribbled. Turner pursed his lips in an expression of 'I told you so!' but Dunster nodded at Mary across the bench, now littered with loose papers, and murmured: 'We shall see . . .'